For Raiden, Cassidy and Drake

Never give up

star struck

Nicole Erdmann

Published in Germany by Books On Demand in 2018

Copyright © 2018
Herstellung und Verlag: BoD – Books on Demand,
Norderstedt
ISBN: 9783748139904

Cover design and artwork by Nicole Erdmann

star struck

Miss Teri's Horoscope

✉ Contacts		♪ Creativity, ideas	
♻ Health		👫 Partnerships, friendships	
♡ Love, relationships		◉ Goals, hopes, groups	
⚖ Horizons		☆ Career	
⌂ Home, family		☀ Energy	
👛 Finances		▮ Travel	

Prologue

December

December ☆♡☼

Out with the old, in with the new? Your life is likely to take a whole new direction this coming year, especially on the professional front, maybe even a new love? Don't be surprised if you even find yourself kissing that certain tall and handsome someone this year on New Year's Eve, Gemini, as you meet someone interesting head on. New beginnings can be scary, and at first this may take the wind out of your sails, but don't give up too quick. Good things are on the horizon if you listen to the signs.

Who writes this crap, anyway? Kissing a tall, dark and handsome someone? Flirting? With whom? Seeing that Joe, my tall, dark and handsome someone was four thousand miles away from me in Amsterdam, well, kissing *that* certain someone was the one thing that would surprise me.

I turned off my phone with a vengeance and tossed it down on the cherry wood side table. This was just another cockamamie prediction from 'Miss Teri's Horoscope', the horoscope app on my cell phone. If Miss Teri is so psychic, shouldn't she know that my handsome prince is far, far away?

It was still dark in the hotel room, its white walls slightly shimmering from the light of the street lamp outside that was still shining and the questions were still rolling in my head

1

when I heard Bree start to stretch and moan in the other corner.

"Morning," she mumbled from beneath her fluffy comforter.

"Morning," I mumbled back.

"It's early."

"Couldn't sleep."

"Oh," she whispered. She must have picked up the irritation in my voice.

"Still haven't heard anything more from Joe?" she asked carefully.

I put my hand over my tightening stomach.

"No," I swallowed, gathering some strength, "and I don't want to talk about it," I said strongly, hoping it would make it real.

"I mean, we didn't save every penny for this vacation, just so he can call from . . . God-knows-where, completely wasted, just to drive me crazy. I'm not going to do it."

My voice got louder as I still tried to process the phone call from last night. "*We just went jogging*," he'd drawled with a drunken slur. Only after we'd spoken for a while did it finally come out that he'd jogged an entire two blocks before he found himself, as the window gods would have it, mysteriously and euphorically in the middle of the red-light district surrounded by skimpily clad women sitting in windows, and well, what was he *supposed* to do?

"OK, OK," Bree backed off, sitting up in her bed. "You don't have to talk about it. I think that's a good plan. I wasn't trying to get you worked up over it, first thing in the morning," she assured me. "Why don't we try to get off to a good start? Let's just wake up Maddie and get to the slopes."

"Right," I agreed. "Good idea. You can go get ready first."

Bree flipped her long brown hair out of her face as she got up quietly and tiptoed around our luggage that was distributed around the individual beds and into the bathroom. We stayed at the Miner's Inn, an old hotel that lay outside a sleepy little mountain town in California which boasted two ski lifts, a café and a rustic bar and lounge. As we'd pulled into the nearly deserted parking lot the night before, I wondered where my cousin Maddie had brought us. I mean, I hadn't expected it to be a luxury five-star hotel, but the place was an ancient wooden construction, stuck in between the highway and the side of the mountain. Fresh snow hung on the faded gray wooden slats on the sides of the box-like structure, and icicles dangled precariously like daggers from what seemed to be a rusted, corrugated metal roof hiding beneath the snow.

"This is it?" I'd asked skeptically.

"Just be patient." Maddie laughed. "You'll see."

I had been patient, but I was still unconvinced.

Despite the large window, it was still dark and quiet, allowing for all kinds of thoughts to go through my head. I turned over in my bed and swallowed, fighting back the gloomy feeling that threatened to take me in its grip and wondered if our dream to have one last "girls' vacation" before we finished college had terribly backfired.

Maybe I took it all too seriously. Maybe I was suffering from burn-out. This last semester at school was a doozy. I had a class that consisted solely of one capstone ad campaign project where we had to come up with an entire ad campaign. Flyers, print ads, commercials, presentations, product packaging... The whole nine yards — alone. My pseudo-client was the distinguished Culpepper Horse Farms. How many horse breeders make TV commercials? Or even magazine advertisements, for that matter? Even coming from Texas, I couldn't remember ever having seen any such advertisements. Anyway, I guess I wasn't doing too well because half way through the semester, Mr. Millington, my adviser, checked my work and advised me not to quit my day job. Maybe he was joking, but if so, the joke was on him since I didn't even *have* a day job. Ha!

In any case, the campaign had taken almost all of my time and resources and nearly drove me crazy. Ads for horses. (sigh). If *this* was what having a career meant, I thought, then

I'd better make the most of it now, you know — YOLO and all that.

"You're going to make it," Bree assured me during one of my meltdowns. "You have plenty of time. I mean, you do realize that graduation is still six months away, don't you?"

I did. Real Life was almost upon us, careers and/or families were right around the bend. In fact, that was exactly the realization that had prompted us to go on this last "girls' vacation" in the first place. Bree and I had skyped with Maddie, my cousin, who lived in Santa Cruz. We started looking for vacations, but with our budget, we had a hard time finding anything that wasn't in the "Scary Category" and after a long and unsuccessful search for an acceptable vacation package, we were getting worn down.

But then, out of the blue, Maddie called with an offer she'd found for us to go skiing in California. The flights left right after Christmas and they were even cheaper than the ski passes at the "little-known, off the beaten path" ski area. We thought about continuing our search, but with dwindling time, budgets and options, we decided we were up for an adventure.

At first, I was apprehensive about what Joe, my boyfriend of nearly two years, would think about our great idea, but to my surprise, he also thought it was a great idea, and right after I had told him about our plans, he announced his own plans to have a "guy's vacation" - in Amsterdam. Amsterdam? I thought. Hmm.

Anyway, we all thought we had great plans worked out and that it would be adventurous and fun, and I never thought there could be a problem, that is until yesterday when Joe called slobbering drunk from the red-light district in Amsterdam, which was where he was spending New Year's Eve with "the guys". At least I think he was drunk. Or maybe he was still baked from all the coffee houses he'd been going on about.

Calm down, I told myself as I held my stomach and rolled over. Surely, they weren't *only* hanging out *there*, I rationalized. Surely, they weren't *only* watching women in windows and smoking themselves completely stupid in coffee houses. Although he didn't really mention anything else.

I repeated this to myself over and over for over fifteen hours, trying to convince myself that he really was just having good, clean and cultured fun with the guys.

"Next," Bree said as she slipped out of the bathroom, and Maddie got up silently and slipped in. I hadn't even realized she was awake. Bree turned on her bedside lamp and broke the morning silence when she started to dry her hair, which only made me curl up tighter in bed, and I promised myself to try not to think about what Joe was doing for the rest of the day. It was almost a new year, a time to make a new start and be positive about the future. And I, for one, was positive that my future included a job in advertising. I dreamt of collaborating with one of those young, dynamic, creative teams of professionals at a major newspaper or in some plush ad agency downtown. But as they say, first you've got to "get your feet wet", "get a foot in the door" and all that.

So, to get my feet wet, I applied at every job I could find that had anything to do with advertising, and as fate would have it, right before Christmas, I got hired to work part-time *selling ad-space* at a local weekly newspaper — the Canyon Beacon. When they told me I could have the job, I was so excited that I actually had a job *in the industry* that I ran home and told Joe that I was finally getting my feet wet.

"Get this! I landed a job at a *newspaper* and I start next month!" I exclaimed.

"What? You got a paper route?" he asked.

"No, smart ass. Really," I said, "at the Beacon, I'll be a bonafide in-training Advertising Sales Representative."

Maybe that should have told me something then.

"Good morning," Maddie sang as she left the bathroom brushing her blond bob. "Your turn!"

"Morning," I mumbled.

I got up, made my way to the shower and miraculously, by 8:30 a.m. we were all dressed in ski suits in varying shades of blue and ready for breakfast.

We went downstairs to the front desk of the small hotel where a disheveled young man wearing a ski hat was sitting behind a dark front-desk, only a few people were milling around in the lobby, where it was mysteriously quiet. From the looks of it, I wondered if there would be anything going on at all here for New Years. I mean, it was way up here somewhere in the mountains. Who would come up here?

"Lilly, are you OK?" Maddie asked me with a look of concern.

"No. Fuck, I'm sorry. I think I already need a time-out," I said as I started walking towards the front door. "Can you guys get direction at the front desk? I'm going to the car and get a breath of fresh air," I called out to Bree.

"Fresh air. Right," Bree called back as I went outside.

Snow flurried around the rustic cafe — The Golden Nugget — that hugged the side of the mountain on the other side of the parking lot. It had the same faded blue stripe running through the middle of the building, hinting to its association to the Miner's Inn. I hurried through the parking lot to Maddie's red Mustang and looked for my cigarettes, which I found crammed and crushed in the glove box. There was one left and it was broken, but I was determined. Despite the freezing temperatures, I steadied my shaking hands to light the last half cigarette that had been spared as I noticed the huge pine trees that cast an early morning shadow over the entire valley.

Beep!

My phone announced a new message, which turned out to be a repeat of Miss Teri's message from this morning.

You meet someone interesting head on...

Yeah, yeah, yeah, I thought. Who am I going to meet head on out here? I turned it back off as I took refuge in the calm quietness that comes when everything is covered in snow. However, being that I only had half of a cigarette, my moment of serenity ended much too quickly and was officially over as Maddie bounced outside, her voice ringing over the parking lot.

"We're ready! Let's go eat! Hurry up!" she called, a tick left over from her glory days as a cheerleader.

"Are they expecting a New Year's rush?" I asked approaching her.

"How should I know?" she asked as she blew her breath into her palms. "Anyway, you're smoking at 9:00 o'clock in the morning. That's disgusting."

"Oh no," I stepped on the rest of the cigarette, "I see you've been out here too long. I can still remember a time when you practically lived off coffee and cigarettes, regardless of the time of day."

"Well, that was then, and this is now. Whatever. They're your lungs," Maddie said, now pulling on her gloves. "Anyway, breakfast is in the cafe and we have to go down the road to get to the ski lifts. That's also where the ski rentals are. So let's hurry, I can't wait!"

We followed Maddie across the snow-packed parking lot to the other box-like wooden building: a tiny establishment that begged you to go in and spend some time chatting and drinking coffee, but no, we were in a hurry to get to the lifts, so instead, we inhaled our scrambled eggs, orange juice and coffee and started down the road to a posher ski resort where the ski lifts were. When we got there, tons of people were already lined up to buy lift tickets and rent ski gear, and after another half an hour, we were on our way.

"The main thing is to try to stay together," Maddie instructed us as we sat on the benches near the counter putting on our gear. "But . . .I mean, you guys do have your cell phones, don't you?" she asked.

"Of course," Bree said, "but just make sure yours are on. I haven't been skiing in decades."

"Well, just in case anything happens, if anyone gets lost, we'll meet back here around noon and again at three. OK?"

"OK," Bree and I said simultaneously as we agreed to her terms and after watching what everyone else was doing with their skis, we just did what they were doing: picking up the skis, hoisting them over the shoulder – and voilà! Like real pros as we hobbled outside and headed for the lifts.

"Make sure you always watch behind you," Maddie said, as she walked behind me, and just as I turned around to catch what she was saying, I bumped Bree's head with my ski.

"Hello!?" Bree cried. "Wake up!"

"That's exactly what I mean," Maddie reprimanded with a fake smile. "You have to be careful with the skis. Remember: there's probably always someone behind you."

"Sorry, Bree, Guess Maddie's just worried that something is going to happen.

"Because it usually does with you around," she teased, although the first near-miss was already at hand.

I saw her point and was now also a little weary myself of what might come as we jumped on the ski-lift and rode up to the top of the mountain. It was beautiful with the snow and the deep blue sky, but I felt out of my element, overwhelmed, even, and thought I might need to get back down quickly to lower elevations, so I checked out the paths, opted for an easy green run and started my descent.

"Look, Mom! No hands!" I called to Maddie as I reached her at the bottom, surprised that I had made it down the slope without plowing someone down.

We scooted back over to the ski lift, now officially into our first ski day. A second run, a third, and to my surprise, they went without incident. Smooth, you could almost say. In fact, the entire day went rather well, and I wondered where was the catch?

Around four o'clock it already started getting dark. We change back into our regular shoes and hiked back to the hotel with all our gear in hand and over the shoulders. As we stumbled through the lobby in single-file, the front-desk guy was still sitting behind the counter and stopped us half way through the lodge.

"You know, there are lockers in the back of the restaurant right across the parking lot." He pointed to the Golden Nugget. "It's first come, first serve, so if you want one, you better go ahead and take one now." He didn't wait for an answer and gave us each a key to a locker to store our things.

"Well, then let's go put our gear in the lockers first," Maddie said. We agreed and walked slowly back to the rustic restaurant, where there was a sign on the door of the Golden Nugget.

"Oh, check this out! Karaoke Rockin' New Year's Eve!" Bree exclaimed, "You guys ready for some soul-sister singing?"

Oh no. Images came rushing back to me from the last time I saw Bree singing drunk karaoke and we had to rush her off the stage before she puked on it.

"Is it the return of the *Inebriated Chanteuse?*" I asked hesitantly.

"That was three years ago. Don't you ever forget anything?" she asked.

"I know, I know. And the image is still with me."

I shuddered as Maddie laughed the silent laugh.

"Come on, party pooper," she said, "It's New Year's Eve. We're here! No need to bring up past horror stories."

"I know, I know. I'm trying to switch modes," I said, acknowledging my less-than-cheery mood. "I'm just not the bundle of energy that you both are, I guess."

We walked into the dark restaurant, which was much louder and fuller than you would have suspected from being outside. The lockers and restrooms were on one side of the restaurant, a lounge area on the other, and a bar was in the middle with a band playing in the back.

We stuffed out gear in the lockers and walked up to the bar.

"It's après ski till seven o'clock. Half price drinks. Should we stay for a beer?" Maddie asked reading a sign on the bar.

In Amsterdam, it must have been around midnight or even one o'clock. I wondered if Joe had called.

"Stupid question," Bree said as she turned and order three draws from the bartender.

"Do you want to stay at the bar or should we go sit down somewhere?" I asked.

We looked around and saw an empty table in the back of the room, and we decided to sit down.

"I'll get this round, you the next one?" I asked digging around for my wallet.

"I'll go save the table before someone grabs it," Bree said. She swung her purse over her shoulder as she picked up the glasses as soon as the bartender put them on the bar, and off she marched to the table, while I dug some more under the watchful eyes of the said bartender.

"Damn it."

"What now?"

Embarrassed, I realized that along with my gear I must have left my wallet in my butt-pack in the locker.

"OK. I'll pay this round," Maddie offered.

"Thanks. I'm gonna go get my butt-pack and I'll be right over."

As I reached the lockers, a guy was crouched down fumbling around in front of his locker which was directly beneath mine. I waited patiently for about a minute before I started tapping my foot and whistling in the direction of the blond hair, but the man didn't seem to notice at all that I needed to get past him. *Are all men so egotistical?* I thought to myself and went forward, reached above him and inserted my key in the keyhole.

"Excuse me," I said loudly, and in a split second, as I opened the door, my bag and a ski boot slid out and hit the guy right in the small of his neck.

"*Au, Scheiße!*" the man yelled and held onto his neck.

"Oh my God! I'm so sorry," I apologized frantically. "Are you OK?"

He looked at his hand, and there was blood on his fingers! And my impatience quickly escalated into near panic.

"My God, you're bleeding," I said hastily, trying to keep my cool while I was really thinking, *oh shit!*

"*Ja.* — I mean, am I?" he asked.

His dark blond, curly hair tousled around his face, and the rest of his face looked chapped and sun-burned beneath a five-day beard.

"Please, let me have a look. I'm so sorry." I straightened his hair over to the side with shaking hands and saw a gash on the back of his neck. Instinctively I grabbed my bag out of the locker and fished around until I found some tissues.

"Here, turn around." I dabbed the gash, which luckily looked worse than it was, I saw after it was cleaned.

"I'm sure it's OK," he said, more to himself than to me. "It's probably really just a scratch." He held onto the back of his neck as he looked up at me.

OK. His neck is still moving. He is conscious.

"I think I'm alright," he said convincingly, but his dark blue eyes, surrounded by skin that was left pale from wearing ski goggles, revealed something else. "Really, it's OK," he repeated. "I'll be alright."

He said "alright" kind of like "aw-rite" with some kind of accent.

"Now, maybe I match my sunglasses," he said as he demonstratively held up a pair of badly scratched goggles that he'd been inspecting. But at least now he seemed to be joking. Relieved, I thought that must be a good sign.

"I, um, I could go get some ice," I stammered. "It might lessen the swelling."

"No, I'm alright, really."

The accent was more audible this time. Swedish? German? I couldn't tell.

"OK, then," I said with shame, unable to look him in the face. "I'm sorry."

I grabbed my pack and quickly pushed the rest of all my gear and my coat further back into my locker. I pressed the locker door hard to make sure it shut and left in a wave of embarrassment.

As I went back to the table, I could hear my phone beeping in my pack. Maybe a New Year's greeting? I thought with anticipation. Maybe one from Joe? There was a nine-hour time difference, so he must have already had the stroke of midnight.

I pulled out my phone.

"Two calls," I announced. "One from Mom and one from Sybille. At least they remember me. Oh, and one message from Miss Teri."

But there was still nothing from Joe. I looked at the time: four thirty-three Amsterdam time. Ouch. This was beginning to hurt. Suddenly a part of me wanted to go back to the hotel and curl up with warm water bottle and tea, but then I got the more realistic vision of me in the bed, crying into my pillow with a bottle of wine and cigarettes surrounding the bed.

No. The risk was far too great, and I was fairly sure, this course of action wouldn't make him call any sooner. I leaned back in my chair and sighed when Bree and Maddie started looking at me with wide eyes.

"I'm sorry, OK? Just give me a little more time; I'll be the life of the party. I think I've just had a bit much for today," I apologized and closed my eyes for a second.

"What's wrong *now*?" Bree asked.

They stared at each other before Bree put on her sweet-talk voice.

"Lil, come...come back to us," she said slowly, hypnotizing me back.

"Yeah, we're here now. Let's try to forget about everything else for now, can we? I mean, I'm sure, everything is fine," Maddie said. "or, is there something *else* bothering you?"

Just then, I spotted the blond guy walking across the room. His head was still intact which was probably a good thing, since, even from this distance, it looked like nice head to keep in one piece.

He went to a table where several other guys in their mid-twenties were sitting and as he turned to sit down, he caught me looking at him and I instinctively sunk in my chair, trying to hide behind my beer glass.

"You are acting so weird! Jesus, Lilly! What are you doing?" Bree asked under her breath, her patience wearing. "You look like you're about to melt into the floor. What is the matter with you?" She was clearly embarrassed.

"That guy over there," I whispered, as if he could hear me.

"What do you mean, 'That guy?' Over where?" She turned around so quickly that it drew even more attention to us.

"Don't look!" I hissed. "He'll think I'm looking at him!"

"You were looking at him," Maddie pointed out.

"Well, he doesn't need to see me looking at him."

"Oh. I see." Her eyes started to roll.

Beep!

My phone. Joe, finally? A bit of relief waved over me at the thought of him finally calling, plus I now had an excuse to stay under the table – out of anyone's field of vision. I tapped the phone's glass, only to find the same new / old messages from Miss Teri:

You meet someone interesting head on.

I hit the exit button on my phone but instead of turning off, the horoscope popped back up again. "Crap. This is so weird. This app won't close." But here, look at this." I showed them my horoscope, hoping it would explain everything quickly. "When I went to get my butt pack, my ski boot fell out of my locker — nearly decapitating that guy. He's from . . . I don't know where he's from. I mean, I think I gave him a concussion. I just hope I haven't caused some kind of international incident. You know, I've been trying to not think about international incidences."

There was a short pause while they still stared on the screen.

"You think *that* guy's in your horoscope?" Maddie took notice. "And you were worried that Joe was going to have all the international fun," she teased. "Here, drink your beer and calm down. At least you don't have to go to the red-light district to have fun."

"Yeah, maybe it'll come to you!" Bree laughed.

"Maybe you're right." I took a big sip. "When I read this, I thought it's kind of funny. I mean, now, I can also say I hit on some foreign guy. Ha ha." I laughed.

"Do that," Bree said.

"Well, by looking at him, he doesn't look hurt," Maddie observed. "But if he is, you should think about making amends with him," she whispered aside.

"Hi there, ladies." A short, tanned waitress appeared at the table and began her memorized lines, "Happy New Year Hamburger and Fries are on special today. More New Year's specials are up on the board. Can I bring you something right now?"

We all directed our attention to the Specials Board.

"I'll take the hamburger and fries," I said quickly.

"Me too," said Maddie.

"I'll have a coffee and a bowl of tomato soup," said Bree. "I'm still freezing."

"And I'll have another beer," I said.

"Me too," called Maddie.

The waitress disappeared and I scooted my chair to position myself so that I could watch the band, conveniently in the opposite direction of my victim.

The waitress came back with our drinks and food, and just as we had finished eating, the music died down.

"We're going to take a break," the singer announced, "so we'll leave y'all to your own devices for a little while here with the Karaoke. Mics are over here. Instruments are off limits! We'll be back after the break."

"Come on before anyone else gets up there!" Maddie urged, grabbing Bree by the arm to go off to the karaoke stage.

"Good idea," I said.

"Any requests?" Maddie teased. "This one goes out to . .?"

"Don't you dare," I warned.

They went to the guy manning the Karaoke machine and requested a song and returned after a short series of 80's One Hit Wonders.

"We're back — *the Inebriated Chanteuses*," Maddie said in my face as they came back just long enough to down a beer and then went back to scan more songs in the Karaoke machine.

I listened as long as I could, then thought I better call my mom back and tossed around the idea of texting Joe or calling him to wish him a Happy New Year.

"I'll be back in a few minutes," I mouthed to Bree on stage as I stood up and gestured to the door to go outside. My coat was in the locker, so I made a quick stop and as I turned, the blond guy was also there, standing in the way again, but at least standing this time.

He managed a cautious smile when he saw me and stepped aside. "You first," he said, holding out his hand to my locker.

Almost immediately, I could feel the heat rise. Why was I embarrassed? I hoped my cowl neck sweater was hiding my blushing, flushed neck.

"I'm prepared to catch any falling gear this time," I announced as I walked past him. I inserted the key and turned it while he stood behind me, waiting, and I could feel him looking at me. I quickly grabbed my coat out of my locker and closed it turning the key.

"OK," I said as I turned, "I think you're safe."

I expected him to open his locker, too, but he didn't. He just stood there, kind of in my way, in close enough proximity that I could smell his cologne, or maybe it was just him. I don't know how long I stood there.

"Well, I . . . um, I have to go and . . . call my Mom," I said as I pulled on my coat and walked by.

"Thanks," he said as I made my way around him and walked out past the bar. I saw Bree watching me, so I raised my phone to indicate that I was going outside, and shook my head trying to shake off the previous five minutes. I turned on my phone to call Mom, but my horoscope popped back up again.

"OK, OK. Shit," I mumbled, closing the app and then dialing home. The phone rang several times before the answering machine flipped on.

"Hello. This is the Dumont residence. Please leave a message after the beep."

"Hi! Happy New Year!" I called into the answering machine. "Just wanted to check back in. I got the message that you called. We're leaving on the second, so I'll try to call back tomorrow. Hope you all are having a wonderful New Year's Eve."

I disconnected and wondered again if I should at least text Joe. But, after *his* last phone call, I didn't know if I wished him a Happy New Year's Eve or not. It wasn't like he had texted or called me, and where he was, it was already New Year's. Probably more like New Year's lunch, even.

I went back inside the Golden Nugget and decided to go into the lounge where it was still kind of empty and sat down at one of the dark wooden tables. There were dimly lit faux candles on the wall and a long, rectangle window where I could still see some of what was going on in the main restaurant area. The band was back on stage, but from here, it just wasn't as loud.

I ordered a beer, answered Sybille's message and considered posting tons of pictures of us all over the slopes having the best time, thinking it might indicate to viewers that I was totally too busy to even look at my phone to know if they had gotten in touch or not. But then I just sent a few pictures to Sybille. Just have a good time, I told myself. Forget the rest for now. Forget it.

The waitress brought me my beer, and when she turned around to leave, I saw the blond guy behind her sitting on the other side of the lounge. He saw me and smiled lifting his own beer glass. Instinctively, I waved back, then I thought I should go and apologize properly, maybe make sure he was really OK. I walked over.

"Hey, we meet again," I said. "How's your neck?"

"Well," he answered quietly, putting his hand on his neck. "It's still there." His smile was crooked. I noticed a scar in the middle of his chin, deep enough to be seen despite the four or five day shadow. Now he'll have a matching scar on the back of his neck.

"Look, I'm really sorry about earlier. I was just in such a rush", I said "I don't even know why."

"It is OK now. I hardly feel it anymore." He pointed to the other chair at the table. "Would you like to sit down?"

"Here? Um, sure. Why not — for a few minutes," I said putting my coat and bag on the back of the chair and sitting down.

"I hear some accent. Where are you from?"

"Cologne."

"Cologne?" I repeated.

"Germany," he added.

That figured.

"Oh, OK." Everything I could think of about Germany was stereotypical: cuckoo clocks, beer, Mercedes. I tried to get a mental picture, but I was caught so off guard and was only drawing a blank.

"So, do you come here often?" I asked, a lame attempt at starting a conversation.

"Not often, but I've been here before, actually. On a school trip."

Again, I was caught off guard. "A school trip?" I caught myself repeating his last statement again and started to feel a little awkward, but I was really surprised.

"Yah, but it's been several years ago", he went on. "I always wanted to come back."

"Is that where you learned English so well?"

"Is it good?" he asked unsure. "Well, there and at school. We all had to start taking English in the fifth grade: See the man. The man is in the van," he recited something he'd learned years ago.

"I guess you have to start somewhere."

"Now they start even earlier, third grade I think."

"Wow. I only speak English, and I have trouble with that. I mean, I had two years of French in High School. I think I can still say my name. Je m'appelle Lilly. But that's all I remember."

"So you are Lilly who learned some French?" It sounded much better the way he said it.

"Oh, right. Yes, well, I'm Lilly, who didn't learn French."

"Have you ever been there? To France?"

"I've never been so far outside of Texas. Just a couple of times to New Mexico, Oklahoma, you know? This is kind of a big thing for me. Actually, this is probably one of the most beautiful places I've ever been."

"That is where you're from? Texas?"

"Yeah," I answered.

"Texas. Ah, yes, J.R.," he replied.

"J.R.? You mean J.R. from Dallas? That's funny. You know J.R.? That's so old."

"The whole world knows J.R."

"And you? You're from Germany. That's somewhere around Holland, isn't it?" I couldn't resist.

He gave me a look that asked if I were serious. Deciding I was, he took a pen out of his pocket and drew a map of the States on a small napkin, scribbled some water on the picture and an amoeba that was supposed to be land on the other side of "the Pond". "U.S., U.K., Holland, Germany." He pointed to an "X" that marked Germany and said, "Here."

"Oh, OK." In the age of instant technology, I thought it was funny that a handwritten map on a napkin was the source of my information to European geography. But I still I felt like I was getting the inside scoop.

"So, I guess they're pretty close then, Germany and Holland?" I asked.

"Well, it's the next neighbor, what is it called? Neighbor country? Right?"

"OK, the next country," I said, somehow feeling the need to explain my lack of geographical knowledge. "It's just that I've never been so far out of Texas. I mean, I didn't do a year abroad in college, and I wasn't an army brat or anything like that."

"Well, it's not like I know where every state is over here, either," he admitted.

His geographical knowledge was obviously better than mine, but he wasn't smug or arrogant about it, and somehow that made me feel better.

I smiled at him, and our eyes met for a stretched second as he also smiled. Embarrassed, I quickly started to scan over the menu, hoping I looked more composed than I felt.

"So, tell me, do you have micro-breweries in Germany?"

"Yeah, well, I guess so. We have a lot of breweries, also smaller ones where they serve beer and special traditional dishes."

"What a stupid question." I looked up at him lifting my hand to my mouth, "Of course you do. I mean, it's Germany! You guys are probably, like, world-leaders in micro-breweries."

He just stared.

"So, what's your favorite beer? Do you like St. Pauli or Paulaner beer better?" I asked quickly.

"I don't know," he answered. "I don't like Weizen, and I don't know St. Pauli. So, maybe St. Pauli."

"You don't *know* St. Pauli?" I asked in disbelief. "OK, now, you're totally messing up my stereotype here. I thought everyone knew St. Pauli. Isn't it like *the* German beer?"

"Not in Cologne."

The waitress came to our table.

"I'll have another one, please," he ordered. "You?"

"Yeah, me too." I said. "OK, well, what kind of beer do you have in Cologne?"

"*Kölsch*, for example."

"I don't think they have that here. I've never heard of it anyway."

"Well, Kölsch is very good. You should try it sometime."

"OK, if I ever see it, I will."

The waitress returned with the freshly tapped beer and disappeared again. He looked at me for a moment in silence before finally lifting his glass.

"*Prost*," he said finally.

"Prost?"

"Cheers," he translated and we both took a drink.

"Oh, cheers."

"So what do you do, when you're not getting hit by ski boots?"

"I cook."

"You cook?" I asked surprised. "OK, so how'd you get over here?"

"I'm on holiday and just — you know, checking some things out," he said rather vaguely.

"So, isn't this, I don't know, kind of boring for you? I mean, you could be in Europe somewhere, with all the coffee shops and the red-light districts and all that."

He looked at me with question marks almost literally flying out of his eyes, and I immediately regretted saying it.

"Why should I go to a red-light district?" he asked a bit stunned.

"I don't know. I mean . . ." I stammered around not knowing if I should say what I knew was about to come out. "I actually have some friends who are in Amsterdam right now. OK, one of them is not just a friend. My boyfriend, actually. Anyway, so far, that's about all they have to write home about. So I just thought, well, that must be the big thing to do over there."

He sat silently with an awkward smile on his face and I was embarrassed that I had brought it up. Were there actually men out there who didn't think that was the thing to do?

"I'm sorry," I said, "I don't know why I'm telling you all this. I just met you. Maybe it's true what they say: Sometimes it's easier to talk to a complete stranger than to someone you know."

"Did you say 'boyfriend'?" he suddenly asked.

"Oh, yeah. We took separate vacations this year for New Year's Eve." I unexpectedly felt a trace of guilt.

He silently looked at me. Was he disappointed? No, get real, I thought. It was much more probable that he was just surprised that someone as awkward as myself would actually have something similar to a boyfriend.

"OK," he went on. "Well, you may just need an objective person to talk to, so, OK, I've been to Amsterdam, but it's not only red lights and coffee shops. I mean, I've been to the coffee shops as well," he laughed a little and looked like he was trying to find the right words.

"They have a good side to them, I admit. But the red-light district? OK, maybe you go down it once to say I've been there, you know, to look. But to hang out? I don't know. No, that's not me."

"Wow. I think you must be the only guy I've ever heard say *that*." I liked his answer, but I also wanted to change the subject quickly. I think he did, too.

"So, how long have you been here?"

"One week so far. There are two left."

"That's a long holiday. I hope your skiing won't be too messed up from my ski boot."

"It's starting to feel better. Maybe it's the beer. But I'm also leaving here in a few days." He showed his crooked smile. "What about you? How long have you been here?"

"Just a couple of days. First, we stayed with my cousin in Santa Cruz and then now we're here for New Year's. We leave the day after tomorrow. Have you ever been to Santa Cruz?"

"No."

"It's a lot of fun. Right on the ocean and all. It's so cool. I mean, I'd never been to the ocean. I'm from Amarillo."

"And where is Amarillo?" he asked.

I was glad that he didn't know exactly where Amarillo was. I saw a chance to regain some of my dignity and took another napkin to draw an "X" by California and another one for Texas.

"Two days by car, six hours by plane. Home to the Palo Duro Canyon." I chimed like the jingle from the ad on television.

"The what?"

"The Palo Duro Canyon — the second biggest hole in America, outside of the Grand Canyon," I said proudly.

"That must be nice," he said and smiled.

There was no way around it. This guy was gorgeous and I was finding it hard to concentrate on anything coherent to say. Or maybe it was the beer. Either way I was starting to feel like a giddy school girl, and not only was I getting tipsy, I also needed to go to the bathroom.

"I'll be right back," I said when I got up to excuse myself. "I have to go to the ladies' room." I reached back for my bag that was hanging over my chair, but it caught on the corner of the table, and in one less than graceful move I tugged on the strap, popping the bag over the corner where it hit his mug, knocking his beer over in his lap. Hastily, I grabbed a cloth napkin from the next table and tried to help him quickly soak up the beer from his lap, when I noticed that I was wildly scrubbing the top of his ski pants.

Stop, Lilly! *Stop!*

It was as if someone had flipped the off-switch on me. I stopped instantly.

"I'm sorry," I said blankly. "Ex. . .cuse me."

I handed him the napkin and walked away feeling the blood drain from my face. I reached the bathroom without any further incident where I sat down in the messy, white and terracotta stall.

You idiot! I whispered to myself. First the boot, now the beer! I was a total Calamity Jane! I could feel my heart beating fast with embarrassment and a lump in my throat. It was hard to convince myself that I still had some degree of sobriety or even some dignity, especially as I sat in the wet stall where I'd been noticeably longer than I needed to be. As I walked out and looked in the mirror I took several long breaths to calm myself down and washed my pale face. After

I'd calmed down, I went back to the table to find the man sitting there with a fresh, full beer.

"You're back." He smiled as he theatrically clutched onto his glass.

"I'm surprised you're still here," I whispered embarrassed. "I've been told that it's a little precarious to be around me. I'm sorry about the spill."

"It's alright. It was good."

It was *good*? Did he just say that?

"Was it?" I laughed.

"I mean, it's alright," he explained.

I sat back down, unable to not notice that he had taken off his sweater, revealing a black turtleneck shirt that stretched out across his broad shoulders.

"Is your sweater also soaked?" I asked, although I didn't really want to hear the answer.

"No. It was just getting too hot in here."

I was thinking the same thing as I strained to make a conscience effort to follow all the small talk advice I'd been reading for years. Keep cool, keep cool.

"Well, I'm really sorry about that," I whispered.

"Maybe we can start over," he suggested.

"Good idea", I was relieved. "Very good idea."

"So tell me, what about you? What are you doing here?"

"I'm here on vacation with my friends. We're celebrating our upcoming graduation. It's in May." I took another sip of my beer. "Actually, Maddie is my cousin, she lives in Santa Cruz. So my best friend Bree and I are here to visit her."

"Is that them?" he asked, pointing through the plastic window behind me where he could see up to the stage.

I turned around and could hardly suppress a gasp when I witnessed Bree and Maddie shaking their hair as they sang their hearts out doing karaoke, as Maddie sang off-key and high-pitched into the microphone.

"*Them*?" I heard myself ask trying to sound as normal as possible. "No. I don't know them." I mumbled as I looked down shaking my head, ashamed of myself.

He didn't say anything, but when I cautiously looked up at him, he was looking at me over the rim of his beer glass with a sparkle in his eyes. A sparkle and a big grin that disclosed he saw right through my story.

I swallowed hard, embarrassed that I'd been figured out, and changed the subject immediately. I checked my phone. There was one new message: "Happy New Year! Have fun and look forward to this new year with all the new chances. From Mom, Dad, Sybille, and Brett." But there was still not anything from Joe. It had been New Year's in Amsterdam for a while now, and when I started to think about it, (boyfriend away, boyfriend pissing me off, me on vacation, gorgeous guy, beer...) I felt all the ingredients of an oncoming royal fuck-up coming together: We talked some more, and before I knew it, we'd been talking for half the night. Despite myself, I was having fun talking with this stranger. That was when I decided I better try to do the right thing, and start some damage control: Go back to the hotel room.

"Are you OK?" he asked.

"Look, I better get going."

"You have to go so suddenly?" he asked.

"Yes, I know. I'm sorry."

I called over the waitress to pay my tab and put the change on the tray and the receipt in my bag.

"Well, it was nice to meet you, . . ."

"Marcus," he said, filling in the blank.

"It was nice to meet you, Marcus," I repeated. "I hope the rest of your trip is safe," I said and put the change and a tip in the plastic tray. "Maybe, I'll see you around."

I grabbed my coat and my bag and walked through the bar area, which was now much louder, and went outside. The temperature had dropped dramatically and it was still snowing. I walked around to the back, and leaned up against the building where it was not quite as windy, cigarettes in hand, the name Marcus going through my head, and I thought how ironic it was that Joe was in Europe supposedly not checking out the girls, and here I was, in California, *totally* not checking out some European guy.

The savory, warm smell of the pizza from the exhaust fan was drifting along between the snowflakes, and I could hear the buzz of the neon sign out by the street mixed with the thumping of the bass from the music inside. I pulled out my lighter, just about to light up my cigarette when I saw Marcus again.

"Are you following me?" I joked, but then instantly felt a pang of panic, because, what if he was? So I quickly tried to be casual and said, "I mean, do you also want to smoke a cigarette?"

He walked over to me, not taking his eyes off mine. "Well, I guess I am," he said, finally.

"Oh," I said, and another second went by. "By the way," I continued, "I just wanted to say, . . . um . . . that I have a . . . um . . ."

He moved in closer to me, and from inside, I could hear in the distance people yelling in the "Three! Two! One! . . .," and he kissed me.

I wanted to say something, anything, but the panic was gone, and anyway, I was breathless. I stood in disbelief that I was kissing him back. I could barely hear the band inside playing "Auld Lang Syne" when he suddenly looked at me softly and said "Happy New Year. "

"Happy New Year?"

I had totally lost track of time and reason. I could feel that my skin was flushed red and my head was telling me "Run!" while the rest of me was frozen in place.

I looked back up at him, and before I knew it, his hands were on either side of my face. I didn't know what to do. His eyes stared into mine, and I knew that, despite the sub-zero temperatures, I was melting. There was only the spicy scent of his tossed hair and the heat of his touch on my cheek as he kissed me again. And he kissed well.

I didn't think about anything else. Nothing. Until I heard Maddie's screeching voice making me jump.

"Lilly! You out here?" she called out loudly from the restaurant door.

"I'll be back in a minute," I answered her in a tone barely audible, unable to take my eyes off Marcus. I had dropped my cigarette in the snow and just from the corner of my eye saw her bounce around the edge of the house and stop dead.

"OK," she trilled when she found me not alone, and turned back.

"I can't . . . do this," I forced out, smiling apologetically, and rushed back to the entrance after Maddie.

Stupid, stupid, stupid! I thought as I tried to make my way through the crowd and across the restaurant, back to our table.

How can you meet someone when it is probably just a complete fluke that they are even in the same country, the same state at the same time as you are? Only to get kissed and have to fight waves of guilt and run off, making you look, and feel, like a complete freak. And this, oh God, is the start to my new year?

January 1. It was New Year's Day.

I woke up in the hotel room and checked my phone: Billy, Jessica, Sybille. That was it. My horoscope beeped, but I quickly turned it off, not needing any more scary impulses. I tried to focus on the day ahead, but I was still wondering what the hell had happened to Joe, and also, what the hell had happened to me.

Maddie and Bree woke up, and we had some breakfast before going to get our lift tickets. In blinding sunlight, loads of people were milling around and buying their ski passes in the crispy mountain air. I got my rental skis and, as I waited on Maddie and Bree to get theirs, I stared into the crowd. Maybe one of these people would be Marcus, I thought. In fact, I couldn't seem to shake off the thought of him. I had only just met him, and here I was looking for his face in the crowd, scared that I would run into him again and at the same time scared that I wouldn't. The memories of the night before were still completely with me, but no matter where I looked, there was no sign of him.

"What's up?" Bree asked when she came up behind me, making me jump with surprise. I was glad I had on sunglasses, hopeful that she couldn't read my eyes.

"Nothing," I answered. "Just waiting on you guys."

1

January

We got back from our trip on Thursday — exhausted and exhilarated at the same time. The bad news was that I never saw Marcus again, so I guess it was time to let him go.

But the good news was that after finally getting into ski mode on the slopes, we had a wonderful time, and I'd actually been able to forget about all the pressures that were waiting on me at home:

1) starting at the Canyon Beacon;

2) the pressure of graduation and

3) hearing about Joe's red-hot vacation in the red-light district.

"Lilly, you need to get up. You don't want to be late for your new job," Mom said as she came into my room.

Post-vacay bliss was now officially over.

"I'm up."

"No, you're awake, but you're not up. Up is up," she said in her stern voice as she closed the door.

Somehow, I couldn't get warm to the idea of getting up to go walk around in the freezing wind. I turned over just as my phone beeped, and I checked the messages — only my horoscope:

January 8 ☆☒☖

The New Year is in full swing! Take some time to look at the changes coming. Look closely at the things that zap your excess energy — maybe it's time to let some things go? Opposites is the name of the game.

I wasn't sure what was zapping my energy, I just knew that I needed some, so I got out of bed and walked down the hall to the kitchen where Dad had already made a fresh pot of coffee.

"Today's the big day?" he asked from behind his laptop.

"Yip."

I got a mug out of the cupboard and poured the coffee.

"It's not exactly the cool advertising firm I'd expected, but you know, it's a start. To get my feet wet and all."

I started my new part-time job at the Canyon Beacon Newspaper on Monday. There was an eight-week training phase where new employees worked on an hourly wage, and after eight weeks went to commission only.

I walked into the building and went to talk to the boss, Mr. Kinkaid, a short, balding man who was both the owner and the editor.

"Here you go, Lilly," he said, handing me a package with a copy of the current issue of the Canyon Beacon along with mock paper supplement.

"Here's the dummy of our 'Next Big Thing': The Easter Supplement. It's still a few weeks away, but it'll be here before you know it. Your job is to go out there and fill up all these little boxes with advertisers just like we talked about in training. Just go around to the local stores and tell 'em how they need to place their advertising dollars with the Beacon. 45,000 readers — all local."

"OK. Thanks, Mr. Kinkaid."

"And, don't forget these." He handed me a pack of generic business cards.

"Just fill in your name on some of the cards. They'll do until you get your own printed ones."

"Oh, got it." I said as I took the package and went back out to my car. I had business cards. Albeit generic. But business cards just the same.

Filled with a mixture of anticipation and doubt, I looked at a copy of the real paper. I was always surprised at how little interest the advertisers took in their ads, with so little attention to white space or balance and absolutely no care for focal points. I wondered how they could do that to themselves, but that, I was told, was not my concern.

"Here you get to experience the industry from another perspective," Mr. Kinkaid had said.

So, despite freezing temperatures, I made a list of shops that I hoped would be interested in advertising around Easter and planned my day of cold calls — no pun intended.

First, I went over to the Sal's Supermarket on Jenkins Street. I knew I'd always seen ads for them, but I wasn't sure if I'd seen the ads in the Beacon since I myself didn't even read it.

I walked into the market and over to one of the check-out lanes.

"Hi. I'm Lilly Dumont with the Canyon Beacon. Can I talk to the manager?" I asked the cashier.

She didn't answer me, but immediately afterwards, there was an announcement throughout the store, "Will to check-out lane 2, please — Will."

I waited, hoping that Will was the manager and that the cashier had not just left me standing there.

After a few minutes, a big guy wearing the rubber apron of a butcher still soiled with I wasn't sure what came up the aisle.

"Howdy, I'm Will. What can I do for you?"

I looked around, felt my neck and chest start to turn red with heat as I was getting a wave of stage fright came over me. I swallowed and gave it my best shot to deliver the lines I'd practiced so many times.

"Hi. My name is Lilly Dumont. I'm with the Canyon Beacon. Are you the manager?"

"That's right," he answered.

"Well, we will be having our annual Easter Supplement coming out in March. The response to this supplement is always big, so I'm in the neighborhood to make sure that local merchants like Sal's Supermarket get the chance to place their Easter ads before the slots are all gone." Then I smiled.

Will, the butcher, looked at me for a second. "Canyon Beacon, you say?"

"Yes, sir." I handed him a generic business card that I had written my name on.

"Lilly Dumont with the Canyon Beacon. I'm the new advertising sales representative." I tried to say it with authority. "If you sign up today for four ads, I'm authorized to give you a ten percent discount."

I upped the ante, sure he would be right back with his check book. He looked at his watch and then at me and said simply, "Uh, no thanks — we've already done all of our advertising this quarter, and I don't think Sal likes that paper."

"Oh. I see." I felt like I'd heard him wrong or that he must not have understood me correctly.

"But thanks anyway," he said as he turned around and walked back down the aisle.

For this response I was unprepared. During training, Mr. Kinkaid had gone over a few points with about what to say when people come up with excuses. They don't have enough money or we're non-profit (and "non-profit doesn't mean no-money," he'd said) but that they "didn't like" the paper was not one of the excuses he'd mentioned.

"Yeah. Um, right," I said, and I also turned around and went back out into the freezing cold, back to my car.

I tried not to get discouraged, but the next two cold calls also didn't really go as I had hoped they would. I was supposed to be getting my feet wet but so far, all I'd accomplished was getting a few nasty blisters on my feet from walking around door-to-door and chapped cheeks from wandering around in freezing temperatures.

So, instead of risking more chapped skin and blisters, I met Bree at the Sports Bar and re-capped to her my first day over coffee with Baileys.

"So, I guess this is it. My dream job," I surrendered.

"Give it a chance. Maybe, it'll turn out better than you think," Bree encouraged.

"Did I tell you I applied at the yellow pages call-center?" I asked.

"Do you really want to do that?" she asked.

"At least, I wouldn't be flat-footing cold calls out on the street."

"True."

"And hey, if the job's in-doors and not on a commission basis, then it's just sitting in a lonely cubicle with a regular pay wage."

Bree looked at me with a "no comment" expression.

"OK, you're right. I know I have wonderful choices: lonely cubicle or flat-footing it out on the street. This was just *not* what I had in mind."

"Don't worry so much about it," Bree reassured me. "There's still five months to go before graduation. Just get some experience, and the right thing will come when it's supposed to."

This was easy for her to say. She'd already had several interviews at the job fairs and even one offer which she turned down, but still, I listened to her not only because she'd been my best friend since fifth grade but also because she always seemed to me to be little more in touch with things and inherently *just knew* certain things. Maybe that was because, on account of her being one sixty-forth — Native American Indian - and had an Indian Card to prove it. That might sound silly now, but when your ten years old, it was impressive, and I still wondered sometimes.

Next week would be the first day of my last semester. Sixteen more weeks, and then I would be free! And then? — And then, I didn't know what I would be doing. Living at home for forever was the one thing that I didn't want to do, but somehow, I kept getting the feeling that I wouldn't be moving out anytime soon.

Of course, that wasn't the only thing on my mind. There was also the issue of Joe, my tall, dark and handsome significant other. His post-graduation plans of working at his dad's garage had been set for a long time. He already worked there on weekends or at least, he did when he wasn't hanging out with the guys from his fraternity, Pi Beta Psi. For the boys of the Pi Beta Psi, turning twenty-one years old came with a rite-of-passage, a time-honored tradition consisting of a first official and legal trip to "The Doll House Gentlemen's Club" also known to some people around here simply as "the local strip-bar". Joe, being a good-standing member of P.B., said he felt an obligation to support his fraternity brothers by attending all the celebrations of their various milestones as they happened. But somehow it was a tradition that didn't set well with me.

"My God, Lil, it's not like you turn twenty-one every day," he would object to my objections.

And then, his trip to Amsterdam had just made things worse.

33

"You're a prude American, Lil," he declared after he had come back, now going so far as to defend their excursions as based on *cultural value*.

Prude American? I thought. The more he went on about sowing oats, the more it bothered me. But I couldn't blame him completely, because while Joe was going on about his European escapades in Amsterdam, the incident with Marcus replayed in my head, so much so that I decided to try to find him on the internet, but I only had the words "Marcus," "cook" and "Cologne" to work with, and I didn't get very far. Finding out that there were thousands of Marcus' in the Cologne area, not to mention however many that were not listed, left me hopeless. And the more I searched, the more I started feeling like a stalker. So, I stopped looking, but somehow that didn't stop me from thinking about him.

2

February

February 6 ☑☀♞

Super Bowl Watch Party at work? Nothing wrong with mixing business and pleasure. Invite your friends over to watch as fresh energy reigns, giving you much needed creative impulses. Watch for clues in conversations with intimate relationships as new ideas pop up. Around the 14th, lovers beware: surprises could be demotivating or cause a setback.

Fresh energy? I needed it! My last semester in college had just started, and I was more than ready to graduate. 15 more weeks — how hard can it be? I thought. The bulk of my work consisted of analyzing ad campaigns, and while Dr. Garfield, my professor, said it shouldn't be all that difficult, I was having a hard time analyzing anything at all. At this point, I just wanted was to make a decent passing grade.

Maybe my brain was frozen due to the freezing temperatures. In Amarillo, where the summers are blazing hot with temperatures easily in the hundreds for months at a time, the bitter, windy cold that comes with February always catches me by surprise.

It was on one of these terribly cold winter afternoons with a wind chill factor around minus twelve degrees that the Super Bowl was to be played. Bobby Brewer was having a watch party later in the afternoon, and Joe and I had decided to go.

I got up around ten, took a hot shower, and around eleven, Joe called.

"I have a lot of errands to run. Would you go over to the store and get two twelve packs and some of that cheese dip and chips? I'll pay you back at Bobby's," he said.

There were lots of other things that I could think of to do besides venture out on a beer run having to put up with party crowds in minus twelve-degree weather, but hey, this *was* the *Super Bowl!*

"And what do I get for this?" I probed.

"Don't worry," he assured me, "I'll make it worth your while."

My dad was already sitting on the couch watching pre-game commentaries on TV while he waited on my sister Sybille and Brett who were coming over later to watch the game with him. I went into the living room when the phone rang again. It was Bree.

"I have news. You're not going to believe this." Her voice loaded with excitement.

"The games have been cancelled?"

"No, seriously," she said eagerly.

"I don't know. Leave out the suspense. Come on, tell me. What's up?"

"I don't want to get too excited too quick," her pause intensified the moment, "but I got the job. Tulsa Medical called this morning and said that I could start at the end of summer."

"Oh my God." I said, as I instantly felt tiny simultaneous stabs of sadness and happiness.

"I can't believe it," she cooed reluctantly.

I couldn't either. Bree had gotten scooped up by a scout for a medical supply company at a job fair.

"Congratulations," I said cheerfully. "I think I'm jealous."

I was happy for her. Really, I was. But at the same time, I was also sad, since this meant she would be leaving. But this wasn't about me.

"Well, I guess, now there's even more reason to celebrate," I said.

"I'll see you later at Bobby's." I exhaled again and turned my attention back to the living room.

"Dad, can you loan me thirty dollars? I'll pay you back later."

He sighed and took out his wallet.

"Should I put this on your tab?" he asked half joking.

"Yes, I'll give it back later, promise."

I went to battle my way through the supermarket, picked up the twelve-packs of beer and some chips and dip and finally arrived at Bobby's small wood-framed house in the university district of downtown around 5:30 p.m. What I thought was a friendly little get-together to watch the game turned out to be a full-blown party, and I couldn't tell how long they had all been there, but everyone was caught up in Super Bowl fever. Everyone, that is, except me. I was all caught up in a sentimental funk.

I walked through the back door which led into the kitchen. My shoes stuck to the beer-drenched linoleum on the floor and I fought through waves of smoke wafting through the air. The big screen in the living room was on and there was a sea of people wearing red jerseys sitting and standing around, all glaring at the television. I instinctively looked around for Bree and Joe who both apparently weren't there.

"Hey, Lil! Can I getcha a drink?" Billy Thompson chortled happily as he came up.

"Yeah, I could use one," I accepted.

I followed him into the kitchen where there were some guys playing quarters and a few girls sitting on the cabinets.

"That Daisy, man, she's a fuckin trip," one of the guys exclaimed."

"You guys are sick," a girl called from the cabinet, "That's some poor kid's dinner!"

"What? You don't know that. Besides, she's a lot lizard," he shouted, laughing.

"Where's Joe?" I turned and asked Billy.

"In the back room . . .," he said.

"Shh!" one of the guys at the table interrupted him.

"What?" I asked, "What's going on?"

"Nothin' Lil. Nothin'," Jack Miller answered, louder than need be.

Piquing my interest, I went down the hall to the back room and found Joe talking to Jake Lowry and a girl with long brown hair who I didn't know. They turned around in silence and were suddenly all looking at me.

"See ya," the girl said. She brushed past me and walked down the hallway, adding to my confusion.

"What's going on?" I took a deep breath.

"Nothing. Nothing, Lil." Joe stood up and kissed me on the cheek.

"Aren't you watching the game?" I asked, my interest now elevated to suspicion.

"Yeah, of course. Come on," he said as he attempted to guide me back through the house. "Why aren't you watching?"

"You know I'm only here for the commercials."

"Mixin' business with pleasure?"

"What?" Did he just say that, I wondered surprised. "I mean, who was that?" I asked, gesturing to the back room.

"Who? Them?" he asked.

"Well, yeah. The ones that were also in there."

"You know Jake Lowry, don't ya?"

38

"I know who he is, I guess."

"Well, that's all right. Don't worry about them. Let's just go watch the game," he slurred, already showing signs of inebriation while he changed the subject. That was when I started to notice more what was left unsaid, the white space. That space around the elements of a picture that pushes your attention one way or another.

We went back into the living room where the sound on the TV was so loud that the commercials seemed to rock the wooden frame of the entire house. In the commercial, there was no white space, at least not in the audio.

"There you are!" Bree beamed as she walked toward me. "It's freezing outside!" Her perma-grin turned to a look of concern as she neared.

"What's up?" she asked.

"Let's go in the garage. Its quieter."

We maneuvered our way through the kitchen and out the back door that led to the garage.

"You first," I said, wanting to hear her news.

"Well, they called yesterday to see if I was still interested, and of course I am, and they emailed me the confirmation this morning. If I still want the job, it's mine." She took a drink of beer. "I can't believe it."

"Me neither," I admitted. "Tulsa. Not too far, but also not too near."

"It's only about five hours. It's not like its cross-country," she assured me, picking up on my insecurity.

"No, of course not." I agreed. "It's just a morning drive, really."

"Exactly."

"So, when's the big day?"

"First of June," she said. "It's incredible. And they all seem so nice."

"Score!"

A loud roar came from inside the house.

"I'm happy for you, really. It's so exciting."

"But there's something wrong with you. What's up?"

"Nothing, really. I just . . . I don't know." I also took a drink. "I just have this weird feeling because I found Joe in one of the back rooms with that Jake Lowry and some girl, and I don't know. I just have a weird feeling, that's all. I don't want to talk about that right now. Let's talk about work."

"OK. How's work?"

"Not my work. I flat-foot half-inch newspaper ads for a dying newspaper, so there's not much to tell. Unless you're a podiatrist." I said, feeling a surge of self-pity. "Your work, - let's just celebrate your good fortune. Maybe some will rub off on me."

Bree rubbed up against me in the cold garage as we walked back towards the kitchen door.

"You'll find it, don't worry. I mean, really, we're not even out of school yet."

"Right," I agreed reluctantly.

After the game had ended, I looked for Joe again and found him in the sticky kitchen this time. "So," I anticipated his next move, "do you want to leave with me, or, you know, pass out here?"

Before he could answer, Jake Lowry called out to Joe from the hallway, "Hey Joe, you comin'?"

"Comin' where?" The tone of my voice went abruptly higher.

"Oh, I told you. Some of the guys wanna go see Mike Schneider off."

"And you want to go, too?" I asked, gritting my teeth.

"Yeah, I know. But Mike's leavin' next week, an' they wanna send him off good. You know how it is," he said, his words increasingly incoherent.

"Come on, Lil, everybody's goin'."

"Everybody?"

"Stop, Lil. We'll talk later," he said.

"I can't believe this. I guess the 'occasional twenty-first birthday party' is now getting stiff competition from life's other milestones. The Doll House: the locale of choice for going-away parties, bachelor-parties and now *Super Bowl Sunday*? Seriously?" I asked, trying to keep my contempt in check.

"Come on, Lil, don't be like that, Baby. I'll be back in no time," he assured me with his sugar-coated voice.

"I don't care where you go," I spat under my breath, trying not to make a scene. "Go see him off. Good riddance to him. You don't need to come back to me either, don't worry about it," I said as he turned.

"There you go again, bein' all goody-goody." He laughed as he walked through the kitchen door that led to the garage.

"I'm the prude American, remember?!" I yelled as I mentally strangle him. "And I want my thirty dollars!" I screamed, but he didn't hear me.

"Hey, Lil. Girl, you are *livid*! You ready for another cold one?" Bobby asked out of nowhere.

"Give it to me," I demanded as my blood pressure rose. I walked straight through the drunken crowd, through the kitchen and the living room, back to one of the back rooms where it was quieter and warmer than anywhere else and sat down on a piano bench when Bobby walked past the room and saw me.

"Here you are, and here you go," he said as he lifted his can to toast mine, and out of reflex, I raised my can to meet his. The cans hit each other with such a sloppy force that half the beer spilled out of them and directly down the arm of my dress.

"Whoops! Sorry, Lil. Let me get that for you," Billy said, sticking his tongue out to lick the beer off my arm.

"What the hell are you doing?" I slapped his head and snatched my arm back, repelled by his dripping tongue and realizing that I was not nearly in the same zone as most of the people here. It was time to go. With a beer-soaked dress, I told Bree good-bye, poured out what was left of my beer in the sink and left.

****

I hadn't seen Joe since the Super Bowl, and I was a little surprised when he actually called nearly a week later to ask me out.

"Hey, Lil," he greeted me on the phone as if nothing had happened. "It's our special day this week."

"What? President's Day?" I asked, trying to avoid the "special" day topic.

"OK, I probably deserve this. But, come on, Lil. You know it's Valentine's Day. How 'bout it, should I come around tomorrow?" he asked.

"Yeah, you can give me my thirty dollars."

"That's not all I can give you," he laughed.

"Get real. Are you sure you're not going to get some urgent need to slip into the Doll House? I don't think I could take that on Valentine's Day," I said, only half joking.

"You're all I need," he coaxed.

"Don't forget the thirty dollars," I said.

On Valentine's Day, around 7:35 p.m., I heard the loud, revved-up engine of his black Chevy Commander jeep from a block away as Joe came by to pick me up — fashionably late. When the doorbell rang, I opened the door to find Joe wearing a cowboy hat and holding some flowers in his hands.

"What?!" I asked surprised. "Where did you get that?"

"The flower shop."

"I mean the hat."

"Well, I read on the cover of a magazine that cowboy hats are supposed to be sexy, so I thought I better get one to make up to you."

"I don't like cowboy hats." I laughed.

"I didn't think so, but I thought I better try something to get back in your good graces."

"You're crazy."

"That's why you love me." He smiled and kissed me, almost picking me off my feet. "Anyways, it's only borrowed. Sorry I'm late. — Hey, Mrs. Dumont," Joe greeted my mom, who was peeking out of the kitchen down the hallway.

"Hello, Joe. Ya'll have a good time," she said, and drew back into the kitchen.

We drove through the sub-urban, grid-like neighborhood before getting on I-40 and zooming over to my favorite restaurant, Patty's Oyster Bar, on the other side of town, that had great views of the sunsets from the Florida room, a jazzy, New Orleans atmosphere, and the yummiest coconut shrimp in cuisine history. It was only an appetizer, but it was huge, so I ordered it with a beer.

"So, happy Valentine's Day," Joe said. He pulled out a small bag that had "Duty free!!!" written all over it.

I opened the bag to find a collection of perfumes — *Hypnotized*, *Lure*, *Free Spirit* and *Wonder*. All 4 ml miniatures.

"Thanks. They're lovely," I said.

"Didn't have a chance to wrap it."

"Oh, well . . . that's OK." I squinted my eyes, giving him my friendliest "don't-B.S.- me"-look. "It's only been five weeks since you got back, but thanks anyway."

"Couldn't help but think of you when I saw them." He gave me his perfect salesman smile.

"Did you try them, too? I mean, do you have a favorite, or should I just put them all on at once?" I asked, teasing.

He leaned in and gave me a kiss on the cheek.

"I don't care which one you wear, as long as that's all you're wearing." His long brown bangs hung in his chocolaty eyes, and I couldn't help but kiss him back.

I hadn't experienced Joe so relaxed in ages, and there I was: sucked back into a hopeful haze.

Despite that school had always come easy for Joe, for the last four months he'd been completely stressed-out from studying for his degree in Business. We had hardly found time to see one another since the onslaught of this final semester. Preparing for graduation had simply taken up too much time. And, OK, conflicting feelings about free-time activities didn't help.

"So, cheers to my favorite girl," he said smiling.

"Favorite?"

"Only!" he said quickly. "Only girl. You know that."

"Thanks," I said hesitantly smiling, scared that I had actually missed him a lot.

After dinner we left Patty's.

"Are you sure you can drive?" I asked. "You know you can't get another DUI."

"Don't worry, it's all good."

He started the jeep, and we went back to Joe's small apartment. I threw my purse and coat on a chair, and we sat down in the kitchen that barely had room for the two chairs and the small camping table that furnished it.

"Here, smell these." I gave him two opened bottles of perfume. "Which one do you like best?"

"This one," he said, handing back the *Hypnotized* " bottle.

Joe went to the refrigerator and got two beers out of the fridge while I dabbed on my new scent. As I noticed how his new red shirt complemented his olive complexion, I followed him.

"Here. Smell." I stretched out my arm.

"Hot," he said, pulling me up to him, and gave me a kiss that was just a bit too moist.

"*Hypnotized*." I corrected, wiping my mouth.

"Come here." He pulled on the low-cut V-neck of my dress, leading me out of the kitchen and into the living room. His dark brown eyes were always easy for me to melt into, and he gave me another sloppy kiss as he pulled me down on the couch. I helped him pull his shirt over his head while when it occurred to me that it had been a while since we'd actually been alone. Happy Valentine's Day. Why did I still want him?

The next morning, I woke up in Joe's arms, in Joe's warm bed. He still had a baby-face and seemed so peaceful. Seeing him like this in the morning, it was hard to believe he also had a shadow side that I despised. Had he sewn his oats? Was he turning back into my ornery but sweet-natured Joe? Joe, the Pi Beta Psi, not the Pi Alpha Psych? Everything seemed so normal as he lay beside me deeply sleeping.

I got up, put on my dress from last night and went in the kitchen where — surprise, surprise — there was no coffee and nothing for breakfast: the typical bachelor pad. Yip, everything seemed normal.

I got the keys to his jeep out of his jeans pocket, wrote a note and left to go to the Quick Stop to do some survival shopping.

Although it was only ten o'clock and freezing, the Texas sun was glaring. I opened the glove box to get out Joe's sunglasses and found the box of perfumes, at which point I became very confused, because I was sure that I had taken them inside last night. The box was still closed with plastic wrap and everything, but I was sure that I had opened it and had even tried it on for him.

I looked in the glove box again. Was I still drunk? I'd had a few beers yesterday but nothing too wild. I looked at the box. There was something else — another present, and this one was wrapped. Did he forget to give me something? I thought how sweet it was of him, and as I took the wrapped present in my hands like a child who'd just stumbled onto a Christmas present, I looked some more and noticed that the present was marked with a sticky note: "for Tayler".

Tayler? I thought completely befuddled. Tayler? Tayler with an "e"? Who the hell was Tayler? I was not Tayler. I tried not to panic, praying that somehow I must have gotten the wrong impression. I stuck the keys in the ignition and sped up to the Quik Stop. I don't know which was going faster: the Jeep's rpm's or my heart rate.

I jumped out of the jeep and ran in, not even feeling the need for a caffeine kick anymore. I wasn't sure what I should do. I bought the coffee and some pastries as if I would go back and just eat breakfast. This would all get cleared up, I thought, and everything would be back to normal, just like last night.

I got back into the jeep and somehow drove back to Joe's apartment complex, parked the jeep in a slot and got back out. I took a minute to try regaining some of my unstable composure, tried to think logically for a minute. I mean, Joe had gone out to the strip bars a few times. And that was only since recently. He wasn't a *cheater*.

My fears obviously had slipped a little too deep into my sub-conscience, I tried to rationalize and even started to feel guilty about me jumping to conclusions without even giving him a chance. Did I really have so little faith in him?

I went back to the jeep and got the perfumes and the present out of the glove box. Whatever was in there probably shouldn't be in the freezing temperature. I took them upstairs with me shaking just a bit. It was probably the cold. Coffee would probably do the trick - I rabidly started to make the coffee, and slammed the plates on the table as I set the table for two. I could hardly stand being there in his apartment looking at the presents and not knowing . . .

"Lil?" he finally called out.

The plate in my hand dropped on the counter. "Yeah?"

"You're making coffee already? Come back to bed!"

"Yeah," I answered. I picked up the present on my way back to the bedroom.

"Hey, can I ask you something?"

"Course," he said rolling over to look at me as I was standing in the door.

"Who's Tayler?" I asked, and my voice shook.

He saw the present in my hand, and I was shocked as his mouth opened but no words came out. The expression on his face was so honest, it was obvious what was going on.

"Lil. I can explain," he almost whispered very slowly. Or was that just my impression? Suddenly, everything he said became like in a dream with barely audible surround sound. I started hearing only sound bites: nothing, some girl, wanted to tell you.

"No need."

I couldn't take it. Couldn't hear it. This wasn't the way this was supposed to happen. Not to me. Not with him. Not on Valentine's Day.

I ran through the living room, grabbed my coat and the keys to the jeep and left the apartment as quickly as I could.

"Wait! Lil, come on, wait!" I heard him yell.

I got in the jeep and hurled the present on the floorboard before driving around aimlessly for a while, not sure where to go when the tears started pouring down my face. I lit up a cigarette, threw the pack in the passenger seat and called Bree from my cell phone.

"Hi Lil. — Lil? Is it you?"

"Are you up?" I asked tensely.

"Yeah. Why? What's up?"

I exhaled loudly.

"Can I come and get you? Can we go to the canyon?"

"It's like nine thirty, but yeah, sure. Are you OK, Lil? What's the matter? Lil, speak to me!"

"I — I'll be right over. Just need to talk to you."

When I arrived at Bree's house, she looked at me with surprise in her eyes.

"Where is Joe?" she asked as she picked up my cigarettes and sat down in the passenger seat in Joe's jeep and then noticed the tears in my eyes.

"Oh God, what's the matter?" she asked, her voice laden with concern.

I wasn't able to look at her. "Can we just go to the canyon?" I forced out addressing the windshield as I drove silently. White space. The space where anything can happen. Bree didn't say anything.

"Not everyone goes to strip bars," I said as I got onto the highway.

"That's true," she agreed without further comment.

"You know, I've even met people who openly admit to *not* going to strip bars." My voice cracked in the middle of the sentence.

"OK." Confusion covered her words.

After half an hour of driving, we ended up thirty miles south of Amarillo on the outskirts of the Palo Duro Canyon. I started driving deep into the canyon and decided at some point I'd gone deep enough. I parked on a scenic turnout and got out of the car. It was freezing outside, but I let myself get distracted from the warn tones of the canyon as

48

the earthy reds rocks mixed with the shadows of the green shrubs.

"What's going on?" Bree asked, knowing something was clearly wrong. "Where's Joe?"

"At his apartment."

She looked at me, still trying to discover the problem.

"Did you guys get into a fight?"

I nodded.

"OK. Do you want to talk about it?" she asked patiently.

"I'm not sure how." I was still in a state of shock and took a few deep breaths trying not to cry.

Bree looked down to the floor and saw the package. She picked it up, read the note and looked at me dumbstruck.

"He has another girlfr . . ." I couldn't finish the sentence.

"Mother-fucker," I whispered.

"He's messing around with someone?" Bree held her breath for just a second. "Son of a bitch," she said dryly in disbelief as she gazed out the passenger window.

"I should've known. I should've seen it coming. He has some . . . Tay . . ."

I couldn't say it. I tried to explain it the best I could. I knew that Bree probably didn't believe that it was over. A small part of me didn't want it to, either. But somehow I knew it was. For good.

3

March

March 4 ◼️🖼️⑥🍎

Friendships blossom when you get in a deep conversation and reveal your wishes. You develop a plan to realize your dreams.

I tossed and turned in my bed while rage, humiliation and repulsion tossed and turned in me. I forced myself out of the fetal position long enough to go outside and smoke a cigarette.

"You need to quit that," Mom said as I walked back through the living room.

"Why? So I can live longer?" I went back to bed.

Joe had called a few times over the past couple of weeks, but I couldn't bring myself to talk to him. Not yet. And what would it be good for, anyway?

Instead, I spent a lot of time in bed. Between cigarettes and REM phases, as my head spun with questions: Did I complete the application for graduation on time? What is Joe doing? Is he also shriveling up somewhere? Did he get a disease that is painful and disgusting and possibly incurable? — Oh, and if so, oh God, please, let it have happened after we broke up!

50

Sybille and Bree came by more often than usual.

"Just try to concentrate on finals," Sybille suggested. "You should try to get a good grade in your last semester even if it is a fluff course. It would be better than messing it all up at this stage of the game."

"Fluff course. Right."

I'd tried that all day yesterday, but in my state of mind, analyzing advertisements was almost impossible. I watched as innocent ads suddenly they began to morph into tools of deceit and seduction. Every headline a shot in the heart. Every tag a mocking lure. And as I thought that, I picked up the 4ml miniatures and through it across the room, breaking the mirror on the wall.

"Or you could, you know, concentrate on work or something," Sybille continued carefully.

"I know. Maybe I should do that."

When I was able to function, my time was spent trying to meet all the many graduation obligations that all seemed to have serious deadlines. But mostly, I just felt sick and miserable. I'd missed so much work. Even Mr. Kinkaid called, wondering if I was OK and if I was coming in. He mentioned that I'd missed out a lot on the Easter Supplement, and after staying nearly two weeks in my bedroom with my head under the covers, I knew that I had to come out and get on with it. I really needed to work on the upcoming finals, not to mention my need for money. So, I talked myself into digging in my heels and make a few cold calls.

"Well, at least the fresh air will do you good," Mom said as I left.

I went in the office where Connie, the layout artist / secretary, stood waiting for me.

"Here is the mock-up of the 'Next Big Thing'."

A mock up. Wonderful word choice, I thought. I looked at the huge monitor behind her, a layout with four columns of one inch ads she had thrown together.

"Is that the supplement?" I asked.

"It is. But, as you can see, it's not filled in yet. Hint, hint."

"Yeah, I got it."

She handed me a paper with the title, "Springtime Home Improvement" printed across the top in seventy-two-point letters.

The four-week supplement will be running through the end of April," she chirped excitedly before pulling me aside and whispered confidentially, "and you kind of need to hit the pavement. These boxes here, they need to be filled!And here's a good chance to show Mr. Kinkaid what you've got."

"Thanks for the tip," I said and snatched the package from her sinewy fingers.

I drove around my territory and finally parked in front of the strip mall on Lincoln St.

Strip mall. My stomach hurt.

I walked down to the end of the shops, put on my best fake smile and went inside Mike's Lawn Mowers.

"Hi. My name is Lilly Dumont. I'm with the Canyon Beacon, Amarillo's local paper with complete metro saturation, and I'm here to inform you about our upcoming Home Improvement supplement coming out in April. The response for this supplement is always good, so I'm in the neighborhood to make sure that local merchants like Mike's Lawn Mowers get the chance to place their ads before the slots are all gone." Then I smiled and waited, remembering the rule that the first one who talks loses.

The beady-eyed clerk looked at me for a second from behind the counter. "Canyon Beacon?" was all he had to say.

"Yes, sir. Is the manager in today?" I asked, "Maybe I could speak to him."

"Well, you can't speak to *her*, I'm afraid. She's on vacation. But you'd have to talk to her, so, maybe you could come back next week," he said.

"Oh, of course," I said crestfallen. "Well, I'll be in the neighborhood all this week, so I'd really like to come back around. She can also call me if she needs anything," I said, handing him my generic card.

Two Guys Plumbing was at the other end, so I walked down the sidewalk and went it.

"Hi. My name is Lilly Dumont. I'm with the Canyon Beacon."

I delivered my spiel, and just then, at Two Guys Plumbing, that's when it happened.

"Yeah, we were just talking 'bout that the other day," the man behind the counter said quickly. "We kinda got behind in all the advertising. Things been kinda busy 'round here, ya know."

"Really?" I asked surprised.

"Yeah, but, you know, you kinda want to keep it that way, if ya know what mean. Even got the little ad from last time still here. I'm mean, it's been a year or two, but we can use this again, can't we?"

"Oh, you bet! Sure. Well, here's your opportunity!" I said, completely unprepared for a positive response. "Then you can just go on to work and not have to really worry about the advertising anymore, you know, 'cause, we've got you covered."

"Good, then let me just get the checkbook, and what did you say, we'd get a copy of that edition, right?" he asked, pulling out his pen.

"Oh, yes sir. You'll get that in the mail if you're not a regular subscriber."

"Well, I'll be looking out for it then. Who do I make this out to? The Canyon?" he asked restlessly.

"The Canyon Beacon, yes sir. That's um, regular fifty-four dollars, but I've been authorized to give a ten percent discount for paying up-front, so then that's, um," I looked at the price list to be sure, "forty-eight sixty."

"Well, then, here you go. And here's the ad," he said, handing me a CD.

"Yeah, great. Um, here's my card, and I think you just have to email the ad to the editor, Mr. Kinkaid. But I'll also give him this, and if you have any questions, just call. Or if they have any questions, I'll just call."

"OK, then," he said just as his phone rang, "Yeah, you do that. I better get this."

He made a gesture that kind of gave the impression that we were finished, so I packed the CD in my bag with the supplement package, waved good-bye, and with my heart racing, I floated back to my car. I couldn't believe I had actually made a sale. How was that so easy? Maybe my luck was changing, I thought as I raced back to the office.

"Mr. Kinkaid," I started, "I've got good news! I got an account!" I exclaimed as I gave him the paperwork and the CD.

"Great!" He smiled from behind his monitor.

"So, I thought I should give you this, although I told Ted, the guy at Two Guys Plumbing, that he might need to send it in per email."

"OK, I'll have a look at it," he said.

Totally motivated, I drove on through the neighborhood and stopped in Martinez Nursery and Curtains and More, but once again, no-one was biting. So, on Tuesday, I went back to the office and into Mr. Kinkaid's office where he sat behind his desk gazing into a computer monitor.

"I went on yesterday and tried several more businesses, but, I don't know, I guess I'm having some trouble getting more store owners to buy an ad."

Mr. Kinkaid stood up and guided me back out of his office and into the office space where my desk was.

"Lilly," he said finally, "this is Theresa." He gestured with his head to a small woman in her late thirties who was sitting at a desk across from mine. She smiled and squinted at me behind the dark rimmed glasses she was wearing. Her dark bangs hung in her face.

"She started working here last week while you were gone. She got two new customers this week. Maybe she can help you out," he finished, passing the buck quickly onto the next new Advertising Sales Representative, who watched me closely with an intensity rarely seen in people not on acid. I wondered if it were true that she already had two new accounts.

"I went to that old discount store," she confided in a tone normally used by people with secret agent status. "They're selling packs of legal pads — four — in — a — pack." She stopped and smiled before inserting a pregnant pause, and then: "Fifty — nine — cents," she continued with a weird satisfaction.

She looked around as if making sure no-one was listening before revealing national secrets as she pulled out her cell-phone.

"Look," she said, showing me a picture of an ad from ABC Discount. Then she continued to clearly and slowly articulate every syllable in fifty-nine cents like "fif—ty", pause for dramatic effect, "nine", pause for dramatic effect, "cents" — stop. She never broke the eye contact. She never even blinked. Maybe she just wanted to make sure I'd heard it correctly the first time, eliminating the need to repeat herself, and effectively keeping national security intact, along with her secret of how to convince people to actually take out an ad in this paper.

"Wow," I said, totally creeped out, "Guess you're really in the know."

"Yeah," she smiled.

"Well, gosh, just keep it up," I said and turned on my heel to leave quickly.

I got in my car, drove around a bit and stopped at the hardware stores, walked over to the paint store and then down the street to the vacuum repair store. I drove by the custom curtain store before stopping to eat lunch in front of the interior decorators store which, of course, was also closed for lunch. I did the same thing over and over for the whole week, and with each cold call I felt my self-confidence withering away in direct correlation to the blisters growing on my feet.

By definition, a Beacon was a symbol of hope, a guiding light. For me, it was a small, dingy, run-down local paper in an equally run-down part of town, that always seemed about two ads away from having to file bankruptcy. And while Theresa went on about the miracles of her newest contacts, I wondered what I'd done in my previous life to have to start my career like this. By Friday, I'd had it.

I called Bree to meet for lunch.

"Just come shoot me, would you? I've been to every fucking store on this side of town that should want to have something to do with spring cleaning and home improvement, but I've only had one sale!"

"Hey, you got a sale? Congratulations!"

"One solitary sale."

"It's a start."

"Yeah, but not enough to keep things going, you know."

"Have you been able to ask that new girl for some tips?"

"Theresa? I can't talk to her. She's a fucking freak! She's on acid or something. You can't even look her in the eyes, or you get trapped somehow." I shivered.

"Well — let's see. drastic situations call for drastic measures, and, I have classes until three, but it sounds like you need some serious pampering to offset all that negativity. I'll see if I can get out early, and then we could go have lunch and maybe get our nails done. How does that sound?"

"That sounds OK."

"OK? Well, how 'bout Margaritas and Mani-pedis?"

"Oh, that does sound better. You're right. Maybe I could walk around the mall for a while, faking work. I don't think I can take any more rejection."

"Margaritas and Mani-pedis. That'll do the trick. At least the girls at Ngyuyen's are usually happy to see us."

"With all the blisters on my feet, we'll see."

"Lil', stop already. I'll meet you in the mall around one-thirty at for mexican, OK?"

"Got it."

I drove out to the mall and walked around. I never noticed the lack of home improvement stores the mall had to offer before now. But to be honest, I was grateful, as it saved me from having a guilty conscious for not getting any ads. At least I showed up.

When I got around to the Mexican Food Joint a line was already formed around the corner, so I by-passed it and went to sit at the bar where the bartender set the complimentary appetizers in front of me.

"Hey there. Here's your chips and salsa. What can I get you to drink?"

"Just a water for now."

I started on the chips and salsa and waited for Bree, who finally showed up half an hour later.

"Sorry I'm late," she said, sitting in the bar-stool beside me. "One of the property managers in Tulsa called about an apartment. I don't know if I should rent a hotel for a while and look when I'm there, or go ahead and rent a small apartment from here."

"Getting a hotel might be cool. If you can afford it."

"Two margaritas and the Cheese Enchilads," she called out to the bartender, "Do you know what you want?"

"Make it two," I said.

"Yeah, I thought about that. I don't want to rent a place, you know, like an efficiency or something, and then it turns out its too small. Or I could get a larger apartment, and then it turns out I can't afford it. I thought about going up there next week-end to have a look around for myself. You wanna come with me?"

"A road trip? I'd love to. But, using what for money?"

"No luck?" she asked.

"Zilch. I even went to that creepy Kirby's Krack-fixer, you know where they fix houses that are about to fall apart with that hydraulic jack thing. Even *he* said no-way, and God knows there's enough houses around there that could use his services." I took a long drink of the Margarita. "You know, I dream of an office with a big window and wearing Armani suits and team meetings, things like that. Instead, I'm just gazing out of my windshield. At this rate, I won't even be able to afford to replace my shoes that I'm ruining."

"Maybe, you should buy a low-cut Armani suit." Bree nodded to the neckline of my shirt. "You know, dressing more 'professionally'?" She bent her index fingers in air quotes as she said 'professionally' and winked at me.

"What?! Um, no!" I shook my head in disbelief at her suggestion. "You can't be serious!"

"Hey, sex sales."

"I'm not selling sex." I said, my jaw tightening.

"Calm down, Lil. Comic relief. Ever heard of it?"

"Of course. It's just not funny. I don't really have a death wish. And besides, have you ever heard of non-existent cleavage?" I winked back with air quotes. "Or is that how you got your job?"

"No!" she exclaimed.

"See."

"OK, OK." She picked up a menu and started looking through it.

"Did I tell you, I have to do an analysis on an Amarillo wine ad? I don't know shit about wine. I mean, I don't even know when I should test it out."

"You do have some hurdles to jump over," she said.

After eating the enchiladas, we went to our double appointment at Nguyen's Wondernails, the mall's fingernail goddess, where I always 'wonder' they're saying behind their masks. In any case, my nails looks good, and I felt a little better.

When Monday rolled around, my nails still looked good, and I had enough confidence built up that I decided to dress a little more professional for work. I thought about which way to go: professional as in career oriented? Or professional as in hooker?

I looked through my wardrobe, only to see that my closet itself was in desperate need of "home improvement". I picked out a dark jacket over a low-cut tank top: career oriented with an optional shift, as the situation required.

Stuck in morning traffic, I smoked a cigarette on my way to work and mentally went over the route and the routine of the day ahead. At the same time, I was thinking ahead to selling the next "Next Big Thing": the Restaurant and Entertainment Guide which would be coming out in May. Maybe that issue would be more promising. Maybe the restaurant industry did more advertising.

I walked through the small dark office and grabbed a cup of coffee before going up to my desk. *Think: home improvement — home improvement*, I chanted to myself.

Theresa was already at her desk.

"Getting any new bites?" she asked.

"Oh, I'm hopeful," I lied. "How 'bout you?" I asked, a polite reflex.

"Duct Tape at Steve's," she answered at barely audible levels before practically mouthing the words "a doll—ar—thir—ty—nine." There was a definite effect in the way she spoke but I wasn't sure the impact it gave was really the one she was going for. Then again, she was the one who had actually sold a few ads.

"You do realize that they're going to *advertise* that, don't you, you know, publicly," I asked her. "I mean, it's not a secret, really."

Right then, Connie called up from downstairs, "Hey, Lilly! Mr. Kinkaid needs to talk to you."

Oh good, I thought, saved by the boss. I went downstairs to Mr. Kinkaid's office.

"Hi!" I said as I walked into his office. He sat behind his desk, concentrating on something important on his computer screen, lifting a finger gesturing for me to wait.

He finally looked up at me.

"Lilly, good that you're here. I wanted to talk to you."

"Oh, me you, too," I started. "I just wanted to let you know that I think I have some good ideas to start selling those spots for the Home Improvement ads, and I'm already looking around for some leads on restaurants for the next "Next Big Thing".

"That all sounds really good," he said, "but now, Lilly, you know that it's been eight weeks, and your initial training phase is over now."

I knew this was coming, but somehow I had sort of forgotten.

"I know. Right, you told me that."

"That means that after the first eight weeks, after building up a clientele, the Sales Reps are taken off the hourly wage payroll, and moved to commission only."

"But I only have five accounts so far, and the commission off these was only fifty dollars."

He looked at me sympathetically; the drawl in his speech lent itself to his sympathetic appearance.

"It's been a rough start, that's true, but you're welcome to stay continue to sell ad space. The commission stays the same, it's just that long-term, well, this position is commission only."

I did the math in my head and it didn't take a genius to figure out quickly that there was no way that I would be able to continue driving around selling ad space for a one-time $50 commission.

"Well, that's a kind offer, Mr. Kinkaid." I tried to maintain my composure. "But I think I'll have to probably just try something else," I said. "I'll guess I'll go back to my desk, and clear out the few things that I had in the drawer."

I left his office and got to the bathroom just in time to prevent another meltdown. *Breathe in. Breathe out.* I collected my composure and went back towards my desk.

"Here's the Two Guys Plumbing account," Mr. Kinkaid told Theresa. "There's a few corrections that need to be made. Maybe you can go by this afternoon?"

My heart dropped.

"Oh, Lilly, I thought you'd left," Mr. Kinkaid said.

I walked by in total confusion over the Plumber's account and collected my things before going back out to my car.

4

April

I looked around the empty room. Nothing. Just white space
and music. Anything could happen. Intimidated but still
curious, I turned and looked to where the music was coming
from. It was loud, and there were a lot of people. Some of
them I knew but most I didn't. They were dancing, talking,
standing around. Fog floated through the air, disco lights
coming out of every corner. It was a small room with one
opening into a hallway, and I could hear Joe's voice in
surround sound singing Happy Birthday song.

"Happpy Birthday to...!"

What was Joe doing here?

My mom came from around the corner, and I immediately
suspected that she and Joe were in on something together.
Mom approached me and handed me a present nicely
wrapped with grass-green paper and a gold ribbon. There
was a sticker from Stella-Marcus Department Store on it
holding the ribbon in place.

Stella-Marcus? I asked out loud.

"I know how much you like it there," she said.

Did she? I wondered. Did I?

"Happy Birthday, Dear." She smiled and gave me a hug. That's peculiar, I thought.

A breeze started blowing through the room, and puzzled, I started to open the present. It was a package of napkins marked with an "X". When I looked up, I saw Marcus. Suddenly, we were back outside that little restaurant at the ski resort where we'd met on New Year's. He put his hands on either side of my face and whispered "Happy Birthday" as if he was going to kiss me but was interrupted when a huge cake with twenty-three big candles was rolled in the room. Marcus was gone, and so was the restaurant. Was Marcus now in the cake?

Before I could process the situation, Joe's voice came in again, still in surround sound, announcing something indecipherable to me, and the entire "gang" ran in pushing me out of the way, each grabbing one of the candles which, upon closer look, were not candles at all but huge joints instead. Everyone started puffing on them. The disco fog had morphed into second-hand marijuana smoke. The cake started to move, and one of those window girls like in Amsterdam with a red wig and a pink bikini jumped out of the cake and towards me. I jumped back, stumbling on a cord to the music, triggering an alarm.

Beep, beep, beep . . .

I woke up with a start, only to find that I'd been dreaming a dream that was so vivid I could smell the smoke. Uneasy, I got up and went down the hallway to the kitchen, and just as I was making my first pot of coffee, the telephone rang.

"What's up?" Maddie asked far too cheerful for that time of day.

"I had a bad dream."

"Oh." She paused for a second, "Am I calling at a bad time?" she asked, feeling out the mood.

"Are there any other times?" I asked in despair. "I think I'm delusional."

"That's my girl: the icon of optimism."

"Seriously, I think I'm going crazy. I think it's all really getting to me. First Joe, then my job, now graduation."

"Don't forget your birthday," she squeezed in there.

"Thank you," I groaned. "As if my waking hours weren't disturbing enough, the shit is now infiltrating my dreams. I can't get away from it."

"Look, you have a lot on your mind right now. You're under a lot of pressure, that's all. I think it's just all coming out in your dreams. Obviously."

"I still have to turn in a paper that's nowhere near finished, you know what I mean?"

"Try to chill out. Go on a walk, or make sure you get enough rest. Just hang in there, Lil."

"Yeah, I know. Maybe I can use my frustrations as a source of inspiration to get the paper done."

"Exactly," she assured, "And, well, if that doesn't work, well, you know what I would do. Tell 'em to fuck off. The whole lot of 'em. Fuck Joe, and fuck the newspaper. Not school, of course, but . . ."

She said it as if it were all so simple.

"Maddie, um, everything has been fucked off."

"Look, there are better fish in the sea, and jeez, you want to *make* ads, not *sell* them. You've got four more weeks of school. It'll go by fast, so give yourself a break. Get your priorities in line, do what you gotta do, and you know what?

Silence hung over the line while she waited for a response.

"What?"

"If nothing works out, you can always move out here," she threw in.

"What?" I croaked.

"Sure, why not?"

"Escapism at its finest? I suppose that would be one way to solve things. I just have this little issue of having to graduate and needing money."

"Well," she finally went on, "look on the bright side. Isn't your birthday coming up?"

"Yes."

"Don't think so negatively. It's not going to get you anywhere! Make a special birthday wish, instead, why don't you."

"Maybe you're right."

"No 'maybe' about it!"

After I'd hung up, I poured my coffee and sat down at the table. The thought of my birthday made me think about my dream again. Even though it was very surreal, the dream seemed so vivid, so real. I remembered the napkin with the "X" that Marcus had drawn for me as I flipped through the newspaper and saw the horoscopes printed on the next page:

April 11 ☒◪☒

While someone far away preoccupies your thoughts — if there's one place where you'll find help right now, it's within your inner circle. A fabulous opportunity may arrive from a close friend.

"Preoccupies?" I laughed to myself. I wouldn't exactly describe two seconds — OK, maybe it *was* two minutes — of thinking about *someone far away* as if they were *preoccupying my thoughts*. And how do they know if he's far away?

Mostly, I considered horoscopes with a great deal of doubt, but in a way, some of this was starting to look familiar. "Fabulous" might be a bit much, but Maddie did just give me an "opportunity" to move out to California. And yes, for a split second, someone far away had been in my thoughts. Was there really some kind of truth in horoscopes? Maybe. But it still did little to change the fact that, at the moment, everything was crap. I needed to hold out for four more weeks, stay the course and keep moving towards graduation.

It will come, I repeated, it *will* come. Oh God, just please come quickly. *Help always comes from my inner circle.*

5

May

Bree sat the corkscrew on the table and poured some 'Canyon Cactus Juice' into each of the glasses. After three weeks of procrastination, fused with arbitrary bottles of different local wines that went well beyond research purposes, we stared into one of the pictures I'd been assigned.

"A single glass of red wine, perched on a cliff with a sunset in the background. What is that supposed to mean?" I asked.

"A singular glass: represents being lonely, unsocial, solitary. Because, you know, sorrows are meant to be drowned alone. Cheers," I suggested.

Bree raised her glass.

"Ugg. I don't like this one. Maybe it means confidence, you know. Able to stand alone."

"And a sunset: because, why wait till it's dark? If you start now, you'll already be wasted by the time its dark. No time like the present," I added, taking a hearty swig. "And isolated in the canyon? Well, because, really, do you want people to actually see you drowning your sorrows? No. Much better to go fifty miles out of the way. Safer for everyone involved."

"No, we don't want that," she agreed.

"And an added plus: when you spill all over? Guess what? No need to worry about the furniture or Mom's carpet → The stone of the canyon is conveniently the same color!"

Bree had helped me with some rudimentary research and God knows I tried to find a connection between the ads I'd received and the actual product, but it was difficult.

Had I made a creditable interpretation of the picture? Had I proven my understanding of the use of lines and depth balanced with asymmetry, tone, color and empty space all jumbled up with emotions, needs and desires? Did the message become clear in different media: print, internet, social media, billboards?

I didn't know. But in any case, I had actually finished my last project, and somehow, turned in some relatively coherent analysises of modern advertising, and somehow, I passed with a "B".

And now, the time had come.

May 13

Step onto the stage, Gemini, for excitement is on the agenda! Fascination falls between you and friends. Your talent for wit gives conversation extra spices. Although it can be fun, stay aware of what you're really saying. A new partner could come into the picture with an exciting new offer, one that requires a good decision-making skill. Stay in tune, and a project or new team may come to blossom. For the next few weeks, you are the brightest star in the room.

Graduation on Friday the 13th. Anyone with an ounce of sense would realize that scheduling a graduation on this day should be an absolute No Go. But there it was.

And on this day, of all days, I was now to graduate. And it was a scorcher. With temperatures well into the 90s, suffice it to say, I was having a bad hair day. My dark curly hair was quickly turning into frizzy spirals around my face. I tried to pin it up, but then the cap didn't fit over it, so I put it back down and put my red sun dress and black ballerina shoes on.

"Here," Mom said, giving me a yellow scarf and my black gown. "Wear this for a while so I can tell where you are. I want to be able to see you."

"A scarf? Are you insane? I'll be the walking puddle of sweat if I put this on."

"And you know Grandma and everyone is coming over for dinner afterwards."

"I know."

"So, we'll meet back here after the ceremony, OK? Don't dilly-dally around too long. OK?"

"You only graduate once," I said, "but, hey, don't worry. I won't dilly-dally. I'll see you late."

I took a quick look in the mirror, and irritated, I drove over to Bree's to pick her up.

"It's about time you got here," Bree snapped at me as she got in my red Honda Civic. "I thought you might wait till next year."

"I said I'd be here."

"What?!" she snapped again.

"Nothing, just get in, and let's go." I rolled my eyes up and down as I lit up a cigarette.

"I look like I stuck my finger in a socket," I said, looking in the mirror. "Do they take pictures at these things?"

"Well, I expect they do. Obviously, your parents are going to want to take pictures of you on your big day and all." Bree huffed, stating the obvious.

"Right, you're probably right."

I kept quiet and drove silently the rest of the way. Despite everyone being on edge, I was actually looking forward to the commencement speech and hearing words of enthusiasm, motivation and inspiration.

"Come here. Let me tuck your hair in your cap," Bree said and shoved some of my untamed curls up under my cap.

"Looks OK?"

"Yeah. Me?"

"Of course," I said before we both took several selfies of us together with our phones.

"OK, then, we'll meet back here afterwards."

The lines were already building when we got to the stadium. We scrambled around to our respective colleagues. Bree rushed off to the Business College and I found my way through the corridor with the other Communications majors. I found Benjamin Dillard and got behind him in the alphabetically arranged line for the procession.

"One more inspiring lecture, and then we're through, huh?" Ben said.

"Yip."

It wasn't long before the music started to play, and we marched into the sweltering stadium and took our seats in the section reserved for the communication graduates.

We listened to the welcome, the introductions, and at around ten o'clock, the Keynote Speaker was announced.

"Please, welcome the author of '*LiFe* — *Lessons in Futility etc.,*' Dr. Ruby Glendale."

I had never heard of her.

"Lessons in Fertility?" Benjamin looked at me and laughed. "This might be good after all."

"Futility," I corrected and smiled.

She walked onto the stage, a short, middle-aged woman with short blond hair and glasses.

"Many times, it seems things in life prove to be futile," she started.

Well, that's inspiring news, I thought.

Her voice was painfully quiet and monotone. Coupled with the uninspiring title of her book, I couldn't tell if she was actually saying anything inspirational or not for most of her speech. Maybe that's why she was so quiet. Maybe she was afraid someone might actually hear her. I watched her mouth move, and after things calmed down, I finally heard a bit of her speech:

"Many things in life prove to be futile. Don't wait." She said, "Look for chances, look all around you," which was appropriate, considering it was a graduation speech, but I still found it disappointing.

"I can hardly hear her," I complained.

"Doesn't seem like much. She is, after all, a futility expert," Benjamin said and laughed.

I listened to the woman up on the stage drone on and on in stifling heat before she finally finished with "Thank you, and good luck," in an audible tone before exiting the stage.

"That was it?" I thought out loud.

"I think I would've liked a fertility speech better," Benjamin chuckled.

I agreed.

After she left, the announcer started the commencement by announcing the "Presentation of the Degrees." Names from the individual colleges were simultaneously called from different corners of the stadium. First the names of the Doctorate Degrees echoed all through the stadium in alphabetical order. Then came the Master's Degrees, and then the Baccalaureates.

"Matthew Laurence Carter..."

I knew, my name was coming up, still, I listened very carefully.

"Benjamin Dillard..."

And then it happened. The dean called out my name.

"Lillian Grace DuMont."

I got up, walked across the stage, took the proffered piece of rolled up paper, shook the man's hand as the photographer snapped a picture and walked back to my seat. Or maybe, I floated. In any case, I'd done it. I had graduated.

My parents and Bree met me outside the stadium after the ceremonies were over.

"Well, it looks like you've done it," Dad said and gave me a hug.

"I can't believe it. All grown up now," Mom said. "Are your parents here, Bree?"

"I'm meeting them at the reception. They wanted to take some pictures of us together and the campus and all."

"OK. I'll see you both at home," I told my parents before I walked back to my car with the rolled-up piece of paper in my hand that had "Congratulations" and "10% off your next purchase of prints from Klinger College Photo!" printed on it. And then, there, in the parking lot, I saw Joe.

"Well, you did it," he said keeping his perma-grin.

"Yeah," I answered, recoiling with irritation.

"You going to Bobby's later?"

"No."

"I figured that, actually," he said and gave me a perfect salesmen smile. "Well, you guys have a good time," he said.

I quickly got in my car.

"No. Just don't look back," I told myself, "just like she said, keep learning and look for chances." I repeated this until I got home, where Mom had almost everything ready for the dinner party she'd planned for graduation.

Just as Sybille and her kids, Jaird and Emmy, came in through the back door We checked off the last of the to-do things from the list before the rest of the guests came over.

"Hey there!" Sybille called.

"Hi there. Your Grandpa's out back with your Great-Grandma," Mom told the kids as they all rushed through. "Here. Put these on the buffet," she handed me a platter of hors d'oeuvres that I placed beside the beers and soda that were lined up on the counter in the kitchen.

I sat down at the table, and my phone started to beep. I checked my messages and saw a notification from Miss Teri.

"Oh, my horoscope again. Do you want to hear it?"

"Are you still reading those?" Mom asked.

"Maybe. Sometimes. I mean, this app beeps, like, all the time and I just noticed several times that they seem to be kind of accurate, you know."

"Accurate, huh?"

"Yeah, although, sometimes it's a little too accurate. And lately, it's going off inexplicably just at the right time."

"Are you sure it's not hacked?" Sybille asked.

"Hacked?" I hadn't thought of that. "Don't say things like that."

"Sounds kind of creepy. Here," Mom said handing me some napkins, "I've got a prediction for you: If you don't help me out, we're not going to be ready when your guests arrive.

"I'm helping," I insisted, placing the napkins on the table and simultaneously pressed on the message.

"Listen," I told them and read part of the horoscope out loud. "Step onto the stage, new projects and partners. That sounds pretty accurate, wouldn't you say?"

"Lil, it is graduation time. Half the country is "stepping onto a stage" and getting ready for new partners and projects. Also you. Take it with a grain of salt, OK?"

"See! It says my wit gives conversation extra spices. Is salt a spice?"

"Lil." Mom was losing patience.

"I swear, it says it right there!"

"That was *my* wit."

"Oh. True. But still.."

The house was soon buzzing. Several aunts, uncles and cousins were floating around the kitchen and Grandma was eating in the living room, re-telling stories to Jaird and Emmy.

"Well, they had that moonshine back there in the barn, stored in the barrels. They never said what it was, but I always knew what was in them."

I sat down to listen.

"Hi, Grandma."

"One party down, one to go, right?" Grandma asked me.

"What do you mean?" I asked.

"Well, you've graduated, but also your birthday's coming up, ain't it?" she asked, eating some cake.

I hadn't even thought about it. "Oh, I'm not sure if I'll have a party this year."

"Well, that doesn't have to mean you won't take a present, does it?" she asked as she slipped me an envelope. "I won't be here on your birthday anyway, so I'll just give this to you now."

"Oh, thank you." Surprise filled me. I gave her a kiss and a hug and put the envelope in my pocket. She had already thought of my birthday.

"Where are you going?" I asked.

"Las Vegas with Grandpa. Got some gambling to do."

She smiled and nudged me.

"Yeah, seems like everyone is going somewhere."

"Now, what do you mean by that?" Grandma asked.

"I don't know. Just seems like everyone has something going for them. You're going to Vegas, Bree's got a job in Tulsa. I mean, she's really leaving."

"Oh, I see," she mused as she took a bite of her cake. "You're not happy about that, I guess."

"Oh, sure, I'm happy for her, of course," I murmured, hoping I sounded convincing.

"Because, you know, sometimes you have to go where you can work," she added. "I had to go with Grandpa all over, back when your mom was little."

"I know. I guess I'm just starting to wonder where I should go, you know what I mean?"

"Well, don't worry too much. When the time is right, you'll know," she assured me.

"Let's hope so."

I mingled around and after everyone had left, I helped Mom clean up the kitchen and then fell asleep with the T.V. on, only to be wakened in the middle of the night with a shot of adrenaline. I sat up straight in bed, covered in sweat from my re-occurring dream. But this time there was no fog, no smoke, no girl.

My thoughts jumped to Joe and our last encounter that replayed in my head over and over.

"It was your idea to go on separate trips! Go ahead, turn it all around, just like you do."

Then scenes from the afternoon, and then my phone went off.

72

Beep, beep, beep...

Miss Teri. I exhaled and picked up my phone from the coffee table next to the recliner and read my horoscope:

. . . stay aware of what you're really saying ...For the next few weeks, you are the brightest star in the room . . .

Was there any indication that there was a light at the end of this tunnel? Well, I was, if not anything else, at least the *only* star in the room.

******

On the weekend, Bree went to Tulsa to look for an apartment. Grandma was in Vegas, and it was my birthday. I spent the better part of the weekend sorting out things that I didn't need anymore. Paper trash, plastic trash, trash trash. I sorted and sorted and then Maddie called. .

"Happy Birthday!" she said from Santa Cruz. "Are you having a good day?"

"Thanks. Um, I don't know, I guess, considering I don't have a job-hashtag-money, no school, no boyfriend," I listened silently. "But hey, at least you called."

"You know what? Maybe you should just move."

"How do you figure that? I just said I have no job and no money. Besides, where would I go?"

"I don't know. Maybe out here. It'd be easy. I mean, you just said it yourself. Basically, you're free. You know you can stay with me as long as you need to. Besides, God knows I could use the help with the rent."

"Hello? Like I said, I don't have a job or money."

"Well, I have faith in you. You'll find a job. I mean, as soon as you move out here, that is."

Now, it wasn't as if the idea had not crossed my mind.

"Seriously, Lilly!" she pressed on.

"You're so confident, but I can't do that," I resisted. "I'd be all by myself, floating around in even more unfamiliar territory. What should I do out there?"

"Look, you already know what's in Amarillo for you." She deepened her voice. "Hashtag-not much. Hashtag-you-need-a-change."

I could almost hear her eyes rolling before her voice perked back up.

"There are lots of jobs around here. It might not be exactly what you're looking for at first, but at least, you'll find something. Come on, we can do this. We're a team!"

Why was she doing this? Why was she so insistent? I sat there silently, contemplating my options — and if moving was truly one of them. *Blink, blink.*

At that moment, my phone beeped again, so I looked at the horoscope entry again: . . . *new team may come to blossom. A new partner could come into the picture with an exciting new offer.*

Her words hit me. It all hit me. "We're a team," she'd said. I quickly considered my dead-end situation in Amarillo and the possibilities of Santa Cruz. The coast seemed to be pulling me in a clear direction, and suddenly, I didn't care why she doing it.

"OK," I said quickly, scared that one of us might change their minds.

"Really?" Maddie asked in surprise.

Did I really just say that?

"Yeah. I'll do it. Really," I answered. "I need a few weeks to get my act together, but I will. I'm moving."

6

June

June 5 🎂💛🏠

In a world ever changing, it's no wonder when some unresolved issues just keep popping up. Does your companion need to talk to you? Think about giving them some quality time. A trip with them might lighten their spirits and give you a chance to practice some patience.

Right. I had no more patience. I had no need to talk, and this was no trip. *This* was a *move*.

"If I start looking through it, I'll be here for hours trying to decide if I want it or not. Just throw it away."

"Here, give me the tape," Mom said, taping up one of the stuffed boxes. "You don't have to make every decision right now. Just pack the things that you don't want to take in a box, and they'll still be here when you come back. You can decide then if you want to keep it or not."

I looked at the last box. Two years of pictures and the presents that Joe had given me. I took the tape and sealed it up.

"OK, then I guess all this can go into the attic for now." I gave her the box marked "Former Life" and continued packing the things I did want to take. I didn't even want to waste time thinking about if I should throw the stuff away or not.

I'd planned out my itinerary just so that my parents could more or less track me every step of the way. I'd bought some maps and studied them. I'd looked for the best route to get me to California by car and had my route and destination programmed into my GPS. I had already shipped most of my clothes, books and my computer out to California, but my Honda Civic was still packed with everything I figured I would need on the way. I made some extra space up front for snacks, coffee and my iPad and packed all my other items that I thought I would probably need on the way out in the back. I carefully placed my CDs up toward the front and tried to find a place where I could make sure to get an overnight-bag. Now, after bouts of frantic packing and panicking, I sat in the drive with a lump in my throat. A disorienting pain sat in my shoulders and neck, tightening them up. I couldn't tell if I was running away or running towards something. Both? Excited and sad at the same time, I suddenly heard the words 'Just go'. I hugged my parents good-bye and before the tears in my eyes could spill over, I drove off.

One chapter closes, another one opens.

I drove over I-40 and got a rush when, not even two hours later, I was in Tucumcari: already over the state line! How hard could this be?

Harder than I thought, as the next thirteen hours were spent between the Rocky Mountains and desert interstates, battling idiots with road rage and dodging dangerous tire snakes from shoddy re-treaded tires that had disintegrated all over the burning highways.

In awe of the scenery, I wondered why everyone seemed so full of road-rage? Maybe because their tires didn't do well at higher elevations? Or didn't like heat?

At any rate, when I got into California and stopped at the Super 8 Motel in Riverside where I stayed for the night. I woke up early, showered and got back on the road around seven as clouds rolled in above and it looked like it might rain. As I pulled onto the interstate, the big green sign informed me: 335 miles to Santa Cruz, and six hours later, dead-tired, I pulled up in the drive of Maddie's small house at the end of Echo Street.

I got out and rang the doorbell, but she wasn't home. I called her on her cell phone, but she didn't answer there, either. There was nothing left to do but wait. I sat outside in the backyard on the small concrete porch for about ten minutes before I started feeling anxious, so I walked down the street and came across the Cappadocia Corner Store on Flower Street, which offered something called the "Bukowski Breakfast" which consisted of a pack of cigarettes and a large coffee. I wondered if this were legal. I thought California was so healthy and it kind of altered my image of it, in a good way.

I doctored my coffee up with milk and sugar, grabbed a newspaper and walked back to Maddie's, where I drank the rest of the coffee which was solely responsible for me being awake. I went back to the patio and was scanning the job ads in the paper for anything in advertising when my phone peeped. I pressed the button to find Miss Teri's message.

June 6 ☆ 👫 🎼

You're making points on the job. Keeping focused may tip the deck in your favor at work. You'll find the time to keep that intriguing new face interested.

Hmm, I thought. Apparently, Miss Teri had little idea about my life. I mean, I have no job, and I am the new face, aren't I? I looked at the icons and noticed the legend at the end of the horoscope. The sun meant radiance, the heart obviously stood for love, and the house stood for beginnings and endings.

I flinched when I looked at the heart icon. If she'd done her research at all, I thought, then she'd know about my non-existent job and about the melt-down episodes in my love life that had finally ended "Lil and Joe". A thought that made me wince. Guess the prediction hit a nerve that was still bruised.

But the next icon meant beginnings and endings. No argument there. The commotion of planning my move had kept me busy over the last few weeks. I wondered if I had over-reacted? Had I acted hastily? Or was it all according to plan? After all, it *did* say it, right there in black and white. I should be ecstatic.

Nevertheless, I could feel the knot in my throat begin to swell and the sting of hot tears rolling down my cheeks. Had I been too impulsive? Was moving out here the right thing to do? Whatever the reasons for my actions were, it was too late now. I was here. I sat down on a lounge chair and buried my head in my knees, wiping the stream of inexplicable tears and snot off my face with the arm of my shirt. I must have been there for a while, because the next thing I knew, I looked up, hearing Maddie's voice.

"Hey! There you are! How long have you been here?"

She had leaned over and thrown her arms around me. Her excitement and cheerfulness were in sharp contrast to my exhausted state.

"Hi! An hour, maybe two, I guess."

"Are you OK?" She looked at me, and her eyebrows pulled tight together. "You look . . . tired? Hope you're not already having buyer's remorse."

Buyer's remorse. That was it. It was just a fleeting case of buyer's remorse.

"Do I?" I asked flatly. "Must've been the drive." I hoped my eyes were not too bloodshot. "I just needed to rest, maybe get a bite to eat."

"Oh, of course you do. Well, let's get your things together and go inside," she said happily.

Her cheerfulness wasn't exactly contagious, but at least it prevented me from sliding down any further into a dark hole, as I was forced to project a demeanor of mere tiredness and being hungry. At least for now, my obscure grief would have to stay parked outside the door.

"A few of your boxes arrived last week," she said as she helped me bring some of the stuff from my car.

My Honda wasn't the largest car and didn't take much to unpack it.

"Here is your room," she said, opening a door. To my surprise, the bedroom already had a bed and a rustic style dresser with a mirror in it. The walls were painted pastel yellow with a border with dark green ivy lined the ceiling, and the natural light was blocked by a large evergreen outside the window. We stacked the boxes along the wall with the others, leaving enough space to walk through the room, and after unloading.

"Sorry, but I don't have much here to eat in the house. Why don't you get freshened up a little, and we'll go get something to for dinner" she said with a smile. "We can unpack your stuff out of the boxes afterwards. What do you think?"

"Sounds good. I'll just need a few minutes," I said and opened my suitcase on the floor.

I went to the bathroom and brushed my teeth, went back to my room and looked around trying to get a feel for it. This would be home for a while. I changed clothes and met Maddie back in the white walled living room. A picture of a map of Santa Cruz hung over the blue leather sofa.

"Well, we can go to Starbucks, or there is a tasty little dive coffee shop down the street," she said letting me choose.

"How 'bout the dive?"

"Dive it is," she agreed.

We got into Maddie's car, and she drove through the neighborhood of one-story single-family homes. Even though they were all mostly built in the sixties and looked quite a lot like the houses back in Canyon Ridge, Maddie assured me that they were all priced way in the upper six-figure league and that California cost much more than Texas, but I didn't realize that it was so expensive.

"Damn, I might have to get two jobs," I thought out loud.

"A lot of people do."

I swallowed silently, hoping that I would be able to pay for my part of the rent. Considering my abundance of freedom, I figured I had time for two jobs.

We drove down Water Street, a larger, tree-lined thoroughfare running through the city as more clouds were covered the sky and it started to sprinkle.

"It's been cloudy since I got here. What happened to 'sunny California'?" I asked.

"Oh, it's an El Niño year," she said, "a weather phenomenon that wreaks havoc on the Pacific coast every eight years, and it was just your luck that you chose this year to move to out here."

"Seriously?"

"Seriously."

The wind picked up as we pulled up to Rick's Café, a greasy spoon dive housed in a small, white-painted brick building that had been plopped down in the middle of a parking lot. The big red letters popped off the grey wall, and when we walked in, the bells hanging on the door frame rang as they hit the opening glass door.

"Look here." Maddie had grabbed a copy of a local paper from the stand by the door and gave it to me as we sat down in a booth.

"It's the local weekly paper. The local job ads are in there. It might be the best place to look for something quick."

I was more familiar than I wanted to be with 'local weeklies', but I took the paper anyway.

"Thanks." I said and waited for my eyes to adjust. Inside the building, it was not nearly so bright as outside. The few windows in the place were up high on the wall, and half the blinds were still closed, obscuring the yellow, greasy walls on the inside at first glance. I opened the pages to the "Job Opportunities" section. "Wait Staff wanted at the Hungry Potato, Starbuck's, Black Forest Restaurant," I read.

The waitress came over and took our order — two coffees and two half orders of scrambled eggs with biscuits and gravy.

"I know it's dinner time, but really, the biscuits and gravy are really the best around here," Maddie insisted. "Actually, the Black Forest Restaurant might not be all that bad," Maddie said. "It's a four-star German restaurant in the pedestrian zone. It's been there for a while. Tips are supposed to be pretty good."

"I don't know. I don't want to mess around anymore, you know? I just graduated in advertising and all. I think I just want to try to get a real job. I want something *authentic*, you know what I mean? I just want something to *happen*."

"Lil, you're here. Something did just happen! You just got here. You've got plenty of time."

"Plenty of time? Then, why am I so anxious?"

"You just have to get settled. That's all."

The waitress brought our lunch.

"Ah! Just in time: Comfort food! You'll be fine after this. You'll see."

I looked at the plate, and although I couldn't tell if I'd be alright in the long run, but the moment, at least, did seem to be saved. The coffee was watered down and the scrambled eggs and biscuits were covered with a thick, homemade gravy. Delicious. A real dive, it was.

****

The next couple of days I spent trying to get acclimated to my new surroundings. I found myself feeling doubts about the job situation, looked in the "Want" ads for a real job which, so far, seemed of the scarce side. Maddie thought that it was far too soon in the game to feel that way and, job or no job, it was time to check things out. So that Saturday, we went to Santa Cruz to look around. The pedestrian zone was lined with little locally owned shops and cafés where I was immediately fascinated by the crowds of people and the street performers. A man blowing up balloons stood on one corner, while a Jamaican contortionist slowly squashing himself into a little glass box on the other, and me and Maddie enjoying coffee outdoors. It was a real change from the strip malls of sprawling Amarillo that were mostly accompanied by a large parking lot.

Beep! Beep! Beep!

"My phone." I took it out. Miss Teri.

"My phone is really getting weird these days. This horoscope app goes off all the time."

"Oh. Enthusiastic algorithms?"

"Hyper-hyper is more like it. It goes off all the time." I re-read her the prediction.

> You're making points on the job. Keeping focused may tip the deck in your favor at work. You'll find the time to keep that intriguing new face interested.

"Now it says the same thing it did the other day. I don't even have a job and certainly don't need any 'new faces'."

"Maybe you could delete it."

"Delete it?" I asked surprised.

"Well, and then you could re-install it. I just mean, you know, if it bothers you."

"Oh. Yeah, right," I said. "I'll have a look when we get back.

On the way home, we walked by an old Victorian-style two-story house.

"That's the German restaurant I told you about, the Black Forest Restaurant from the job ad," Maddie said.

Sure enough, there was a "Help Wanted" sign for waitressing in the door of the restaurant. Maddie stopped at the entrance. "Are you sure you don't want to just pick up an application? I mean, it's not far from the house which means it's easy to get to. You could even walk or bike to work," she added enthusiastically.

"I did waitress and do some bar-tending, you know, back in the day. Maybe I will. Doesn't mean I have to turn it in or even that they'll hire me," I replied, sure to leave myself an exit strategy, just in case.

I walked in and through the foyer where signed pictures of what seemed to be local celebrities hung on the walls. Past that was a rustic, but formal dining room with heavy, dark furniture and deer antler trophies decorating the walls. and a big fire place in the corner. And scrumptious, savory smells drifting from the kitchen.

"Good morning." A short, stable lady with her blond-gray hair pinned up in the back and wearing a traditional German dress came out from a small room to the foyer where I stood.

"Good morning," I replied.

"We open at 11:30 for lunch, alright?"

"What?" I asked, stopping in my tracks. Her "alright" sounded like "aw-right". Just like Marcus.

"We open at 11:30," she repeated.

"Oh, that's OK," I said. "I just saw the Help Wanted sign in the window and wanted to know if I could pick up an application."

"Of course." She went behind the bar, and when she came back, she handed me two pieces of paper. "Have you been a waitress before?"

"Yeah. Well, in Texas where I'm from, I used to wait tables when I was in college." I said it like it was so long ago. "I just graduated, but I live out here now, so, you know, we'll see what happens." I tucked the papers away in my backpack.

"I see. Well, we are open at 11:30 through to 10:00 in the evening every day, except Mondays, you see, and also of course not during the mid-day between three o'clock and five o'clock," she explained in heavily accented English.

"Um, right. Well, I'll bring them back when you're opened, of course." I closed my backpack and turned to go.

"You ask for Liesl, that's me, when you bring them, alright? What is your name, again?"

"Lilly Dumont. Thanks," I turned and walked back out through the foyer where Maddie was waiting.

In light of the job situation, I figured, every application might count and that I might just have to fill out a lot of applications, and therefore I might need the practice. So, I filled it out as neatly and professionally as I could and returned it directly on Sunday. To my surprise, one day later, on Monday, I got a phone call.

"Can you come in on Thursday for an interview?" asked the voice on the other end.

"Of course, I can." I agreed immediately.

So, on Thursday, I walked into the restaurant and was greeted by a tall, thin, elderly woman in an orange and brown German dress with an apron tied around it. A white napkin hung over her forearm.

"Good afternoon, welcome to the Black Forest Restaurant. How many today?" The lady's eyes squinted tightly above her forced smile. Maybe she had just forgotten her glasses, but it gave me a feeling of fake friendliness, as if she were doing her job. Not more.

"My name is Lily Dumont," I started, "I have an appointment with...Lisa?" I stopped, unsure how to pronounce the name. To me there seemed to be a vowel missing. "Um, Liesl? For an interview," I said, hoping I had pronounced the name correctly.

"OK. You can wait in here. I'll come and get you when she's ready," the woman assured me before she turned around, and her eyes were still squinting. "It shouldn't take too long."

I walked behind her into the bar area and sat down at one of the tables. There was also another girl waiting. She was quite plump and had dyed black hair and a serious Gothic-look about her. I tried to imagine her in one of those dresses. Maybe that's what they were going for. Maybe a Gothic or Transylvania look was what they wanted, and then the whole issue would solve itself. In fact, now that I thought about it, the tall, grey-haired, squinty-eyed hostess also seemed to have a gothic look about her.

I starting to get a strange feeling about all this, hesitant even about turning in the application, but then she came back.

"Kayla?" she called out. "Liesl can see you now."

Gothic Kayla got up and followed the tall waitress into another room. Before long, the door re-opened and the uncertain looking Gothic girl walked back past me.

A few minutes passed, and the original blond and grey-haired lady came out and called me in to interview. I followed her into a casual dining room and sat down, ready to show off my interviewing skills.

"My name is Liesl," she introduced herself, again, "I am one of the owners of the Black Forest Restaurant. So, you are here from Texas, and you have experience in waiting tables in a restaurant?"

"Right, exactly," I answered confidently.

"Very good. We have our own training program, because this restaurant is different from every other one. Everybody who works here has to learn this, how do you say? From scratch. Is that OK for you, Lilly?"

"Oh, sure. That's not a problem at all." I hoped so.

"And you have just graduated from the university?"

"Yes. Finally."

"Very good. That's very important for your life, you know."

"That's what they say."

"Lilly, do you know very much about the different kinds of wines there are?"

A vision of a solitary wine glass came to me.

"Not a lot, I'm afraid. Just a little." I wondered if that might be a deciding factor. "But I'm a quick learner, you know. I could definitely try a lot of wine and get caught up on the whole thing, you know," I blurted out, immediately regretting it. I sighed and waited for the next question.

"It's OK, Lilly. It may be better if you are not that experienced in alcohol at your age." Suddenly she sounded like my mom.

"Oh." I sighed again, this time relieved. "Right."

"Can you work on week-ends, Lilly?"

"Oh, of course. I'm totally flexible."

"And lunches, evenings?"

"I'm free," I said.

"Very good. And math? You are good at math?"

"Um, yeah. Sure."

"OK, Lilly."

She gathered up her papers and turned to the wall. Then she picked up a dress, similar to hers, that was hanging on a coat hanger on the wall. She walked over to me and held it up.

"Oh, this will be very nice," she said, somehow pleased.

I watched her, slowly getting the picture that she meant it would look nice *on me*. I, on the other hand, couldn't really think of anything that would make it "nice."

"Do you always wear your hair like this?" she asked, pointing to my pulled-up hair.

"Well, not *always*," I answered honestly.

"I like your hair like this. You should always wear it like this," she instructed as she held the dress directly up to me this time. "This is a real Bavarian dress: a dirndl," she explained. She was sizing me up, murmuring "wunderbar" as she went about pinning and altering the dress on the spot. "It's still a little long, so I may have to alter it another time. But you will need it right away. I think this will be very nice, Lilly. You come back tomorrow for looking and signing some papers. We will start then. Be here at two o'clock, yah?"

"Uh, yeah, sure. Great," I said upbeat, but somehow it all seemed very surreal. "But I just wanted to make sure you read that I just got my degree in advertising, so, you know, I also have interests in that area. You know, not that it turns into a conflict," I told her. Somehow, I thought it was fair to make sure she knew that I had bigger plans.

"Very well, Lilly. Take the dress. You need to iron it, and come tomorrow in uniform, at two o'clock, yes?" she said as she handed me the dress.

"OK. I'll be here at two. Thank you so much."

I let out a sigh of relief, relieved that we understood each other. It wasn't until I was outside that I got a surge of second thoughts. Was this it for me? Was Liesl too sure?

I rolled the dirndl to a bundle to fit into my backpack, walked back down to the coffee shop where I bought myself a consolation Vanilla Latte and called Maddie.

"Guess what? I've got good news and maybe bad news."

"OK." She hesitated. "Good news first."

"I got the job."

"That's wonderful!" she exclaimed. "So, what's the bad news?"

"I think I have even more buyer's remorse."

"Stop already! What's the matter?"

"I can't help wondering if I'm trading in my dream custom tailored suits, an office with a window and California sushi for schnitzel and a dirndl."

"A what?"

"A dirndl. You know, those authentic dresses from Germany?"

"Oh. Well, so maybe it's not that bad. You always said you were ready for something authentic."

"I did. Only mine has a little more of an 1800's-slash-pioneer-prairie look about it."

"OK. Well, is there anything else on the table for you to choose from?" Maddie asked.

"Right now? Nope. No Plan B," I admitted.

"Well, then, maybe it's alright, you know. At least now some of the pressure's off. You can still look around for something else."

"OK. I know. You're right. And you know what? There's more good news: now that I think about it, I'll make nearly twice as much as I did selling ads."

"Super! See? Your stay in California might actually have a chance at being a little longer than a few weeks."

Maybe she was right there, too. But just to be sure, I thought I better go home and quickly apply for a real job.

87

****

On Tuesday, I got ready for my first day of work at the Black Forest Restaurant, the four-star restaurant that enjoyed a great reputation due to its authentic food and décor and in a weird sort of way, even because of the uniforms.

I put on the dirndl, pinned my hair up as Liesl had suggested — or was that instructed? — and looked at myself in the long mirror in the bathroom, and froze.

The dress, being very low-cut, was obviously designed for the sexy women in Oktoberfest pictures carrying fistfuls of beer mugs. But despite Liesl's tailoring attempts to make it look more fitted, the dirndl hung on me like a curtain all the way to the floor. And an 1800's pioneer-prairie style curtain at that. Not exactly sexy.

Beep! Beep! Beep!

Ok — this time, the timing was not bad. I read Miss Teri's prediction, curious to see what it had to say:

June 17

You never get a second chance to make a first impression. Or do you? If that first impression didn't go as well as it could have done, remember that taking a little time to pamper yourself can also lift your mood, making you beautiful, inside and out!

On account that I still didn't know anyone here, first impressions were about all I could make. I imagined myself walking down the pedestrian zone to get to work and suddenly, I couldn't do it. I couldn't even walk out of the house like that. I quickly took the dress back off, folded it, and stuffed it into my backpack before getting back into my street clothes and setting off for work. No sense in getting off to a bad start, I figured.

Shortly before two o'clock I walked in the front door and found Liesl with the dirndl-sporting waitresses in the server station rolling silverware in napkins.

"Hi there. I'm here," I announced as I approached them.

Liesl, in a blue dirndl with a vest, looked at me with a friendly face, but with wide, questioning eyes. She walked towards me, giving me the once-over the whole time. By the time she got to me, her look had turned into a twice- and thrice-over. She had the sweet, fresh powdered smell of a grandmother.

"You are not dressed!" Liesl shot back, her voice high, filled with confusion.

"Oh, I have my dress in here," I said, lifting my back-pack.

"OK, of course," she finally said, as she took my arm and guided me in the other direction.

"Here is the bathroom. You can change, and then we get started showing you around."

I slipped into the restrooms and quickly changed into pioneer-woman, then I took a deep breath and walked back out, relieved that I was still the new girl and that there was no chance of me running into anyone that I knew.

"Girls, this is Lilly. She will be working some in the restaurant and also at the bar. — Lilly, this is Gerri and this is Johnney," Liesl said, introducing me to the other waitresses.

I recognized Gerri from the other day, the gothic hostess was apparently a waitress. But her eyes were still squinting, her smile still plastic. She had hair that had been recently dyed and was in stark contrast to her pale face color.

"Gerri will show you today what you need to do. You go behind Gerri and watch today. Only watch, *ja*?"

"Good morning," she said, still wrapping the silverware. Although her voice sounded soft, she seemed very no-nonsense.

"Hi there," said Johnney, a shorter, blond-bombshell kind of woman with a pink and green fairy tattooed on her bare shoulder blade and plenty of cleavage to set it off. She must have been around thirty years old, which left me as the obvious youngster of the bunch.

"Hi. I'm Lilly, the new girl."

"Well, I suppose you will," Gerri said. "But there won't be much goin' on 'round here for a while, so you can just help us out with this silverware that needs wrappin'." She handed me a cloth napkin.

"You just gotta lay the silverware down like this," she said with an accent more country than mine. She demonstrated how to lay the cutlery properly on the dark blue cloth napkin, "then fold it over and give it a roll," she said, rolling it up in one smooth roll and laying it inside the drawer of a hutch.

"We do this till about four, four-thirty, till the first customers start to come in," Johnney said. "That's usually just a few business guys coming in early for drinks, you know, happy-hour stuff, so I guess that's your department, if you're at the bar," she continued, straightening the top of her blue lacy dress.

Although she looked like she should be twirling and singing on top of a mountain somewhere, she actually looked good in her dirndl. She definitely won in the *décolletage* department.

"*Ja*, but you don't need to worry about that today, you're only following Gerri," Liesl instructed. "Even if you work the bar, you still have to go through training."

"No-one gets around *the training*," Johnney whispered and smiled.

I walked up to the large wooden hutch to get some more silverware and noticed my reflection in a mirror on the back of it. I shrunk at seeing myself. Me, in a dirndl. The orange lace sewn around the edges of the apron part of the dress and deep cut shirt bothered me. I instinctively looked away quickly, grabbed more silverware from the tray on the counter of the hutch and started rolling.

We stood there, huddled in the nook rolling silverware for quite a while, when a door from the adjoining kitchen slammed.

90

"Where the hell is the garlic?" came a deep, accented voice from the kitchen. "How can you cook beef tornedos without the garlic?" the man roared throughout the building.

"Beef tornedos?" I asked as I had a vision of cows flying through the air.

"That's Fritz," Johnney explained just above a whisper. "He's always like this." She shrugged and rolled her eyes just as a blur of a man thundered past us. Fritz, dressed in white and black, marched quickly through the kitchen, through the nook and on through to the bar, shouting the entire way.

"That's Fritz, Liesl's brother," Gerri informed.

"That's her *brother*?" I asked, disbelieving every word.

"That's him, the master cook of this place," Gerri said.

"He's always in what you might call a 'serious' mood," Johnney muttered with air quotes.

"That must be some serious garlic," I said, but I meant that he sounded seriously mental. In fact, for a first impression, he seemed nothing less than mad. He was tall, had graying hair, sported a graying mustache and had a graying mono-brow over his determined blue eyes. He wore white leather shoes with a cork sole and hound's tooth black and white cook pants that made me think he was probably more from Sweden than Germany. I didn't know if he was intimidating or laughable.

He caught up to Liesl in the bar, and they kept talking loudly, but since they were speaking in German, I couldn't understand a word they were saying. Soon, he thundered back through the nook, and when he saw me, he stopped.

"Ah, you must be the new one," he said, almost through clenched teeth.

"Hello." I answered hesitantly. Too hesitantly, I guess, because he didn't wait and just started to walk off.

"Does she know the rules for here?" he asked, looking back at Liesl.

She mumbled something in German in response, then turned back to Gerri and Johnney.

"Later, he will meet with the new event manager," she whispered, as if she were trying to excuse his demeanor. "Maybe that will help change his mood."

Johnney then turned to me. "Fritz has to go to court today, so he is not very happy, as you can see."

"Make sure you tell her about the 'no fraternizing policy'," Fritz suddenly yelled from the kitchen. "No fraternizing or . . . or that's it!"

"The what?" I asked, deciding he was more on the intimidating side.

Liesl turned to me. "Lilly, come with me." She led me back to an office area with a big window that gave a complete view of the kitchen and server station. "You understand that here, at the Black Forest Restaurant, it is not acceptable to *fraternize* with other employees. I do not think that it is a problem, but we have to say it, *ja*? It's in the policy."

I looked at the people standing in front of me: gothic Gerri. Sexy Johnney who should be on a mountain – but was not my type, grandmotherly Liesl and Chaos Fritz. I honestly didn't see where this could remotely be a problem for anyone and held back a laugh as Fritz suddenly looked to the window, and at me expectantly.

"I think I understand what you're saying, and I am totally fine with that;" I stated as convincingly as I could. Apparently, he was satisfied enough with my response.

"Don't forget to bring back the work policy," he repeated before going back into the kitchen to yell at his apprentice.

"You will get a copy of the work policy before you go," Liesl told me after her brother had disappeared in the kitchen. You just have to read through it and sign it before your next shift."

"That's fine. No problem." I held back an urge to salute.

"He is not himself today, with the court thing coming up and everything," Liesl said, "He's just under a little time pressure, but he is hiring a new event manager soon," she assured me. "He just has to find the right person," she explained as if this would justify his tirade to me. "But that is not important for you, Lilly. Now, you must come with me," she added. "Do you have your napkin? You must always have your napkin." She grabbed a white napkin, draped it over my arm, and I felt like a total dork as she guided me through to the dark dining room where all the tables were still empty.

"You know how to lay the table?" she asked. "No matter," she went on without waiting for an answer. "Now you must learn how to lay the table at the Black Forest Restaurant. Every table gets one white table cloth and one colored." She got a pile of folded linens out of a hutch and demonstratively covered one of the tables in the dining room. "The table is like a clock," she explained. "The plates go in the middle. The silverware for the desert go at twelve o'clock." She laid the silverware above the plates.

"The water glass goes at one o'clock. The red wine at one thirty and the white wine at two o'clock. Coffee rests at three o'clock. Now you. Just like this."

I copied her every move, taking the dishes from the trolley and the glasses from the hutch, placing everything exactly where it belonged: two table cloths, one salad plate on top of the dinner plate. Salad fork to the far left, then the dinner fork. On the right: the knife, the teaspoon then the soup spoon. At one o'clock: a water glass, then the red wine glass, then the white wine glass.

"Very good, Lilly. Now you finish the tables. Every table just like this one," she instructed and left the room.

I stayed in the dining room where I worked on setting the tables. After almost half an hour, Liesl came back, and to my embarrassment, I still wasn't finished. She inspected each table, moving some dishes around that apparently were not in *just* the right spot.

"Very well, Lilly," she finally said, giving me the responsibility of setting up the *Jägerroom*. "When you are finished, you come back to the station to help with the silverware. This is what you must learn today, setting the table and silverware. OK?"

"Sounds good," I said.

I looked at the tables to see what she had moved, but I couldn't really see a difference. I finished the last of the tables, hoping that they were alright, and made my way to the bar as the first customers were coming in.

The entire shift consisted of rolling silverware, bussing and re-setting tables. After three hours, the shift was over and as I was putting my silverware away, Liesl came over to me.

"Lilly, you can order a portion of the Daily Special if you would like to eat something. Next Rule: Employees are allowed one meal per shift. Today, the special is *Geschnetzeltes in Rahmsoße mit Bratkartoffeln.* That is strips of pork with roasted potatoes, OK? You put in your order and employees can sit in the lounge at table 15 to eat. They'll bring it to you."

When I went back to the kitchen, it seemed nothing worked up an appetite more than seeing and smelling all the dishes come out. But now I was sure that I was absolutely starving, so I quickly took the opportunity to try one of the dishes. I put in my order and went to table 15. When my plate came out, it was just as perfect as a dinner for any other guest: an over-sized plate with soft pork strips covered in a creamy sauce, accompanied with roasted potatoes and vegetables. The plate was decorated with a raspberry sauce and oranges and looked *almost* too good to eat. But it wasn't. It was delicious.

I finished up and was about to leave when Liesl caught up to me.

"Lilly," she said, handing me an armful of documents, "take this home and learn the menu. Tomorrow, we will begin work in the kitchen, so you have to know what we offer. You must be able to make suggestions and explain. And also the work policy. Here you are."

I went to change back into my street clothes and shoved everything into my already stuffed back-pack. I wanted to show Maddie the menu and the dress, but when I got home, the house was empty.

I read through the strangely worded Work Policy and decided again that I was glad that job this would only be

temporary. I signed it, put it back into my backpack, and then opened the heavy, leather-bound menu. I couldn't even begin to pronounce half the stuff in it and began to wonder how I should be able to make any suggestions at all. I looked at the appetizers, stumbled through the heading: *Fleisch und Hähnchen* before deciding the food menu was too daunting. So, I skipped to the drinks, thinking it would be easier. I read the heading: *Bier, Wein und Spirituosen:*
Bier: *Weißbier, Weizenbier, Malzbier.*

No, I thought. That's not easier at all.

So, I looked at the wine list: *Liebfraumilch, Silvaner, Gewürztraminer* ... What?! Haven't they ever heard of Chardonnay? Merlot?

Survival strategies of how to get through my first shift started to creep into my thoughts: I could:

A) feign laryngitis until I was able to say something
   properly, or
B) I could simply show the menus to the customers with   no
   comment, or
C) learn one or two entrees well, and the rest was up to
   them — the ole "fake it till you make it routine."

Panic attacks threatened to break through when, luckily, I saw the spirits section: *Jägermeister*. Bingo!

Finally, there was something I recognized. I looked at the non-alcoholic drink list: Coca-Cola, ice-tea, sparkling water. Here was something I actually knew. I exhaled and thought, maybe there is hope.

****

The next day, uniform safely in my bag, I snuck in through the front door, slipped into the bathroom and changed into Pioneer Woman. When I came out, there was Liesl.

"Good morning, Lilly," she greeted me. "Do you have the work policy?"

"Yeah, I do," I said, fumbling for my backpack.

"You go in the lounge area and look over the menu. The specials for the day are on the board. Read over them, and then we will go into the kitchen where you can learn them."

The thought of having to "read" the indecipherable menu, combined with having to go into *the kitchen,* started to make me twitch, and I hoped it wouldn't develop into some kind of neurosis.

Boeuf Tournedos, Gemüseliebe, Spätzle. I tried to read it out loud, but it came out more like *Bofe Tornedos, Gemooslibe, Spatzel.*

It sounded much better when Liesl said it.

I labored over the menu and I could feel my neck starting to flush as she came back in.

"What is the matter with you? Have you been too long in the sun?" Liesl asked, noticing my glow.

"No, just trying to pronounce these...dishes."

"Do not worry about the pronunciation just yet, Lilly. We will have to work on that over the next weeks. OK?"

"Oh. That sounds good," I said, honestly relieved.

Thank God.

Exhale.

"So, now, you must come with me for training in the kitchen. Only there can you see the different dishes."

I could already hear Fritz, even if I couldn't understand him. I followed her apprehensively into the kitchen, the domain of Fritz — the lion's den.

"Two salads," Gerri called hanging up her order ticket. She didn't seem scared, so I started to suspect that it might be OK.

Maybe Fritz's bark was bigger than his bite. I hoped.

We stood out of the way and watched the plates come out. The orders not only smelled wonderful, but they were each beautifully decorated with different kinds of sauces and syrups and garnishes that made them look like special creations, just for that person.

"This is the *Sauerbraten mit Spätzle*. *Spätzle* are authentic German noodles," Liesl explained.

"Noodles," I repeated, although I couldn't understand half of what she was saying.

The next plate came up. A dessert.

"Oh, here, this is the *Apfelstrudel.*"

"Oh, I do know what this is, actually." The familiar apple pie kind of dish made me feel a little more secure as Liesl put on a healthy helping of whipped cream over the hot apple-cinnamon dessert that was tantalizing my nose, convincing me I must be hungry.

Even if I couldn't pronounce the names of all the dishes or even remember them for that matter, I started feeling a bit more confident.

Fritz still spoke to everyone in military commando tones, but for some reason, he didn't speak to me at all. He didn't even acknowledge my presence, to be honest. Was that part of the No Fraternizing deal? If it stayed like that, there might be a chance that I could deal with it, who knows? Maybe it wouldn't be so difficult after all.

"Good. Now you have seen the specials for tonight. You can go back and help with the silverware."

"OK." I said and went to help Gerri and Johnney.

"How are you getting along?" Johnney asked.

"Good, I guess. It all looks tasty enough," I said.

"Oh, it is. That, you never have to worry about."

I picked up a spoon, knife and two forks and started rolling them up when my phone went off.

Beep! Beep! Beep!

Gerri shot me a look of disbelief. I took my phone out of my apron and looked quickly at the message.

You never get a second chance to make a first impression....

"Just my horoscope," I explained. "It must be messed up. It keeps giving me the same one. Says I should pamper myself and try to look good. Maybe it's right, you know, good for business and all." I hoped they saw the benefit of my app. "See, look." I showed Gerri the prediction, sure that it held more weight.

"Well, here you do get plenty of opportunities to make a first impression," she said.

"Oh, you know what," Johnney added, "I heard something about that just the other day. Something about first impressions and how guys are subconsciously taking everything in from the size of your limbal rings to the manufacturer of your shoes, all within the first twenty seconds of meeting them.

"Your what?" I asked.

"Your limbal rings. You know, those dark rings around the color part of your eyes."

"What does that have to do with anything?" Gerri asked in disbelief.

"Well, apparently, the thicker they are, the better."

"Well, hallelujah!" Gerri exclaimed. "Finally, something gets to be thicker."

"Gerri!" Fritz called from the kitchen.

"You girls make all the first impressions you want. I'm more than happy to have my return customers," she said as she smiled and left the server niche.

"And hey, you never know when you're gonna meet Mr. Right," Johnney said.

"What about the No Fraternizing thing?"

"Well, I don't think that counts for customers!" she laughed.

I silently wondered about my own limbal rings and if they were noticeable, not that I could do much about it if they weren't. Shoes, however, were a different story. At least theoretically. Seeing that my dirndl went all the way to the floor, my shoes would never even make it into the equation. Besides, I wasn't going to be there forever. And the last thing I was looking for was Mr. Right.

"Don't forget to bring back the policy!" Fritz called out suddenly, reprimanding me as he walked through the server niche.

"I won't," I answered, almost like a reflex as Liesl walked up behind him.

"Everything is fine. He's just a little on edge," she said, then whispered "you know, because of that trial. But you start next week on your own, so please make sure that you bring it."

"I will. Don't worry, I will."

So, this was Fritz "on edge"? I wondered what kind of trial it was and if there was another side to Fritz. Until now, I hadn't seen it.

*****

June 28 ⭐🎴🎵

Rashness effects a bond or a relationship to a colleague. Couple instinct with expert advice to get further. A money issue works out.

Friday morning at 9:42 a.m., I woke up to the sound of crows cawing in the woods behind the house. Again, the house was empty. I hardly ever saw Maddie. Our jobs had different hours of operation, so while she was usually ready and gone by 7:30 in the morning, I didn't leave until around two in the afternoon.

Today, though, was a special day. I had to be at work at four o'clock. After two weeks of training, it was my big day. I was flying solo.

In the morning, I did my laundry and cleaned up around the house. I took a shower, got dressed, made coffee and toast and sat down to the paper. I checked the want ads for dream jobs and, upon finding none, read my daily horoscope. Rashness, relationships and money issues . . . Rent, food etc. — I *did* have enough money issues, that was true enough. Could there be any real meaning behind what it said? If there was, I hoped that my money issues, at least, would be taking a U-turn because, starting today, I'm graduating from waitress-in-training to official waitress — my second graduation in as many months. I had followed Gerri and Johnney around for the last week, and I was finally earning my stripes, or at least my apron strings. No more training, no more bussing tables or sharing tips. Tonight, I was on my own. This was it. I had my own section.

I got to work early, changed clothes in the restroom as usual and clocked-in. I knew I wouldn't remember everything, especially not on my first night, suffering from stage fright, so I walked over to the specials board and wrote down the specials for the day on a cheat sheet.

"Lilly, you will really have to remember the names. It doesn't look good if you are reading," Liesl reminded me but apparently was willing to let it slide for today.

I looked around my section, which was the little one in the back of the restaurant, and then went to help Gerri with rolling the silverware.

"Slow down there, Lil. Are you tryin' to beat a record? You're rollin' three napkins to my one. That silverware ain't goin no-where."

"Oh. Just want to be prepared. That's all." I had waited tables before but never like this. Never with the white napkin over the arm which, incidentally, was not an accessory to the uniform but rather a "very useful gastronomical tool", proving useful in many varied situations from setting down hot plates to wiping up spills. Never before in any waitressing job had the tables properly been set with both red *and* white wine glasses *and* with every size fork accounted for — and never in a *dirndl*. I was nervous.

Finally, my section got seated. I looked at the three individuals that were sitting down at my table. For the record: two women, probably late thirties or early forties, one older teen boy. I smoothed out the ironed napkin hanging over my forearm, took a deep breath and approached the table, picking up three menus on my way.

"Good evening," I greeted my guests, "my name is Lilly. I'll be your server. Our specials tonight are the Beef Tournedos with Julienne Carrots, and homemade Spätzle noodles. For dessert we have a fresh homemade Sacher Torte. Can I bring you a . . . a . . ."

I couldn't think of a wine sort to offer, "a glass of wine while you look over the menu?"

Liesl hovered around behind me, making sure that I said all the specials and that I did everything correctly. It was strange to feel like I was being tested on something like *waitressing*, but I was.

"I'll have a Riesling," said one woman.

"I'll have the same," said the other.

"I want a coke," ordered the teenager.

"Very good. I'll be right back," I chimed, content with how well that went.

I brought the guests their drinks, took their order, turned it in and went to the server niche to wait for my name to be called out. I couldn't go anywhere else, scared that they would call it and I wouldn't be there, and then the food might get cold. So, I waited. And waited. And waited.

After a while, I didn't notice Liesl around anymore, and I figured she must have gotten busy doing something else. I almost began to relax when one of the ladies gestured for me to come over to their table.

"I'm sorry, but we are sort of in a hurry. Do you know how much longer it is going to take?"

My heart rate sped up. "No, you know, I'm kind of new at this. I mean, to tell you the truth, you're my first table. Kind of a *premiere*, you could say," I said dramatically for effect. "I'll just go back to the kitchen and ask how much longer they think it will be, and, . . . and then I'll be right back out, OK?"

I quit stammering and went back to the kitchen where I asked Fritz himself how much longer it would be for my table's order and told him that they were in a hurry. Asking

101

for time approximations seemed harmless enough to me, but as it turned out, I'd made a near lethal mistake.

Without missing a beat, Fritz went off on a rant.

"*Scheiß* fast food! They want *fast food*? Tell them next time to *go get* fast food!"

He underscored his sentiments by slamming a butcher knife into a cutting board. I walked back out of the kitchen, stupefied. What was *that* for an answer? How could he say that?

Flashbacks from my first job as a waitress came flooding back to me. Mottos that brainwashed all new employees of The Lobster Bake, like "The customer is the life-blood of every business," "The customer is always right," "I'm here to serve," "The customer is king."

It was always the same drill, and after a while, I'd internalized every customer service motto there ever was. *What* was *he* saying?

Scared that my customers - my *kings*, would consider doing the unthinkable and might prepare to *complain* — an act that would be reflected in my tips, potentially could cost me my job and that I would no doubt probably take quite personally — I got a basket of pretzels from the bar and walked slowly back to my table.

"They said it will just be a few minutes. I brought you some pretzels in the meantime," I said flatly before I turned and went back to hide in the station, absolutely bewildered. I'd been side-swiped in my first shift. This was a completely unacceptable response, especially coming from the boss.

After nearly twenty more minutes, their dinner was ready, and I served it to my famished, time-pressured customers.

Thank God, I only had three tables the entire evening. When the shift was over, Liesl said that for my first shift, it hadn't been too bad.

"You mean it can be worse?" I asked.

She smiled silently.

I cleaned my section and still tried to figure out what had exactly happened. I got the feeling that I didn't know my schnitzel from my bratwurst. Fritz had a total disregard of customer service as I knew it — as I'd *lived* it. How could the other waitresses and cooks deal with his rudeness? Was it a California thing? Was this a German thing? In Amarillo, if you weren't already in the midst of having a heart attack, you'd be lucky if you didn't get shot for acting like this.

I sat down with a coke at table 15, and waited on Liesl to check me out, as Johnney walked up and sat down at the table.

"Man, that trial must really have Fritz on edge, huh?"

"What trial is that?"

"Oh, you don't know yet. There's some trial going on, and somehow, he's involved. Had to go in for a deposition and all. Must have pissed him off pretty bad, as you can see. That's all I know." She sipped her coke. "But you know, maybe I shouldn't say anything. You didn't hear it from me."

"No, of course not."

Liesl finally came to us.

"So, Lilly, what do you think?" she asked me.

"Good. I think everything was OK."

"Yes, me too." She smiled.

To celebrate, I went home and grabbed a beer from the refrigerator, as this was my one last weekend before having to work almost every Saturday and Sunday.

"How'd work go?" Maddie asked as she walked through the door.

"Bizarre. My view of the restaurant world has been shattered."

"How so?"

"Because, it's like, the customers are not kings, the life blood or anything else at this place. I don't get it." I took a drink. "He actually screamed loud enough that *the customers* could hear him! Johnney said he's more uptight that usual — something about the court case that he has to deal with."

"Oh, the intrigue," Maddie said sarcastically. "Any idea what it's about?"

"No. I think he is just a witness. Anyway, because of this case, they have the absolute 'No Fraternizing Policy', especially with the kitchen personnel which makes it kind of difficult to communicate, if you know what I mean."

"But you're not into fraternizing anyway, right?"

"No, I'm not," I said determined and looked deep into her eyes.

Maddie watched me for a second. "OK, you're not fraternizing, but what are you doing?"

"Checking your limbal rings."

"My what?"

"You know, your limbal rings. The circle around your iris. The bigger, the better, I was told today. I'm just checking.

"And, how are they?"

"OK, I guess. It's just not something I ever thought about. I'm going to bed."

"Great. Now I don't only have to worry about circles *under* my eyes, but also *in* my eyes."

"Have a good night." I went to my room and turned on my computer, updated my resumé and applied at an insurance office in hopes that I might find employment somewhere more civilized. And quick.

7

July

The first week flying solo at the Black Forest Restaurant went by fast, and I felt like I was starting to get the hang of it. Liesl had scheduled me only in the afternoons and had alternated my shifts between working behind the bar and waiting in the smallest sections. But in the mornings, I had time to read the paper from cover to cover and looked fruitlessly for a real job. As I skimmed over the jobs-wanted page of the newspaper, my phone beeped — announcing a message from Miss Teri.

July 1 🝰🔆🎼

Surprise, Gemini! As the saying goes, we meet people three times in life, and Mercury just went retrograde. Is there someone from your past who might be in for future?

Oh, God, I hope not. As I read it, and for a nano-second, my not-so-distant turbulent past came crashing back before my eyes. I was just starting to get adjusted to my new life, and the last thing I wanted was a blast from the past just as things were starting to feel like they might be alright.

Well, almost everything. We were deep into summer, and I thought that I would know the menu a bit better, but as it turned out, it was the Daily Specials that were ordered most often. And, as the name implied, they changed daily. I tried them as much as I could, but despite being seriously delicious, most of them were still very unfamiliar, dishes that I had never heard of, with names difficult to recall and impossible to pronounce. I tried to remember names like *Schinkenbandnudeln mit Pfifferlingen,* but they always seemed to slip through my short-term memory like water through a sieve, gone before I even reached the table. Cheat sheets became an indispensable crutch.

In the kitchen, there were always boxes of groceries, filled with things like blackberries, wild mushrooms or freshly picked herbs from the garden behind the restaurant. Fritz used nothing but the freshest ingredients in his dishes, ingredients that had a wonderful, enticing effect when cooked together, and with the weather still so warm, the doors and windows of the restaurant were kept open, letting the rich aromas drift beyond the restaurant, outside to the pedestrian-zone where they lured passers-by to stop and come in.

And come in they did. Seduced by wafts of deliciousness that floated out of the open windows, every afternoon, the place filled up with hungry, curious customers. I mean, they must have been seduced by the smell, because it certainly couldn't have been due to Fritz's unique charm. For all the magic he could do with food, he was still Fritz, and I figured it was a very good thing that he was usually confined to his kitchen. Especially now since he had been acting particularly neurotic. His voice was higher, his outbursts more frequent. Liesl rationalized that he was just so nervous because he was working with some event manager, planning an upcoming event. I thought the event manager was supposed to help him calm down, but it didn't seem like that was happening.

On the flip side, after several weeks of working there, I noticed that it was also not unusual to have local celebrities come in as well as regular tourists who swore by the place.

Many people came here not only for the food, but also for the drinks: authentic German beers, wines, or spirits that, lucky for me, weren't exactly cheap. As the restaurant had four stars, the prices themselves were high, so it didn't take long for customers to accumulate substantial tabs, and after all that beer, they were often in a good mood and very generous. Translation: great tips. So financially, I was keeping my head above water, but being the new girl, I had only been scheduled to work lunches, which meant less money which equaled no Girl's Night.

Maddie must have been reading my mind, because, just as I felt a hint of yearning for fun, she called.

"There's a concert on Saturday. You want to go?"

"Do I want to? Sure, but I can't."

"Oh. You have to work on Saturday?"

"No, I don't. Liesl said it's supposed to be busy, and I probably wouldn't be up for it yet. That being the case, I really don't have the money to do anything."

"Oh, too bad." She hesitated for a second before going on.

"What do you think about just going to Rick's then? I mean, I've been wanting to introduce you to Silvia and Brooke, anyway. It's not expensive."

"I don't know. I don't really —"

"It's on me. It's settled," she insisted.

"Uhm, well, OK. I guess that sound's great," I said, unable to refuse.

Rick's had become the personal hang out for me and Maddie when it came to having the occasional brunch. I had hardly hung up the phone when it rang again.

"Hello?"

"Hello, may I speak to Lilly? It is me, Liesl, from the Black Forest Restaurant restaurant."

Oh no. Her voice had a sense of urgency in it, and I instinctively straightened up.

"Hi Liesl. It's me." I wondered if I had done something wrong. "Is everything OK?"

"Yes, Lilly, dear," she answered quickly. "We need you to come in tonight because Gerri is very sick. Can you come in for the evening, Lilly, to work at the bar at three thirty?"

"Tonight? Sure. I can jump in. I'll be there in the afternoon," I said.

"It's not a busy night, so you shouldn't be here too long. Usually till around nine, Lilly. We see you in a little while."

The last sentence stuck in my head. *We see you in a little vial.* I knew she meant "while", but somehow I saw myself in a small, glass laboratory bottle like in a scene from *"Honey, I Shrunk the Kids."*

I hung up the phone, glad that I could go in, and also glad that now, I could also go out – guilt free. I started to put my phone down when my horoscope beeped, again. Is this some kind of joke?

July 1 🔆☀🎼

Surprise, Gemini! As the saying goes, we meet people three times in life, and Mercury just went retrograde. Is there someone from your past who might be in for future?

Ha! I thought. Jokes on you, Miss Teri! I don't know anyone out here from my past!

When I got to work, Fritz was setting up in the kitchen, still in "mildly-irritated" modus; Johnney was setting up the server station, stocking and, folding napkins; and I got to work setting up the bar. Some glasses from last night were still on the counter, ice needed to be put in the ice bins and the beer needed to be re-stocked. I finished setting up the bar shortly before four o'clock and felt relieved that I'd been safe from the choleric lunatics when I heard Liesl in the dining room chattering away to someone, in German. I could hear her voice getting louder by proximity, and I turned around to see her walking toward the counter with a guy who looked just like Marcus. She walked away and into the kitchen, leaving the doppelganger at the bar.

Stunned, I jumped back and saw that the guy looked just as surprised to see me as I was to see him.

"I know you, don't I?" he finally asked.

Know me? I'm the new girl. I don't know anyone out here, I thought rationally, but right then, I realized it wasn't someone who *looked* like Marcus. It *was* Marcus who was also doing a double-take. I couldn't believe it, but yes, I was sure I knew him. Speechless, I instinctively started scanning the place, checking to see if any choleric bosses were around.

"Lilly, right?" he repeated.

"Right." I said, just as Fritz's voice carried all the way from the kitchen. Although, it wasn't his normal yelling, but was loud nonetheless and I got so startled that I dropped the glass from my hand.

"Two cokes," Fritz ordered without looking at me, then he started talking to Marcus in German, but in a notably friendlier tone.

I quickly swept the pieces of glass to the side and fumbled around for two new glasses when it struck me that Marcus was conversing back. With Fritz. I hardly ever saw Fritz speak in a normal tone, a normal voice, using normal gestures. As far as I could tell, he was actually having a conversation — with Marcus. In German.

I carefully placed the drinks on the bar. Fritz took them, gave one to Marcus who looked at me smiling before they both walked off, as my heart pounded inexplicably, which gave way to a lovely domino effect of my chest starting to flush and then beginning to sweat.

"What's the matter with you?" Johnney asked as she came up to the bar.

"What do you mean?"

"You're standing there with a silly smile on your face. I just wonder what you're smiling about."

"Am I? Maybe you like this better," I suggested, giving her my best go-to-hell smile. "What do you want?" I asked, side-stepping the question.

"Two Rieslings."

Stupid fucking smile, I thought as I internally cursed her and the thought spiral threatened to accelerated out of control. I mean, wasn't there a mountain somewhere she should be twirling on? How was I supposed to work like this? I wished for a cigarette and cursed Gerri for being sick, as I read the ticket. Two Rieslings.

Then I exhaled, realizing that she'd actually placed a really simple order. One I should be able to handle without too much risk of screwing it up. What was the matter with me? *Just stay focused.*

I rung up the white ticket and poured wine into the glasses.

"Anything special going on out there?" I asked, trying to sound casual. From the bar, I couldn't see the dining room, and I wondered where Fritz and Marcus had gone.

"By 'special' you mean — especially dead?" she asked flatly.

"Oh, is it dead? I thought it must be busy. I thought I even saw Fritz seating someone," I mentioned calmly.

"Oh, you mean the guy he's with? He's not a customer. He's the event manager."

"He's *what?*" I gasped. "The *event manager?*" I asked unbelieving.

"Yeah, I think so. Kind of a hottie, you know, but kind of weird, too," she said aloud but more to herself and then adjusted her cleavage. "Wonder what they're doin'," she said as she took the two glasses and turned to leave.

"Don't forget that 'no fraternizing' policy!" I called after her, my voice getting higher as I wondered who was weirder.

No-one was sitting at the bar, but there was a steady flow of orders from the floor. Liesl came up periodically, then Johnney, then Liesl. A lot of the orders were for Fritz and Marcus, and after several hours of this, it was a miracle that they were still able to stand, let alone work.

"Two Bitburgers, please," Liesl ordered. She didn't say anything else, but there was a nervous energy around her.

"Everything OK?" I opened the bottles and set them on a tray.

"Everything's OK, Lilly, everything's OK," she answered quickly and left.

It was quiet again for about half an hour, and then she returned. Same order. This kept up for the next two hours until it was almost closing time.

She returned to the bar.

"Lilly, dear, pour me two whiskeys. One with water and one with ice," she said with a hint of relief in her voice. She walked up behind the bar and got some pretzels, I guessed, for them.

"You can go ahead and close up afterwards. There is nothing more to do here. Tuesdays are often kind of slow, you know. Only Fritz and Marcus, planning for the fall, and this could go on for a while."

Relieved and anxious to leave, I quickly closed down the bar and tabbed out. I skipped changing back into my street clothes and exited out the kitchen into the ally.

Was *he* the event manager? Was this the blast from the past? Curiouser and curiouser, I thought as I lit up a cigarette, and I heard my name.

"Lilly?"

Immediately recognizing the voice with the accent, I stopped and slowly turned around.

"Hi." I tried to sound as normal as possible.

"Hi."

After an awkward exchang of monosyllabic greetings, we simultaneously started to talk again.

"What are you . . ." I started. — "How are you?" he asked.

Why was this so weird?

"You first."

"Well, I just saw you come out here, and I wanted to say I'm sorry about the glasses."

The air filled with the scent of whiskey, and the smoothness in his voice had morphed into one long slur.

"I guess we're even," I said, remembering the ski boot in his neck.

"Ha! Yeah, I maybe so," he laughed. "So, how are you?"

"Good. I'm doing well. And you? What are you *doing* here? I thought you were only on vacation," I asked.

"I'm working here for a while. And you? Aren't you supposed to be in — where? Texas?"

"Good memory," I cut in.

"But you're still here in California. And here, at this restaurant..."

" I was thinking the same thing. So it's true. You are working here. Small world, huh?"

"*Ja*, well, kind of for Fritz. He needs some help with organizing the festivals in the fall, and . . . um, how do you say . . . wine tasting fairs."

"Wine tasting fairs? That sounds fun. So, you're here for a while?"

"*Ja*, for a while."

We stood silent for a few moments. He grinned, swaying, trying to keep his balance.

"Looks like you've had a bit too much to drink."

After the amount I'd served them, I was surprised he was still able to speak or stand at all.

"And you? You are now wearing a dirndl?" He asked, not attempting to hide his smirk at the low-cut v-neck of the dress.

"It goes with the job. But I hear they're all the rage next season."

He looked at me puzzled.

"I'm a trendsetter, you know, like a fashion trend . . . setter." I couldn't think of any synonyms for trendsetter.

"Ah, right." He let the thought sink in. "Let's hope not," he added with a skeptical smile.

"Does it look that bad?" I asked.

"No! I mean, um . . .," he stammered around the subject, "now, I probably can't say anything right, but . . . um, *na ja,* I

112

mean, for a dirndl, it looks good — on you. I'm just surprised to see you in that. I mean, to see you at all. Not only in the dress."

"Yeah, me you too."

Johnney came out through the kitchen door. She looked at me, looked at Marcus and then back at me with a smile.

"Bye-bye, Lilly." She said, giving me an extra knowing smile. "See ya tomorrow?"

"Yeah, I'll be here."

"So, I saw you, of course, earlier," he picked up our conversation where we'd left it off. "But I only want to say hello, and that, um, I'm around here for a while. I mean, I *will be* around here for a while," he corrected his grammar.

It had been six months since I'd seen him. His English was still broken, but he'd made some major jumps.

"So, I guess we probably see us again, then," he added.

"If you're around here, I guess wewill."

"Good. Then, I wish you a good night."

He sounded so polite, almost formal. It was hard for me to imagine him and Fritz being from the same planet, let alone the same country.

"Right. OK. You too, Have a good night. I'll see ya around, I guess." At least I hoped.

He disappeared back through the kitchen door, and I continued through the alley behind the restaurant.

When I got home, Miss Teri beeped again, and I read the prediction with cautious, hesitant belief.

Well, maybe there was someone from my past that might be in my future . . .

******

113

July 9 ▣▣▣

A little water-cooler chitchat could end up zapping the whole morning before you know it. So much for your plans to be productive, right? Actually, a little extra socializing could be a key career move, particularly if that last meeting ended on a frosty note.

Weekend! Liesl said I didn't have enough experience to work a Saturday night, so I had the night off — lucky me! In the afternoon, I went down to the pedestrian zone and had lunch and coffee at a sidewalk café where I sat and people-watched for hours under a grey sky. The style of dressing was different out here. There were many more hippy and organic types than in Amarillo. More than I was used to. But now that I saw it and thought about it, I wasn't really sure if a dirndl would stand out here or not — not that I was willing to try it out.

Later, Maddie and I went to Rick's around nine o'clock and found her friends. Brooke and Sylvia sat in a booth at the back of the restaurant and were just ordering some drinks.

"I'll have a tea. Do any of you also wanna one?" Brooke slurred, pushing her glasses up her nose, and her reddish bangs out of her eyes.

"Tea?" Maddie asked knowingly before turning to me and whispering '*the Long Island variety*'. "What's up now?"

"You already know: Leon," Silvia answered. The petit woman with a dark ponytail sat in the corner of the booth. She wore in a sleeveless tie-dyed dress and beads around her neck. "He broke up with her — again," she said with an eye roll.

"Um, I think I'm just going to have a beer," I told the waitress who was still standing next to us, waiting.

"Me too," Maddie said.

"They've only been together for six months and broken up about as many times," she explained, letting me in on the details.

"I never know what you see in him, anyway," Silvia said.

"You're one to be talking. You're in love with your professor," Brooke argued.

"Your professor?" Did I hear that right?

"He is *so* hot," Silvia gushed and drank her beer. Were her large green eyes beaming with happiness?

"And he's not my *professor*," she looked to me, "he's a grad student," she clarified.

"Oh," I said.

"But he will be," she added with a mischievous laugh. "Anyway, it's fate. I know it. Did I tell you he called me over after class today? That *has* to mean something."

"Well, I don't know if it means it's fate, but you're right. It probably means *something*," Maddie said.

"It just means he knows you have something for older, guys," Brooke hissed before gulping down her drink. "And weird older guys who wear tailored scarves in seventy-degree weather at that. You better be careful, is all I have to say. She turned and asked at me expectantly. Would you start dating a man from work?"

Yikes. We had just arrived, and the level of openness in this conversation already in progress left me feeling uncomfortable and embarrassed. For a moment, I even thought I heard someone say "Tayler", but that cannot have happened. I watched them all with their relationship problems and was increasingly glad that I didn't have one. I came out here so I could concentrate on my career, and I could see that *that* was exactly what I would continue to do.

The waitress returned with our drinks as I thought about the crew at work. "Well, actually we have a 'no fraternizing' clause in the policy at work, so I guess there's no chance of something like that happening there." I took a drink of my beer.

Silvia gave me a look of disbelief. "Clause, schmause," she muttered. "You want what you want. No-one has *control* over that. No *clause* is going to change that."

"Maybe not," I said, "But I don't really want to be on the next bus back to Amarillo just yet. So I will just have to try to control myself."

"*No* control?" Maddie asked, "Che será, será?"

"Sure, why not? And besides, he's not *that* much older. I believe in the universe. Leave it all up to fate, destiny," Sylvia said.

"Screw fate," Brooke said solemnly. "Like you said, you want what you want! Sometimes you get it, and sometimes you get it and lose it."

"Then maybe it wasn't meant to be. But you were probably meant to learn something by it, don't you think?"

"Oh, fuck off." Brooke shot back, her eyes now watery.

"I just..."

"Ok, guys, come on," Maddie cut in. "Let's not talk too much about this. I think I sense the need for a happy spark in the conversation here. Otherwise we'll all be crying before the next round."

"Oh, of course she doesn't want to talk about this." Brooke looked at me. "She has the perfect boyfriend, the perfect relationship, the perfect job."

"That's not fair," Maddie defended herself.

"But true," she said, "No, I'm happy for you. At least someone has a normal relationship."

"I just think, if you want something, you have to make your own way. You can't just leave *everything* to chance, you know. Not everything is a coincidence, don't you think, Lil?"

"Um, maybe not everything, but, well, speaking of coincidences . . . I had a strange one today," I said. "You'll never guess who showed up at work."

"Someone from Amarillo?" Maddie asked surprised.

"No. Do you remember that guy when we went skiing?"

I could clearly see in Maddie's face that she did.

"He came in today."

"To eat?" she asked surprised.

"No." I paused. "He works there."

"What? No way!" Maddie exclaimed. "That *one*?"

"Yeah, that one."

"What's he doing there?"

"I don't know. Somehow, he works there. Organizes festivals or something like that. Anyway, it was a pretty strange thing for me today."

"And you think *that's* a coincidence?" Silvia asked.

"Well, I think so. I mean, I certainly didn't know anything about him being here. On the other hand, now that you mention it, my horoscope did say something about 'someone from my past'." I drew the air quotes around the words with my fingers.

Silvia smiled with satisfaction.

"Don't forget the 'no fraternizing' policy," Brooke said in undertones.

"No, I mean, he just started working there. There is absolutely no risk of anything happening. Besides, I'm not going to be there that long," I repeated. "But it's all kind of strange, you know, having a *no fraternizing policy* in a restaurant? I've never heard of that before. I asked Gerri about it the other day. She just said it had something to do with someone Fritz used to know — they had to close their restaurant and he had to go in for a deposition, and it kinda freaked him out, so now he's taking extra precautions."

"Sounds a little paranoid," Brooke said.

"Yeah, now he's all like 'you get caught fraternizing — and you're fired!'" My arms started to spontaneously fly around, as I composed myself again. "I mean, his restaurant is fine. It's just kind of weird, the whole 'no fraternizing-Marcus-big case thing' you know?"

"If it's meant to be, it'll be. The universe can get pretty creative sometimes, when it wants to," Sylvia added after her next sip.

I couldn't see anything happening. And after watching all this, I knew my time there, once again, wasn't forever. My real job was coming. Hell, this wouldn't even be but for a few months. Actually, it could end any day.

******

July 12 🗓✉♥

Discover a whole new area of interest this month, for it's never too late to discover something (or someone) new to love. Explore your creativity more, perhaps with a class.

Although I was running late to get to work, I stopped by the post office to get some stamps for my resumes. I went to the philatelic counter and picked out some stamps that I thought would stand out, walked briskly down the mall.

When I got to work, Carlos, the apprentice, was turning out homemade *spätzle* noodles from a noodle maker. He smiled politely without saying anything when I walked through the kitchen and into the bar. Instinctively, I almost said "hello", then stopped. No fraternizing.

Tuesday was inventory day, so I pulled the beers out of the refrigerator, counted the bottles on-hand and noted down the brands that we were short on the order form.

From the kitchen, I could hear voices speaking in German. I recognized both Fritz's and Liesl's voices. But then there was the third, and my ears strained, for a moment to listen to the deep, low voice, as if I would understand anything.

Quit eavesdropping and get to work, I said to myself as I lost track of my beer count. I started over just as the distracting voices became louder, and the three of them walked out of the waiter niche. Liesl and Fritz walked off, leaving Marcus alone at the bar.

"So, this is where you are working today?" he asked, switching languages.

"This is it. Do you want anything?"

He looked at me, his eyebrows raised.

"A coke? A beer?" I emphasized.

"Ah, no. Thank you. We're leaving in a few minutes."

"As you wish."

We stood there, on opposite sides of the bar, until I broke the awkward silence that filled the space.

"So, where are you two off to?" I asked.

"We're at Summer Festival in San José. Didn't they say anything?"

"To me? They never say anything to me. Except telling me when I'm supposed to be here."

"Oh."

Fritz came back around the corner with a large bag in hand, and they walked off.

"Bye." I called, noticing a wobble in my voice. Why did I just say that? Why?

I started to re-count the bottles of Weizen beer for the third time.

"Are you finished with the order yet, Lilly? I have to send it over," Liesl reminded me.

Was it already so late? I kept losing track of my count. How many bottles were there? The first customers were coming in, and I hadn't even started with my bank.

******

July 29 ⑥⚪⬚

Wash, rinse, repeat. Wash, rinse, repeat. If at first, you don't succeed, try, try again! With Mars retrograde in Jupiter, everything might feel a little backwards.

Eighty-four degrees. Light breezes from the west and cloudy. Summer in Santa Cruz. The crowded mall meant that most people would be enjoying the day outdoors. Not like me. I would spend most of it alone behind the dark bar as it had been for more than two weeks now, getting fairly accustomed to my job. Fritz was gone to some food festivals. That left Liesl to work with Carlos, in the kitchen, which suited me fine, since the mood of the entire restaurant was generally calmer and lighter.

"Good morning, Lilly," Gerri said when she walked by me.

"Everyone is gone already, huh?"

"Yeah, looks like it," I answered.

She was hummed a tune as she walked back to the station, just as Liesl walked out and gave me a to-do list of duties, along with some cleaning supplies.

"I know that there is not a lot of business right now, but here are some things for you to do. The health inspectors come around regularly, so we always need to be ready."

I read the list, which confirmed that I wouldn't be standing around bored all day.

Clean ice bins: check.

Dust the bottles: check.

Take the mats out, clean the floor: wait until later.

Dust the fixtures: OK. I tried to reach them, but I was too short, even with the duster. So, I went back to get a step ladder through the conspicuously calmer kitchen. No screaming. No tantrums. So strange.

I couldn't say that I missed Fritz, but I did find myself wondering if Marcus would ever come back. I hadn't seen him in weeks, not since the last time his presence had interfered with my bottle counting. But just as I was thinking that, just as I returned to the bar with the step ladder – lo and behold: there he was, standing right behind me in the walkway to the bar.

Flustered and surprised, I nearly dropped the ladder and flinched, but he didn't. I started to feel my personal space being intruded upon and moved backwards towards the ice bins, but although I didn't actually see him move, somehow, he was still near and right beside me. My heart rate accelerated, but I decided not to move anymore and to stand my ground.

"Hi," I said tightly.

"Hi." His voice sounded low and velvety.

"I just need to fill the ice bins and I'll be finished." I heard my voice waver.

"Take your time." He smiled but still didn't move, and I started to get the feeling that he was enjoying this.

I filled the ice bins and then returned the buckets to the kitchen. Then I went to the dishes and got a tray of tumbler glasses to restock while the no fraternizing policy kept going through my head. Be serious, I thought. Stay focused on ... .what was I doing?... dusting.

I walked back to the bar. He was still there going through some logs. I got the step stool again and put it down. Stepping on it, I tried to reach the fixtures, but I was still not high enough to reach them.

"Darn it," I said quietly to myself and got down.

"Shall I?" He looked at me, gesturing to take the duster. He stepped up on the step stool and easily reached all the fixtures. He swooped over them, causing dust to rain down below which reminded me of my next duty that I had put off before. At the same time, I was caught off guard by his willingness to help.

He jumped down and gave me the duster.

"Is there anything else you need?" There was that look again, and though I believed I must be imagining things, I instinctively looked away.

"I think I'm fine," I said. "Thanks, though."

"Enjoy your afternoon." He smiled and walked past me, and I didn't see him for the rest of the day.

But I didn't really enjoy it, as my thoughts turbo-ed through my head for hours.

"So, he's a space invader?" Sylvia asked later as I told about my proximity issues.

"Yeah, but you know how usually it's weird when someone gets too close. You get nervous or pissed off?"

"Yeah."

"Yeah, well, I didn't. I don't know why. But I was just, like, paralyzed."

"Maybe your amygdala got kind of high-jacked?"

"My what?" I asked, fearing the worst.

"Your amygdala," Sylvia said, twirling a necklace around her neck, "it's the part of the brain that get strong reactions to personal space invasions. You know: fight, flight or freeze mode. It sounds like you froze."

"Oh, so I'm not crazy? My amygdala is working fine?"

"That, or he is a psychopath."

A *psychopath*? Yikes!

"Here," she said, handing me a bracelet with some greenish rocks, "It'll help against fears, you know, strong reactions."

I wasn't sure it would do the trick, but I put the bracelet on, willing to give it a try, seeing that the reaction was so strong.

Only I wasn't sure it was all in my brain.

8

August

August 6 ▥☆▥

The August full moon will shine in your house of adventure and work, which can intensify emotions and add an element of unpredictability. If stress shows up at work, don't be so quick to think it's all about you. Other people have their own problems, so a friendly word could make your life — and theirs — just a little better.

None of my potential future employers had, as of yet, called me back, so I decided to up the ante on my resumes: I invested in specially chosen postage that corresponded with my correspondence. The Philatelic Center had just opened when I walked into the post office. "Wonder Woman" and the "Grand Canyon" were the stamp designs of the month, and as there was no need to fall any deeper, I opted for a page of "Wonder Woman", hoping that this little detail would scream my love of graphic arts, my ability to pay attention to detail, and, of course, that this was the resume of a wonder woman. Hopeful, I put the stamps on the envelopes and sent them off with good wishes, before going to work, where Fritz, in stark contrast, was verbally abusing the Julienne Carrots, while Carlos watched closely. By now, the outrages were pretty predictable, actually, but this time I knew why. It was Deposition Day, and I really couldn't blame him for not being so cheery.

"Can I get another draw?" Mike, one of my regular customers who was sitting at the bar, asked.

"Sure." I filled the glass.

"Gotta do something to beat the heat, ya know?" he smiled.

"Well someone's got to this bar up and running. Looks like everyone's at the beach. They probably want to take advantage of the good weather before it gets bad again."

Heat. Who would have thought that Santa Cruz could get just as hot as Amarillo? And out here, there weren't air conditioners everywhere, so people seemed to just walk around trying to find a breeze or cruised in their cars with the a/c on. El Niño, "the baby", had been sleeping for a few days, giving us a break from all the storms and leaving sweltering, humid heat in their place. I tried to accommodate my few customers by keeping the doors opened so that a breeze could blow through, but for some reason, Liesl would inevitably go back through the restaurant and re-shut all the doors. Gerri said that she was afraid of drafts.

"Then why did she open a bar?" I asked.

"As in breezes. She's afraid of breezes."

Sometimes I thought I would never figure these people out. I spent the morning doing inventory and cleaning behind the bar where I found some board markers and a black neon-board. I wrote the drink specials in neon blue, red and yellow markers, and drew flowers and borders on the board when Marcus walked by.

"So, you're an artist?" he asked as he stood close behind me, watching over my shoulder.

"An artist? Me? No. I mean, I've had a few classes, but I'm just trying to liven this thing up a little, you know? Maybe put it outside, try to get some customers in here."

"Um hmm."

"Or at least I'll have an excuse to go outside where there is a breeze."

He raised his eyebrows like he was in deep thought but then only said "OK" before he gathered up the logs that were stored behind the bar, and as he walked by me to leave, he winked.

I continued drawing on the neon board but found myself perplexed. Did he just *wink* at me? I drew flowers and borders around the edges of the neon board and, for a good part of my shift, wrestled with the wink question and why was it bothering me when my phone beeped again, reminding of me of the full moon. Of course, it was the full moon. That's what it was.

****

August 26 ⬚ ⬚ ⬚

Eenie meenie miney – Flow! Need to express yourself? Need to let go? Find a way to let your creative juices flow! Even if work and personal time seem to be co-habitating well, be vigilant to keep the balance, even in the eye of the storm.

The eye of the storm. After teasing Santa Cruz with a couple of weeks of hot but lovely weather, El Niño woke up with a vengeance. Gusty winds and rain beat down on the city, and for once, I was happy I had dry clothes to change into when I got to work, even if it was the dirndl. But however, annoying the rain was in terms of clothes, it seemed to be good for business. There was a light, almost fun mood in the air, which was partly because Fritz, who was scheduled to be at several food festival through August, had not been there for a couple of days.

I got some ice out of the ice bins, said "Hi" to Carlos and went back behind the bar where Liesl was working, talking to Mike and some other regulars who were sitting there.

"Good, you're here," she said. "I have to go to the floor. You take over."

"Ok. Can I get you guys anything?"

"Not yet. I'm still good." Mike said.

Some mail had been piled up on the counter. A box with business cards and new table tents with an Oktoberfest theme were mixed in with the usual bills and advertisements. I started to peek at the table tents when Johnney came up to the bar with a huge drink order.

"Have you seen table 12?" she asked exhilarated.

"No."

"Oh my God," she said fixing her hair in the mirror behind the bar and adjusting the lace on her dress, "He must be poor, 'cause he sure is beautiful,"

"What do you mean?"

"Well, you can be rich or beautiful — you can't have both. Least that's what my Daddy used to say."

"Really?" I asked, opening the bottles. "If he keeps drinking these, maybe it'll up your chances with him."

"Ha ha." She fake-smiled as she scooted the tray over her forearm to steady it and left back for her station.

In the midst of making iced teas and opening Weizen beers, Marcus appeared in the main door, carrying the neon board with the "Specials" sign that I had drawn on it the day before, the letters now smeared and streaming down the board.

"I guess you want to have this cleaned? Because the rain is doing a nice job." He held it up for me to see with a smile.

"Crap," I sighed. "El Niño strikes again. I'll re-do it later."

He placed the board behind the bar and didn't seem in a big hurry because he leaned up against the cabinets where he stayed, presumably looking for something. He looked through the mail and through one of the new menus that had arrived. He turned up the music from the receiver behind the cabinet and German "Volksmusik" pumped a little louder through the restaurant, the kind of oom-pah music that relied heavily on the use of the accordions, and somehow reminded me of a mariachi band.

I placed all the drinks on a big tray, rung up the ticket and pushed the tray over the bar for Johnney to pick up.

"The sign out front seemed to be a good idea, anyway," Marcus said suddenly.

"Oh?"

"Ja, well, I wasn't sure at first." He paused. "But it seems to work," he gestured to the customers sitting at the bar.

It was true. Several people sitting at the bar were actually drinking the specials that I'd advertised outside on the neon board: proof that my idea was a success! (as least as long as the weather lasted).

"Well, I guess this makes me happy." I said, barely able to look into his face.

Then he winked, and walked off.

"Thanks," I turned, only to see my reflection in the mirror behind the bar. I stood there stumped with a stupid smile. What was the matter with me? I was even wearing the protective bracelet!

Know my neck would soon be glowing, I pulled up the top of my dirndl as Liesl walked by, still doing her floor manager routine.

"Another beer, Mike?"

"Sure," he accepted automatically.

"Mike, why do people wink?" I asked my regular.

"Aren't I supposed to ask you the questions? You're the bartender." he replied jokingly.

"Probably. That just tells you how messed up I am." The *Amygdala* and *psychopath* debate raced through my head as I gave him his beer. "No, seriously. What does that *mean*?"

"I don't know, maybe it's just a friendly way to communicate?"

"Maybe." I thought, washing out some tumblers. "But to communicate what? Who winks?"

"Well, that one man who comes in here sometimes with the little boy. He winks."

"Yeah, but usually because he wants you to go along with one of the stories that he's telling his little boy."

With Marcus, this wasn't an explanation. So, what could it mean?

Later, I posed the question at Girl's Night, which had about equally clarifying answers, and mostly more questions:

"Did he have something in his eye?" asked Maddie.

"Was it a platonic, friendly "hello" or "good-bye" message? You know, maybe a cultural thing?" asked Sylvia.

"Or does it lean more towards the 'Hey there, I'd like to fuck your brains out' message?" asked Brooke.

I didn't know, and besides, wouldn't that be fraternizing?

9

September

Autumn had arrived! And Maddie had gone to a seminar, so I had the house to myself for the week. I sat out on the back porch, smoked a cigarette, drank my coffee and read my horoscope.

September 22

You've got your foot in the door, but now where to go? Don't worry — travel and adventure are on the radar! A change in your routine can help you to think outside the box and get you moving in the right direction.

Traveling and adventure sounded nice, but honestly, I didn't have the money, time or inclination to travel at the moment. And besides, I felt like I *was* on an adventure, relieved that I was finding a routine and was getting used to things at home and at work. The upcoming Oktoberfest had also sparked some curiosity in me, but I sent out two resumes anyway, just to be on the safe side.

The local harvests were in full swing, and El Niño must have been taking a fall nap, because the weather was great for most of September. Fritz and Marcus were away at outdoor food festivals, and The Black Forest Restaurant was filled with friendly weather and friendly customers, who poured into the restaurant. In Fritz' absence, the apprentice, Carlos, came up with one masterpiece after the other, and as business

129

boomed, and so did my schedule and the tips. I even got promoted to better sections every now and then.

But this afternoon, when I got to work, there was a huge commotion. Great, I thought, Fritz must be back. I tried walking undetected through the kitchen, when I saw that it wasn't Fritz making the commotion, but Liesl, who was on the floor as Gerri, Johnney and Carlos hovered above her.

"I can not move it!" Liesl cried.

"It's her ankle." Gerri went for the phone. "We'll need to see if we can get you to the emergency room."

"I can not go to the emergency room!" Liesl protested.

"You're not going to be able to do anything with an ankle like that." It was swelling even through her shoe.

"I have to be here!" she cried. "Everyone go back to work!"

We cleared off and left Gerri alone to handle the situation, and before long, she came up to the bar and asked me if I had any interest in going to Santa Barbara.

"Santa Barbara?" I asked hesitantly. "What should I do there? How will I get there?"

"Fritz is going to have to come back. There's no other way. We'll order a train ticket for you. Once you're down there, Fritz will pick you up, so he can come back. But they need someone there fast. Can you go?"

I wasn't exactly sure of what it entailed, but it sounded like there were probably worse things I could do.

"It pays 100 dollars a day."

"Sold," I said before she could retract the offer. And, best of all, I didn't have to wear the dirndl! It looked like I would be traveling after all!

I went home, packed my bags and could hardly believe it as I stowed my luggage above the seat on the Coast Starlight, the train that traveled down to Santa Barbara. The train took of slowly, sped up along the coast, slowing down in the towns and cities. I'd never been on a train, and it seemed like I must be dreaming as I looked out the window to the ocean and through the stations.

When I arrived, nervous and starving, Santa Barbara, Fritz appeared out of nowhere on the platform in his hound-tooth pants and white jacket.

"How is Liesl?" he asked shaking his head.

"Well, she seemed to be in a lot of pain. I guess she'll be happy when you're back."

Fritz was obviously not happy, grumbling most of the time in a muddled voice, which I was happy not to understand.

We drove speechless to the festival which was down by the beach. Palm trees floated above a labyrinth of white tents lined up next to each other, mostly distinguishable but for the big number hanging on the outside of the tent. The sea breeze blew between the crowds of people that were milling about from tent to tent, testing and tasting the wine and food, and as we walked along the gravel paths in pursuit of Booth 39, I noticed, there was even more sun. Several bands played upbeat music in a jazzy atmosphere, and I tried not to seem too impressed with the venue, but found myself quickly getting into it, thinking, "Yes! This is the kind of life that suits me: a chance to run around in the sun, listening to music, having a glass of wine...and get paid to do it!

No wonder Fritz was pissed off that he had to go home.

We reached Booth 39, and for some reason, when I saw Marcus, I stopped, feeling a wave of awkwardness. He was laughing and talking with some customers and somehow you just knew he was in his element. But was I?

Fritz waited a moment until Marcus had finished talking and then approached him with authority. By the tone, I imagined they were words of warning: no fraternizing with the customers! Or the employees! Or anyone!

Marcus's smile was replaced with a serious look. Fritz also looked serious when he switched into English.

"So, here is my replacement," he said. "Yes, it's you." He handed me a white button-down shirt and a long, black apron.

"OK. Here. You need to wear this. You can go to the bathrooms if you need to." he said, pointing up the hill.

I took the shirt and walked up to the public restrooms, where I put my own folded clothes in my over-sized bag and returned to the tent.

"I'm back," I said quickly, "so I guess you're free to go now."

"Nice that you think so," he muttered as he gathered up some of his stuff, and with a simple "good-bye" to Marcus, he left. And suddenly the mood lifted.

"Well, I guess it's just you and me now," Marcus said with a cautious smile.

"Looks like it. What should I do?"

"First, just have a seat," he said, gesturing to one of the two swiveling bar stools behind the counter.

I sat down and looked at the different wines but didn't see anything that looked familiar to me. No Chablis. No Chardonnay. No Merlot. The thought of having to learn yet another new assortment made me nervous, and Marcus must have picked up on my hesitancy.

"Don't worry. I'll explain it all," he said in a low voice. Or maybe his voice was just being drowned out by the bands, because he spoke in a such a low voice, that I found myself leaning in just to hear what he was saying. Or maybe it was my hearing that was going. Maybe my hearing was in cahoots with my amygdala. Maybe it was my entire brain. Maybe it was my *whole* head.

"You can do this," he said and patted my shoulder. It was only a pat, but somehow I froze.

"You have lots of experience. And remember, it's not brain surgery," he continued.

"*Brain* surgery?" I coughed back.

And there was the onslaught of something like panic:

Had I been walking, I would have stopped dead in my tracks.

Breathe

Could he read my mind or something?

I got an urge to call Sylvia instantly.

Breathe

I needed to know more about the whole dysfunctional amygdala issue - now, and if there was anything I could do.

Was I brain damaged?

GET A GRIP!

"Your vote of confidence is encouraging," I managed to mumble.

"OK, here is a *Spätlese*," he picked up a green bottle. "It is what they call a semi-dry. And this is the *Auslese*. It is sweet. And this is called a *Riesling*. It's a dry, white wine. And this is a *Spätburgunder*." He lifted another bottle up high for effect. "You see — it is red."

The way he explained everything, it seemed as though it should be easy enough to grasp, but really, whatever happened to good ol' White Zinfandel, or Cabernet Sauvignon? None of the Napa Valley regulars were here. I was that much more relieved when I looked over his shoulder and saw the chalk-board sign with the wine prices on it, and the description! Yes! I thought. A cheat-sheet! This, I could use!

He went on explaining the wine selection, but while his voice sounded calm, he was constantly twisting a beer coaster in his hand.

Did he not really think I could do it? Or maybe it *was* more the psychopath theory. I wondered about Sylvia and remembered, luckily, at least I had the bracelet on.

A rush of people came up and I watched more than anything else. Wiping down the counter, taking the money. During the next slow period, he pulled out wines with names that were real tongue twisters. Words like *Liebfrauenmilch* or *Gewürztraminer, Spätburgunder* or *Trockenbeerenauslese* that showed no resemblance to the subject of wine as I knew it.

Was I seriously supposed to be able to say this? Maybe we should give them some nick-names, I thought. Something a little less intimidating. Something like Liebi, Trami, Spati and Trocki? No. They sounded more like cartoon characters. Anyway, before we could discuss it, there was a rush of

133

people. Was it the after five crowd? There were so many around that we didn't really have time to talk anymore. Training was over.

Some customers stayed at our booth for a long time. They listened to everything that Marcus had to say about the wine list as if it were the latest breaking news. He had this way of commanding an audience, and time seemed to fly and stand still all at once. Several hours passed, when it was starting to get dark, and all at once, it slowed down. I gathered the wine glasses off the bar and washed up as Marcus put the supplies away and locked down some of the containers for the wine bottles.

I noticed that each of the bottles had little icons on them, and I wondered what they were but felt too stupid to ask. The entire day, I had tried to figure them out and wished that I had been able to help more. But for some reason, I didn't want him to know that I didn't have a clue what it meant. I guess Marcus must have picked up on this, too.

"Here, try this." He handed me a glass with a taster portion of a Riesling. "I think, the best way to know the wine is to try it yourself, don't you?"

As he handed it to me, our elbows touched, sending an electrical shot up my arm. And I couldn't move.

I held onto the bracelet, wondering if it was my arm? My brain? Again, I didn't move.

"Imperial research is the basis of all advances in knowledge," I finally said quickly, gulping the drink.

"What?" he asked puzzled.

"I mean, the wine — researching the wine. Just drinking it is probably the quickest way to learn about it."

"Oh. Right, of course," he said, handing me a different glass. "I think, you already know this one. It's the Riesling."

"Sounds good to me." I took the glass, needing it by now.

"Hmmm," I said, trying to decide if I liked it or not, but also not really caring, as long as it calmed me down.

He handed me some crackers and poured tasters portions of white wine in a glass. "And now . . .," he said with some space between us, "this is the *Gewürztraminer*."

Dare I try to say it? "Gewoh . . ., Gewurtstra . . . What? Do you have to be drunk before you can pronounce this one?" I asked.

"Sometimes I think, proper pronunciation is extremely overrated." I took a sip. "This is good. Kind of fruity. Kind of orangy?" I tasted again, letting the taste swirl around in my mouth. "But also kind of, I don't know . . . cinnamony?"

"Ja, that could be."

Of course, now, I'm going to have to learn to say this properly, so I can order it." I took another long drink. "This one is definitely more for me."

While I stood there, testing and tasting, Marcus sat reserved on one of the bar stools. He didn't stare, but I got the feeling he was observing me. I guessed it was getting to start closing down. He didn't say very much after that.

After nearly half an hour, I finished up. Marcus and I went to the car together. With the remote, he unlocked the doors of a silver SUV with a sign on the window that revealed it was a rental car. We got in and drove through the night in silence. Palm trees hovered overhead like giants the entire way, and almost all the buildings along the road were white and orange with terracotta roofs. The atmosphere was very different from Santa Cruz and worlds apart from Amarillo, and my thoughts were all over the place.

What had happened to my arm? Why was he so close? Was it a cultural thing? Maybe the amount of personal space allotted each personal was different in Europe. The countries there were smaller. Or maybe, he had some form of brain damage.

"I'll pick you up tomorrow morning at eight o'clock, OK?" Marcus said when he pulled up to the front door of the hotel, obviously ready to pull back out.

"What? Aren't you coming in?" I asked while I got out of the car.

"No," he answered, not elaborating.

"Oh, OK, then. I guess I'll see you tomorrow at eight. So, you'll pick me up here?"

"Let's say around ten. The morning wine drinkers are on their own," he smiled.

I gave him a thumbs up, shut the door, and when I got to my room, I turned into a wine detective. I opened my notebook and stumbled through several websites on German Wines and was overwhelmed by charts and matrixes used to explain the intricacies of German wine-making. There was no shortage of German words as long as freight trains or diverse pyramids to further fog up any areas of uncertainty. Maybe this *was* like brain surgery.

The motto "fake it till you make it" kept going through my head, when out of nowhere, I heard Bobby Brewers' voice say ". . . but you can't bullshit a bullshitter!" Words of wisdom that I should probably heed.

After doing my best to get as informed as I could on the subject in the time that I had, I finally quit my research and turned off my computer. I looked at the flyers that I had picked up and thought about the Oktoberfest that was coming up at the Black Forest Restaurant. The printed material that they had ordered was OK, but it didn't really catch my eye. Here, the quarter-page fliers and menus that were all around gave more examples at what was common for this industry, this crowd. I looked them over again, packed them back in my backpack and went to bed.

The next morning, I went downstairs to the hotel dining room, computer in hand, and tried to do some more research. For some reason, I wanted to be seen as half-way competent. I didn't want Marcus or the customers to think that I was completely ignorant of wines altogether. I mean, what was I doing there? At least I wanted to be able to participate in the conversation.

I concentrated on the different kinds of wines that were made and took in as much as I could from the whole wine culture. Packed with all my newly acquired knowledge-delvino, I quickly made myself a cheat-sheet and hoped that I could help out a little more at the festival today.

I used the cheat-sheet regularly but found myself trying to figure out what I had written down. At least I could decipher the labeling system that was typical of German wines which indicated the sweetness of the particular wine: yellow meant "lieblich" and was sweet, green meant "halb-trocken" was semi-dry, and wines with a red label were "trocken", or dry.

I tried to advise potential customers, but when I wasn't sure, I had no choice but to ad-lib or start reading from the menu.

"This is the Auslees," I said to a dark-haired woman. "This means that it is really quite good."

She looked at me, said "thanks", and went on.

Apparently, I was making some pretty bad mistakes. Marcus looked expressionless at me with my cheat-sheet.

"Aus-lay-*suh*," he finally said in undertones. He was correcting *me* this time.

"Aus-lay-suh," I repeated.

"It just means the grapes were harvested later than some of the other kinds, and this one is actually a bit dry." He pointed to the bottle I still had in my hand.

"Keep trying. You'll feel more confident if you know you're saying it right."

I followed his lead and learned the descriptions and the selling points of the wines they offered. But most of the time he took over most of the duties — taking orders, explaining and giving advice — while I took over the pouring and washing up. At last, it became increasingly comfortable to work with him, and by three o'clock, we were actually working as a functioning team.

It was just my luck that, about the time I really started to be able to have fun, the festival was coming to an abrupt end in the afternoon. After a while, the live music had stopped. The smiling, happy people had all but gone, and in their place were napkins and trash blowing across the grounds, outrunning the street cleaners behind them and leaving the fairgrounds looking empty and dirty compared to just a few hours ago.

"There is not much more to do. It's probably a good time to go get your things and all, so I'll drive you back to the hotel."

We walked back to the SUV, and when we arrived, the entrance was blocked by several cars, so Marcus pulled around to the garages to let me out.

"I'll be back here at eight o'clock to take you to the station, OK?"

"Sure, thanks." I wondered how he was getting back to Santa Cruz, but he didn't offer any information, and I felt like I would be prying if I asked.

"Bye," I said as I grabbed my purse and got out of the car. He was already driving off when I realized that I had left my back-pack in the car. Fuck, but OK, he'll be back in a few hours. I walked through the garage to the side entrance and went up to my room where my bag was lying on the bed. I lay down beside it, thankful to have a few minutes of quiet before I checked out and headed out the side door that I had come in through so that I could meet Marcus back at eight o'clock.

I hadn't gotten too far in the garage when I suddenly had a strange sensation. I could hear the "psst, psst psst" of someone whispering behind me, and any doubts that I'd had concerning my amygdala vanished instantly. The whispers got louder, and I knew someone was close behind me. I felt a warm breath on my neck when the feeling of danger became so overwhelmingly strong and a sudden wave of panic encompassed me. With no time to think, I balled up my fist, ready to beat, kick and scream at whoever was behind me. I swung around with all my might, only to instantly try to break my punch mid-swing. There, standing behind me, looking almost as surprised as me, were two *boys*, one a little taller than the other, both no older than twelve. One was carrying a pocket knife and pointing it clumsily at me!

"What the hell are you doing?!"

They quickly realized that I wasn't going to do anything except scream. They looked at me like *I* was crazy and actually started to laugh at me, when suddenly, a much older kid, came at me from behind the trash dumpster. He ran straight toward me, yelling at the younger ones, and with all his might, pushed me to the ground, tore my purse from my shoulder, all the while giving the younger ones orders.

"Get outta here! Get outta here!" the older boy commanded.

My purse had vanished. Probably, he had given it to the younger boys, and they must have run off while he pushed me to the ground again.

"Lilly!" I suddenly heard my name being screamed and wondered for a brief second how did the boys know it.

The older boy looked up.

"Lilly! — *Scheiße! Du Schwein!*" I recognized that it wasn't the boy's voice but Marcus's voice, despite that there was something indecipherable to me in the scream.

The teenager who was holding me, let me go and ran off, and a second later, Marcus was by me.

"Are you OK?" he asked, catching his breath.

"I'm not sure. I think so. Did you see them? They were just little kids."

"Yeah, damned little kids." He was shaking his head and helped me up off the ground. We went to the car together which he had left at the entrance near the street. "Get in," he instructed, holding out his hand for me, looking around and keeping watch. I got in quickly and shut the door, and we pulled out of the garage onto the street.

"My purse is gone."

"Oh, *verflucht*," he answered. "We can go back, but I suppose it's no use. — Are you OK? I saw him push you."

"I think I'm alright."

"*Verdammte kleine Arschlöcher!*"

He was rambling off something that sounded like he was really pissed off.

"What?" I asked confused.

"Sorry." He pat my knee with his hand. "I'm sorry, it is not about you." His voice changed back and forth, one second very calming, but a moment later, he was screaming, probably going on about those kids, but all I could make of the scene was the two of us in the car and him going crazy with anger.

"Look, Marcus," I said when he made an odd pause, "I'm so sorry about bothering you with this crap, but if you're angry at me with —"

"No, Lilly, not you", he cut me short. "I'm sorry. I can't say . . ." He pulled to the side of the road and stopped the car. There, he rambled some more, hitting the steering wheel every now and then. "I should have . . .," he began again, turning to me.

He took a deep breath. "OK, let's think first, now," he said finally. "You are OK, but your purse is gone. What was in your purse?" he asked, obviously making a plan.

I tried to think clearly, but my head was still spinning because of what happened. I swallowed hard before answering, "Everything. *Dammit!* My phone, my tickets, my wallet. Oh shit! My I.D. *Everything.*"

I was about to start crying. Maybe thinking clearly was not the proper way to deal with the situation.

"What the hell was that?" I asked. "I mean, it's not exactly like we're in a bad part of town, or are we?"

"I don't think so," he said looking around. "OK, I think, first, we have to go to the police or some security personnel and let them know, and I will think about the rest afterwards."

Marcus pulled back into the garage, and I got out to look around the building to see if they had thrown my purse down or maybe thrown it away, hoping to find anything. But I didn't.

We went into the lobby of the hotel and reported the incident to the hotel security.

"They were just little kids," I told the security.

"Yeah, little kids with older people hiding 30 feet away," the security man said. "You know these big festivals. You gotta be careful. Now more than ever."

140

He took my details and said they would have to report it to the police. They would contact me if they found the boys or my purse.

"We'll look through the security cameras and see what we come up with. Just between you and me, though, don't hold your breath." His remarks stung, and we turned to leave, when he went on, "I don't want to be mean, but they're minors, ya know. Not a lot can be done."

A sickening feeling started to well up in me with the reality of the situation starting to sink in. As we got back into the car, I noticed my backpack in the back seat.

"My backpack!" I held back tears while I took it from the back seat as all the way while we drove to the fairgrounds and down a gravel path that lead back to Booth 39.

"I want my things back," I said clutching to my backpack, still under shock.

Marcus stacked some boxes and sat me down on them facing the ocean.

"Try to calm down for a little while. I can get this," he said and packed the wines and equipment back into the boxes.

I sat under an overcast night sky, wondering what was going to happen to me. How would I get home? How could I cancel my credit cards? Was this the end or just the beginning? My driver's license, bank cards, pictures. Everything.

Marcus went about cleaning up while periodically muttering angrily under his breath. Probably expletives. He kicked some of the boxes that were still lying around.

"I wonder what the penalty is for beating up little kids," I said redundantly. Actually, the look on the boys' faces in the garage wouldn't leave my head. Nor their laugh. It disturbed me that I almost punched them. And it really disturbed me that I might not have been a match for them.

"You don't want to do that," Marcus answered.

A few of the flyers were still on the ground. I picked up one from one of the competitors and put it in my pocket while Marcus called Fritz and told him what had happened. They spoke for a while, and Marcus acquired a very assertive tone in his voice. After a few minutes of talking, he hung up and turned to me.

"I have to talk to you," he announced.

"OK," I said, still shaken, wondering what was coming now.

"I don't think —" he started and stopped, struggling with his words before he started up again. "I don't think it's a good idea for you to go back by yourself," he said slowly, carefully thinking about what he was saying.

"I was thinking — you could go back with me."

I tried to consider my other choices for a moment. Were there any? In my present state of post-traumatic shock, I weighed my options. Going back with Marcus sounded better than sitting paranoid on a train back to Santa Cruz, not to mention I didn't have a ticket back, so I decided to go with my fate and take him up on his offer.

"OK. No objections. Might be better . . ."

I borrowed his cell phone to call Maddie, the only person whose number I could think of, only to get her answering machine.

"Hi Maddie, it's Lilly. I've had a bit of a mishap. Looks like I won't be home tonight after all. Please give me call back when you get this."

Marcus had packed the last of the supplies and equipment into the trunk of the SUV in the meantime, and we pulled out of the fairgrounds, but I got a little confused when he pulled onto a road leading to a different direction than the highway.

"Where are we going?" I asked, fighting a surge of anxiety. I wasn't really up for more surprises on this day.

"I have to unload the equipment before I return the car. It's rented."

I had known so much, but still more questions arose.

"Unload it? Where?"

"At the dock."

Before I could go on asking, we pulled up into a road with a sign leading to the Santa Barbara Harbor. Would our equipment be *shipped* home on some barge? He finally parked by the docks and got out of the SUV.

"It's just down here a ways," he said. I followed him down the dock, where he stopped at a boat possibly bigger than Maddie's house. However, this was definitely not a barge.

"Here we are," he said.

I looked at him in disbelief.

"What do you mean — here we are?" I was completely confused now. "Please, just tell me what is going on," I begged.

He grabbed on to one of the ropes tied around the boat and jumped on board.

"Come here." He just smiled and offered his hand. "Foot over the rope," he instructed. "You will be alright." He was almost laughing! At me!?

I cautiously looked around to see if anyone had followed us, then took his hand and swung my foot over the ropes and railing, the whole time feeling like I might get caught doing something I shouldn't be doing. He unlocked the hatch and led me below deck.

"Please, sit down." He gestured to a small table with a green, cushioned, booth-like seat. "Would you like a coffee?" he asked.

"A coffee?" I asked skeptically. "You've brought me here, and now we're *just* going to have coffee?"

"Yeah. Something wrong with that?" he countered cooly.

I, on the other hand, was not so cool.

"Well, maybe instead, you could first explain to me where we are and how or when we're going home?"

I could literally feel the air leaving my sails, completely overwhelmed at the situation and the possible consequences.

"OK, I'll try to explain." He poured water into a kettle and lit the gas stove before he sat down on the opposite side of the green booth.

"This boat," he started, "belongs to my uncle. I was to bring it here for a repair, and — how do you say, advertise? And, *na ja*, to have some fun. I rented the car so I can get around while I am here, and now, I have to put this stuff on board and take the car back. We would sleep on board tonight and go back with the boat to Santa Cruz tomorrow. There is an extra — um — sleep cabin, with a door over there." He pointed to a door that was ajar, and I could see the bed through the open cabin door.

"I'll sleep out here. There is another bed." He paused, running his fingers through his hair as if still choosing his words carefully.

"Lilly, you know, you didn't look well earlier." The thoughts finally came out. "Like you should not be alone. But if you wish to go by train, I can take you there. It is not a problem, really. We could get you a ticket."

Suddenly I needed to talk to someone. "Can I use your phone once more?" I asked.

"Of course," he answered, handing me his cell phone.
I thought about who I should call. Mom? Maddie? Sybille? Next joker: I decided on my sister and went out on deck to call her.

"Oh my God! Are you alright?" she asked in shock.

I was glad and relieved to hear a trusted voice with genuine concern.

"Yeah, I think. Except my purse was stolen. I'm OK. I'm just, you know, wondering about going back by boat now or not. I don't really have a choice, but I wanted someone to know where I am. Just in case."

"A boat? What kind of boat?" Sybille asked.

"Does that matter?" I was surprised at the question. "I don't know. Big. I've never been on a boat." I looked up. The mast was like a very long flag pole.

"It's like the *Black Pearl* or something," I said finally.

"Wow — and you're sure he can sail it?"

"Well, I hope so. I've got to get home. Sybille, I'll call you when I get there."

"Don't worry. I've got this cell number. I'll track you down if I don't hear back from you soon, OK? Take care of yourself!"

"Hey, Sybille? One last thing. Can you call my bank and cancel my credit cards? You can get the information from Mom, but don't tell her. I don't want them to worry."

I went back downstairs. Marcus was still sitting at the table.

"Coffee will just take a second," he said, still waiting on the water to cook.

"I don't know how much caffeine I need, but sure. Why not?"

I sat down on one of the green cushions. The interior of the cabin was surprisingly neat for a bachelor pad, and someone's good taste was evident in the furnishing and décor. There were cubby holes built into the sides, and windows above the table with lights shining through on the dock side, and pitch black on the side of the water.

Water heated up on one of the tiny plates on the stainless-steel stove which was noticeably greaseless and polished. A spice rack was hanging overhead. It all kind of reminded me of a mixture between camping and vacationing in an efficiency apartment with a kitchenette. Like a floating mobile home.

"Here," Marcus said as he handed me the cup, "please."

"Thanks," I said, hoping I'd made the right decision. We sat there for a few minutes until he broke the silence.

"I have to take some stuff to the car and then return it. I'll get a taxi back here and then we can eat something. Would that be alright? — Or would you like to come with me?"

"Um, no. I can stay here, if you don't mind," finishing the coffee.

"OK. No problem," he said as he got up and disappeared up the stairs.

I listening to his steps, heard him moving things around up on deck, shifting things onto the boat or off the boat. Until finally, I heard his footsteps getting quieter on the dock as he walked away, and it was then, as I sat alone, that I heard all the unfamiliar sounds of the harbor, the ropes that hit back and forth with a clang in the wind against the mast, that the muscles in my neck and jaw started to tense up and I realized that I was alone on this boat, and I was way out of my comfort zone and didn't feel at all well in the unfamiliar surroundings. My heart started pounding in my chest, and in a near state of panic I ran up the stairs and through the hatch.

"Marcus!" I called the moment my head was outside in the breeze, hoping to catch him before he was gone. I didn't know which way he'd gone or even which way to look and I couldn't distinguish anything through the jungle of boats, masts and sails blocking my view.

"Marcus?" I said again, swallowing the crack in my voice, before quickly going back down the stairs, and then I heard his voice.

"Lilly?"

"Yeah?" I answered quickly, relieved to see he was standing back on the deck of the boat, looking down the hatch at me. "Um, are you sure you won't come with me? It's a nice evening out here."

I exhaled and crawled back out of the cabin.

"Yeah. On second thought, I think I will. "

He locked up the hatch and we drove the car back to the car-rental, dropped it off and sat down on a bench as we waited on a taxi to take us back to the marina. The events of the day were swirled through my head.

"How long does a taxi take here?" he wondered out loud.

"I don't know. I don't usually take taxis."

I didn't say it, but my patience was wearing. "I should have gone out the front door. Why didn't I just go out the front door?" I commented, unable to hide my aggravation.

"Was there another one?"

"Not in the rental place. I mean today. Everything."

"Don't be like that to yourself. It happened. Now you just have to figure out what to do."

"Like what?" I asked, ready for some big epiphany.

"I don't know, really. But you'll have plenty of time to think about that, once we're out of here." He looked at his watch before changing the subject. "You are probably hungry, *ja?*"

"I don't kno-" I started, but he cut me off.

"A good dinner might make you feel better. What would you like to cook?"

"Fuck," I said, feeling my exhaustion, "Oh, sorry. I just mean, I can't really cook. I don't have any money..."

"Oh. Right. I invite you for eating, OK?"

There wasn't a lot I could do, except to accept the offer and try to be gracious about it.

"Thank you. I owe you one."

His long blond bangs covered his face so that I couldn't fully see his expression.

"Schon wieder," he said with a satisfied smile, looking in the other direction.

"What?" I asked of the unintelligible remark. "What's that mean?"

"It means we need to get some food and then get gas."

"Get gas? I thought you knew how to sail," I said nervously.

"There is also this crazy thing called a motor on this boat. We can also use it."

"Oh. Right. I knew that."

The taxi driver stopped at the entrance of the parking lot, and Marcus paid him as we got out. There were some restaurants lined up along the harbor, but only a deli was still open.

"Would you like to eat here or rather take it to the boat?" he asked.

"Could we get it to-go?" I asked. "It's getting late."

"Of course — your wish is . . . how do you say it? Your wish is my. . .?"

"Command," I helped out.

"*Ja*, exactly. That's what I wanted to say. 'Your wish is my command.' We can order here and take it back with us."

We took the two hot ham and cheese sandwiches with chips to-go and made our way back down to the dock to the boat, where I noticed "Star Struck" was painted in cursive blue letters on the side. First, I had been on the Coastal Starlight, and now the Star Struck. How weird was that? I decided I liked the name.

It was getting cool outside, as we climbed over the railing and went back below deck where we sat down again at the green and black table to eat.

The clang of the ropes and pulleys hitting the masts bounced through the cabin and Marcus turned on the small, brass table lamp which was now the only source of illumination. The soft glow provided was quickly soaked up in the dark wooden paneling and the warm scent of hot ham and cheese quickly filled the air.

Simultaneously trying to digest the events of the day and the sandwich, we ate in more silence.

"Thanks for the sandwich," I said when I was finished.

"You're welcome."

"So, I guess I'll go to sleep now," I said, pointing to the small doorway that separated the dining niche from the bed and bathroom.

"*Ja*, that's fine," he said, getting up, too. "Wait here just for a moment, I want to get some things out of there."

He disappeared through the doorway and returned with his arms full.

"Here. Maybe this is OK for you." He offered me a T-shirt that was obviously too big.

"Oh, thank you."

"I thought you might want something more comfortable than the work clothes to sleep in," he said, rubbing his hand over his forehead, "I am going to sleep here, and you sleep in there," he said, calmly, controlled even, as he guided my shoulders and turned me towards the bedroom.

"That's . . . Thank you," I said exhausted.

"Good night," he answered.

"OK, then. Good night."

I went through the small doorway and closed the door behind me. The double bed was wedged up in the niche in the front of the boat, cluttered with bedding, clothes and books, but it was clean. I changed into the over-sized T-shirt and was relieved to be able to lie down on the bed, where I laid down, wrapped up in an unfamiliar smell, and the scenes from earlier in the day kept replaying in my head. Those boys screaming at me mixed in with the water that was lapping on the side of the boat.

I opened the window above my head for some fresh air, and watched as clouds intermittently crossed with the stars above. Normally I would have thought that this would put anyone to sleep in no time, but I was still too wound up to to sleep. After thirty minutes of lying restlessly in bed, I decided to get back up.

"Marcus?" I called.

"Ja?"

"I can't sleep." I felt like I was ten.

"Um. OK." There was a long, pregnant pause. "What should I do?"

I looked up as he appeared in the doorway. I hadn't heard him open the door. I hadn't heard anything.

"I think I'm just still a little wound. I can't sleep."

"Have you ever been on a boat?" he asked.

"Oh, sure," I said.

The truth was that I'd only been on a blow-up boat once or twice, and that had been about ten years before. This boat, however, was something entirely different. It was some kind of a mixture between a big sailboat and a yacht. I'd never been on a sailboat or yacht. Unfortunately, the glamorous feeling I would have expected from being on a yacht was drearily over-shadowed.

"Can we talk a little — just till I get tired?"

"Of course. Come on out. Maybe I have something for you."

I got back up, pulled my jeans back on and went and sat down at the kitchen table. He was already opening a bottle of wine and had two glasses set on the counter.

"Not being able to sleep," he said knowingly, "is nothing that a glass or two of Spätburgunder can't help."

"OK." I hesitantly took the glass.

"Prost," he said.

"Oh, I remember that."

The words were out before I realized what I'd said. We had never mentioned New Year's Eve.

"Prost," I followed quickly, and we clicked glasses.

"This was kind of a rough day for you, huh?"

"You could say that," I said, still over-whelmed by the subject. "I'm trying not to think about it all right now. It's too much."

"I see. So, we talk about something else?"

"Yeah, we can do that." I took a drink of the red wine and watched as the lights reflected in the glass. "So, how did you get here? I mean, why are you still here?" I asked.

"Well, you see, the food festival is just over, so..." His look suggested that I wasn't getting it.

"I know that. I mean, why aren't you in Germany?"

"Well, I had just finished school, and while I was here, I applied for this job. I got it, so, what should I do?"

"Wow, that's cool. What did you go to school for?"

"Gastronomy — Culinary Arts, I think you say."

"Oh. Restaurant business kind of stuff?" I asked.

"And what about you? Aren't you still in school?"

"Nope. I also just graduated. In advertising."

"Advertising?" He looked puzzled. "I think you mentioned that. So, what are *you* doing here?"

"I just… moved out here." I thought about why I'd moved, and then didn't want to think about it. "Life just wasn't really going anywhere in Amarillo. My Grandma says, 'you have to go where you can work', so, when the opportunity came, I took it, you know. See what else is out there."

"So, you had a job in advertising?"

"Well, no, actually," I said, not exactly wanting to go into the whole drama that had helped to catapult me out here.

We both took a drink as I inspected the bottle on the table.

"And, what kind of wine is this?"

"Spätburgunder," he answered in authentic German that was impossible to replicate. "I told you," he said, mimicking me.

"Touché," I said. "Shpayt-boorg-dah. Does that mean anything?"

"Something like 'Late Burgundian'."

"Which means . . ."

"Which means . . ." He paused, looking for an explanation. "It is a kind of Pinot Noir."

"That explains it." I said dryly.

"Well, you can serve it with many different kinds of food. A good, what, a general wine. Good for cooking. I mean, if you like, we could cook something together tomorrow that would go nice with this."

"I told you I can't cook." I said.

He glanced up at me with a look of disappointment, like he'd confused me with someone else. Maybe for an accomplished cook it was inconceivable that someone would not really know how to cook.

"Oh, well, yes, you did say that, . . ."

"I mean, I can do the basics, you know, like hamburgers, tacos... ."

"She can't cook..." He posed the thought to the air, like he wasn't listening to me anymore, before adding "Then maybe you just have to sing for your supper."

"Oh no!" I laughed. "I'm sorry. I can't sing either," I protested, and now feeling very unaccomplished. I almost suggested washing the dishes as, I guess, he was contemplating what on earth I could be good for.

"Then you'll just have to dance," he concluded.

Whoa. Did he just give me... *a look*?

No fraternizing, No fraternizing!

151

"Maybe I could just wash the dishes?" I asked, trying desperately to side step any more weird developments.

"Dishes?"

"Yeah, well, I think maybe I am getting tired. I might try to go to sleep." I quickly drank the rest of my wine.

"As you wish."

"Good night, Marcus."

"Good night, Lilly," he said with a hint of disappointment.

I went back to the bed in the niche and opened the window where the sea air and tone of his voice were all swirling together, soothing my frazzled nerves. I don't know how long I lay there until, as the water lapped against the side of the "Star Struck", I finally fell asleep.

*****

The next morning when I woke up, I saw a wine list from the festival in the niche above the bed. I looked it over, noting the names of the different kinds of wines that had been offered, and wondered about Oktoberfest and the carnival that Liesl had mentioned. But the not-so-unfamiliar scent kept floating by me. *It's just a scent. He's from Cologne, for God's sake! Go back to sleep,* I told myself.

Right. Just a warm, spicy, *relentless* scent, a scent that was lingering in the room, on the pillow…

The pillow seemed to pull me into it, into the dark, spicy, sea-salty scent, where I reluctantly inhaled, and, when I opened my eyes, I saw Marcus himself standing in the doorway, looking at me with raised eyebrows.

"I forgot to tell you, there is breakfast out there for you. I thought maybe you're hungry," he said with a knowing smirk on his face. "We'll be pulling out in just a little bit," he added as he turned around again and left.

I heard him upstairs, moving things around, doing… captain-things, but I couldn't bring myself to show my face, until later, when, as the ropes and masts chimed with the wind and the boat rocked back and forth, I peered out of the window and saw that we were gliding, almost silently, down the fairway.

I crept up the stairs, saw the houses and other boats floating by and Marcus at the helm, steering us out of the harbor.

"Morning," I said, feeling dizzy.

"Good morning," he replied. "Are you OK?"

"Yeah. I think so. Why?"

"I don't know. You just look... pale." he answered. "The sea might be a little rough this morning. So, you know, you can go lie back down, if you don't feel well." And winked.

Oh geez.

I went back downstairs and crawled back into the niche.

I don't want anyone. I don't want anyone. I don't want anyone.

****

Later in the afternoon, the wind died down and we anchored the boat not far off shore to stop for lunch. We went downstairs and inspected the kitchen and the food situation.

"I'm not getting a connection," he said, putting his phone on the counter, and put a tape in a tape deck in the wall.

"There is only this tape player on board, and so far, I've only found this one tape, unless you have something with you."

"My stuff got stolen," reminded him.

"Right, it did," he said, as he pushed play and soft music began.

"Do you like Spanish music?" I asked.

"I think it is Italian," he said. "At least that is what my aunt told me. It's her tape."

"Oh. I don't think I've ever heard anything Italian. Well, maybe 'O sole mio', you know, but nothing outside of food stuff, like the spaghetti, ravioli, Mama mia."

"Italian is supposed to be the best language to sing in. At least that is what they say."

"But if you can't understand the words?"

"Do the *words* always matter."

"I think they do to me," I said. "Sounds like 'drove through some rice', so I'm sure that's probably not what it's saying."

He unpacked a loaf of bread and set a bottle of wine on the table as the tune played on.

"I think there's also a feeling," he said, waving his hand in the air. "*Wein, Weib und Gesang.*"

"And what does that mean?"

"It's just an old saying." He smiled a little embarrassed. "It means 'wine, women and song'… well, at least in older times they used to say that – until the fifties. Then it became 'sex, drugs and rock 'n roll," he growled with a Billy Idol undulating lip.

"Oh, really? That's where that's from?" I asked. I didn't know that.

"Yeah, sure."

"But you seem to be more the 'wine, women and song' type," I ventured.

"Ah, OK," he said thoughtfully, "I guess if I have to pick, you are probably right. I might go with 'wine, women and song'. Here," he said, handing me food from the small refrigerator, "I have some bread and cheese and fish, if you like some."

"Sure. Cheese sandwich sounds good."

I sat down at the table and Marcus pulled somethings out that smelled very bad. I wasn't sure what it was, but what he pulled out was not the kind of groceries normally used to make a cheese sandwich. In fact, I thought he could have used it as fish bait, but instead he was going to eat it himself.

"Eewww! What *is* that?" I gasped. "Bad fish?"

"Cheese," he replied matter-of-factly.

"What kind of cheese is that supposed to be? — It's not Swiss or American."

"No, for sure not. It is a camembert with — what are they? — mushrooms. Like to try it?"

The pungent smell took my breath away, even from across the table.

"I don't mean to be rude, but I can't imagine that *that* was meant to be eaten."

"This? It's just a little mold," he said, defending his gooey mass. "This is very good. With the wine? It is really very good. You should at least try it."

"I'll take you up on the wine, but I have some serious reservations about your moldy cheese."

I picked up the cheese and inspected it skeptically. The mold alone was already enough to make me cautious, but the putrid smell of the oozing glob was starting to make me nauseous. How somebody could willfully eat it was beyond me.

"Maybe I'll just have a piece of bread and a glass of wine."

I poured myself a glass of the Spätburgunder and took a big sip as I read the description on the label.

"So this is 'full bodied and fruity'?" I asked.

"Do you like it?"

"It's not bad."

"It is actually not *that* full bodied. There are many other wines that are much heavier that this one," Marcus explained.

"But it's fruity."

"Yes, I think you can say it is fruity." He took a sip. "But it has some other tastes that aren't there so much, also."

He sipped again. "Maybe a touch of vanilla? Maybe caramel? I'm not sure."

I had never thought about wine tasting like vanilla or caramel, so I tested it again.

"I don't taste either one, if I'm honest."

"Well, maybe it will come. Keep trying."

Was this really what people were looking for when they tasted wine? I thought for a moment maybe he was trying to get me drunk. Or maybe I hoped?

We sat at the small green table with the sunlight glowing above.

"I'm sorry you don't like the cheese. There is a café in the marina. It's just a few hours away."

"That's OK. I'm not all that hungry. Not really."

"OK, then. We better get going. They said that there might be bad weather coming in. Luckily, so far only a few clouds."

****

Big, rolling waves lifted the boat high up and then brought it back down, giving my empty stomach elevator tummy. Wave after wave. I went out on deck to get some fresh air, and at one point I was almost sure that I had seen a dolphin or two. At least I hoped they were dolphins. Finally, we stopped in San Morrow, a small marina between Santa Cruz and Santa Barbara. It was not as big or well-equipped as Santa Barbara, only a small café and showers were available.

As we sailed into the marina and pulled into a slip, I threw the fenders back into the water to prevent any damage to the boat, while Marcus hooked a rope around a post and tied the boat to the dock.

"Good work," he said affirmatively, but somehow there was a coolness in his tone.

He hooked up an electrical cord to the boat and went downstairs, where I followed.

"We'll stay here for the night. Have to have something to eat. You must be very hungry, or?"

"Or what?" I asked, not getting it.

"Or not hungry?" he answered impatiently, as if it were only me that didn't get it.

"I guess I am."

"*Ah ja*," he said, not looking up. Obviously, he had remembered something. "After all that happened yesterday, I forgot this." He got up and went back downstairs but returned a second later with an envelope in his hand. He sat down beside me.

"Here. — I needed to give you this. Fritz asked me to give it you before you left."

"Give it *to you*." I corrected like a reflex.

156

I opened the envelope and was shocked to see three fresh, crispy hundred-dollar bills.

I was slowly grasping that my situation had just improved dramatically. I now had three hundred dollars. At first the same thoughts kept going through my head: I could have bought a ticket home. I could have rented a car. I could have gotten a toothbrush, but of course. "I... I could have gotten another train ticket. I could've been home by now." I kissed the envelope as my mind was racing and Marcus was looking at me very intensely.

"I didn't think about that at that time. I couldn't - just let you — go. Not after that," he said, obviously contemplating his words.

"I could be home." I sighed to myself again.

"Look, I'm sorry if you needed to be back at home already, but I talked to Fritz. He knows where you are, and I'll get you back there, safe. Promise," he said, somehow sounding slightly spurned.

"It's just, I need to make a lot of phone calls when I get home. Cancel all my cards. Get new ones."

"Well, we're in the marina. There's reception here, so why don't you call your sister again. Maybe she found out something."

Good idea, I thought. I took the phone and called Sybille.

"Just checking in. Well, kinda. Were you able to cancel my cards?"

"Yeah, but there was already a few transactions. Nothing too much, about three hundred dollars, but you should be able to get that back."

"Oh my God." My stomach sank as I tried to think of exactly what was in my purse. Any other cards? Anything else?

"I went up to the bank," Sybille said, "They said that you actually have a theft insurance on that card. But it'll take some time to clear it up. In the mean-time it's been canceled and they're sending you a new one, so I'll send it to you as soon as it's here."

A kind of relief fell over me, and the urgent need to be home lightly alleviated, so that I could think a little clearer.

"I have some money. I could rent a car."

"Not without a credit card," she said.

"True."

"Maybe I could go by train."

"I don't know. Are the ticket offices open this late at night?"

"I don't know, either. But I think, as long as the card is canceled, that's the main thing. Thanks, Sybille."

There was so much that I needed to do, and I considered going back as quick as possible,

But for some reason I didn't.

Marcus patted me consolingly. "I'll get you home as quick as possible," he assured me with a slight irritation resurfacing in his voice as he spread out a map on the table and studied it.

"So how long have you been sailing?" I asked, trying to make polite conversation.

"About ten years," he answered quickly.

"Do you have your own boat?"

He waited a few seconds. "Had one," he finally said without going into detail.

I picked up that his mood had changed and that he was intentionally being vague.

"Had one. OK." I echoed. He obviously didn't want to talk too much about it. For some reason, the more I tried to have a conversation with him, the less forthcoming he seemed to become.

He didn't say anything, only looked down. So, I got up and went outside to the deck. At least, there would be a sunset. I turned and started to walk up the stairs to the hatch.

"Wait," he said suddenly.

I acted as if I didn't hear and kept going up the stairs.

Marcus got up and followed me up to the deck.

"Look," he said, louder this time. "I have a girlfriend."

"OK . . .," I said slowly, as it sounded definitely like he was trying to tell me more than just that he had a girlfriend, but I didn't know what. At the same time, the news hit me like I'd just walked into a wall, and I instantly wanted a cigarette. I grabbed my backpack and unlocked the gate of the rails. I clumsily started to get off the boat when I slipped on the small pole of a step and lost my balance. Trying to steady myself, I slipped even more and screamed when I heard a crack and knew immediately that something was very wrong.

Pain and fire raced from my ankle up through my entire leg, and I fell over the edge of the boat into the water, screaming in pain.

"Shit!"

"*Ach du Scheiße!*" Marcus appeared over the rail and yelled for me from the boat. "Where are you?!"

"I'm stuck! Oh shit!" I yelled back from the water. "Help me!" I continued screaming.

Marcus got out of the boat and quickly accessed the situation. He got down on his stomach and caught me under the arms, scooping me up out of the water, fished out my backpack, and sat me down on the dock.

"Oh shit! My ankle!"

"*Verdammt!*" he yelled, back in his angry voice.

"I think it's broken. My God! It hurts. Shit! It got completely twisted between the dock and that . . . and that thing."

I sat down, dripping wet, on the dock, about to cry in pain.

"Hold on just a second. I think of something. *Scheiße!*"

By now, there were a few people gathered around from the other boats. A large man with light blond hair and a Rangers baseball cap appeared.

"What're you kids out here doin' this time of night? Is everything OK?" he asked walking down the dock.

"No," Marcus answered.

"You OK, ma'am?" he asked me again, giving Marcus the once over.

"No, I think I broke my ankle!"

"You need to use a phone? Maybe call a taxi... or an ambulance?" he offered.

"That would be great," Marcus said quickly.

The man dialed the phone to get a taxi.

"Just going to the café," I said, hobbling on one foot, holding back tears and holding up my backpack, still dripping wet.

We sat on the dock and waited a while until a taxi pulled into the parking lot of the marina.

"Thanks," Marcus said to the man as he picked me up, "Hold on to me," he said, one arm behind my back and the other under my knees, as he carried me to the waiting taxi, which took us to the local hospital. When we arrived, a nurse came out with a wheel-chair and brought me back into the emergency room where I filled out some papers.

The hospital wasn't crowded. In fact, for most of the time we were nearly the only people there. We sat in the small waiting room. Not even a T.V.

The room was silent, but my thoughts were screaming. Sybille! Three-hundred dollars! Girlfriend! Credit Cards! Driver's license! Go Home! But any thoughts of leaving now were over.

"What did you —" he started and then stopped, shaking his head.

"I don't know," was all I could say.

"Miss Dumont?" A short, stocky man in a white jacket called out my name.

Thank God. Saved.

"Over here," I said, holding up my finger.

"Hello, I'm Dr. Morten. I guess we need to have a look at that ankle."

****

Two hours, five x-rays and three coffees later I was all wrapped up in a fiberglass cast and ready to go. Dr. Morten gave me a prescription for pain pills, a few extra in a bottle for immediate use, and put three extra pills in a plastic medicine container. He gave me some plastic bags to take along for the ride, so the cast wouldn't get wet and dirty so quickly.

"Take one of these tonight and one tomorrow morning. It looks like it's a hairline fracture. Should heal up just fine." Dr. Morten said, handing me a small bottle with a few pills in it. "Make sure you get to a doctor in Santa Cruz as soon as possible. You still wouldn't want it to grow back wrong with complications."

"Will do." I said, exhausted. "Thanks."

Marcus wheeled me back to the counter in the waiting room where I picked up the papers that I needed to take back with me.

"Fritz said don't worry too much. It's a workman's compensation case, and you need to bring him the report from the hospital when you go back to work."

Upon hearing that Fritz knew, I was humiliated and didn't want to show up back at work to give him the papers or for any other reason for that matter.

Finally, around 11:30 p.m., Marcus and I waited together for a taxi to come and pick us up to return us back to the marina. I took one of the pain pills, hoping it would soon kick in.

Marcus got up and went to the water dispenser.

"Here, for you," he said, handing me a cup. "For the pill."

"Thanks," I whispered.

I could feel him looking at me, analyzing me.

"What?" I asked.

"It's not boring with you, is it?" he said almost smiling and shaking his head.

"Boring? My life? You know, sadly enough, it actually is. This is probably the most excitement I've had in the last couple of years."

"Years?" he asked.

"Um, maybe not 'years'," I admitted, and got a shiver in the cool September night.

"Are you cold?"

"Freezing."

He stood up and took off his jacket.

"Here. Put this on."

My clothes were still damp, and the rest of any energy reserves that I might have had were starting to get zapped, but the pain started to let up a little bit. I looked through my backpack for my cigarettes but found the entire contents were just as wet as my clothes. Cigarettes ruined.

The taxi pulled into the drive-through bay and Marcus helped me up and half carried me to the taxi before pouring me into the back seat. As he got in and sat down beside me, he looked at me and scooted a little closer, putting his arm around my shoulder.

"Body heat," he said.

"Yeah, right."

"Where to?" the taxi driver asked.

"To the marina," he replied, still looking at me.

Embarrassment, shame and fluttering in my stomach mixed in me, and I didn't know which emotion to deal with first, so I closed my eyes and leaned my head on his shoulder, where I kept it until the taxi driver stopped at the marina. We got out and I sat down on a bench outside the café. Marcus looked around the marina.

"What are you looking for?"

He thought for a second. "A *Schubkarre*," he said.

"A shoe what-ah?"

"A . . . shovel with wheels." His words trailed off as he was still looking around the property. "*Ah!*"

A wagon leaned up against a big tree between the showers and the café. Marcus jogged over and steered it back.

"Is this a 'shovel with wheels'?" I asked teasing. "Very resourceful."

"Don't know what it's called."

"How'd you know it was there?"

"They always have them here, for transporting food and stuff to the boat. Come."

With that he scooped me up from the bench and lowered me in the wagon.

"Seriously?" I asked in disbelief.

"Yes. Ready?"

"For what?" I asked.

"I guess you can't walk like this, so somehow you must get back," as he started slowly pulling me in the wagon down the sidewalk until we arrived at the boat where he helped me out.

"OK, now, just stand here and hold on to the rope. Don't let go. OK?"

He swung his leg over the rope and climbed on board, kneeling on the side of the boat.

"It's going to rock a little," he warned, looking down at me. "Don't get scared, OK?"

Scared? Too late. The boat was rocking, the chains were clanging, and it was dark. I *was* scared. I was petrified.

Still holding on to the railing, Marcus leaned over and positioned his shoulder into my stomach. He wrapped his arm around my knees and lifting me up over his shoulder like a bag of potatoes. He turned at the waist and deposited me on the seat cushion next to him.

"Hope that wasn't too bad," he said, looking guilty with his eyebrows raised.

"I'm alright." I straightened out the still damp shirt and jacket. Just cold."

"Oh, yeah, let's get you inside."

He jumped in the cabin and turned around to awkwardly lift me off the stairs and placed me on the bench at the table again, apprehension showing in his eyes.

"Wait here. I have some dry clothes I can give you."

Marcus went into the bedroom and came back out with a pair of sweats and a T-shirt.

"Sorry, it's not fresh. It's all I have." He handed me the half-folded clothes. "But they are dry."

"Great. I'll just go into the bedroom, where I can change. Can you give me a hand?"

"Of course."

He got up, and I put my arm around his shoulder, so I could hobble back to the bedroom. I sat down on the bed as he turned and walked out of the room, shutting the door. I heard him as he left the boat, picked up the wagon and walked away with it.

"Would you like a tea or a coffee?" he asked loudly from the kitchen when he returned just a few minutes later.

"Do you only think about food and drink?" I thought out loud.

"*Was?*" he asked louder.

"Sure!" I called back, changing the damp, cold blouse for the warm gray T-shirt. It smelled just like him. The warm, soothing, spicy scent. With just a hint of salt.

Stop, I told myself. Don't start this again. I fought with smells that seemed to grab my attention. *Get a grip on yourself and just change out of these cold clothes!*

"Tea or coffee?" he a called from the table.

I stood up for a second to unbutton my jeans, when I almost lost my balance again and sat back down on the bed. I pulled off the damp, right jeans leg and began to inch the left jeans leg down, but it hung up around the cast, so that I had to wrestle with the leg to try to take it off. But it didn't work. It was stuck. Then I tried to pull it back up, which I now couldn't manage, either.

"Lilly? Are you OK?"

"Yeah. I'm OK," I lied.

The more I pulled on the jeans, the more it pulled on the cast. I got the gray sweats and put them on my right leg, but my ankle hurt so bad now that I was scared to even touch the jeans of the left leg, and I slowly sunk into panic mode.

"Lilly? You want a tea?"

"Shit!" I whispered to myself, cursing the jeans and the pain.

"Lilly?" he pressed on.

"Yes, tea. Tea is great!" I snapped back, trying hard to hold back tears.

I couldn't think of anything else to do, so I delicately pulled up the left sweats leg over the cast, with the jeans tucked in the pants leg around the cast, which now looked like it was pregnant and swollen to three times its original size.

Sitting on the bed, looking at the large cast, I felt my eyes start to water and my throat tightened.

"It's ready!", Marcus called again.

I looked around, trying to find a tissue.

"I'll be there in a sec." I tried to say it loud, but my voice cracked.

"Lilly, can I come in?" Marcus asked, slowly opening the door to the wedge-bedroom.

He looked around, and his eyes widened.

"Oh." He looked at me, obviously unsure about what to say.

"I'm alr-r-right. Really. You can come in. I just have... something in my eye."

"Yeah, I see. Um, I don't have a handkerchief. I can offer you a toilet paper."

"That would be great," I sputtered, now almost going into uncontrollable sobbing.

He went into the lavatory, got some toilet paper, and handed it to me as he sat down beside me while I blew my nose and tried in vain to dry my eyes.

"Is something else wrong with your foot?" he asked, gesturing to the bloated appendage.

"I c-c-can't, get it, o-o-off," I mouthed, unable to find enough oxygen to actually say the words.

"I don't think you are supposed to take it off."

"No. Not the c-cast, the jeans." I pointed to the crumpled-up jeans, half on, half off.

"Hm, wait. Just relax. I think I can . . . help you." He stood up.

"Give me your foot."

I lifted my foot up, and he inspected the condition of the cast and clothes.

"You know this would be easier without the sports pants," he commented, tugging on the pants leg.

"Without what?" I gasped, still drying my eyes.

"Only joking. Just trying to see you smile. I can get this off."

"Really?" I asked relieved.

He successfully pulled the sweat pants over the bunched-up jeans and inspected the situation anew. He tugged and pulled on the jeans, trying not to knock the cast.

"This one is a little harder." He looked up at me with a clinched jaw.

After analyzing my foot for several minutes, he got up and went to the kitchen.

"Scheiße," I heard him blurt under his breath.

"What does that mean?" I asked him.

"Shit," he blurted back.

"What?"

"It means 'shit'." He came back with a strange contraption in his hand. "I have to cut it."

Cut it?! I thought to myself. My eyes widened. My favorite pair of jeans! They cost me eighty dollars - on sale! I winced at the thought, but the pain was so bad that it didn't seem to matter too much that my favorite jeans now seemed destined to be shredded.

"I don't think I can get it off like it is. This is a special tool for sewing. I can cut through the seam of the pants, to make it big enough, so that it will come off. Should I do this?"

I didn't know what choice I had.

"Go ahead," I said, grieving quietly for my jeans.

He took the special scissors and started cutting along the seam of the left leg, finally pulling the clammy jeans over the cast, freeing me.

"I didn't mean for it to end up like this."

"You can probably get the pants sewn again when you get home. I just go get you a pillow from the kitchen for your leg, OK? You can then hold it up better."

I was just happy to have finally gotten them off.

"Can I borrow your phone? I'd like to call Maddie."

"Sure." He gave me his phone and turned around to back to the kitchen.

I pulled the sweat pants on and scooted up the bed, leaning my back against the wall beside the wedge-bed. My backpack was lying beside me, and I grabbed it and pulled the content out to dry. I put the envelope with the money beside the bed in a cubby hole and laid my journal out so that the pages would get some air, before turning on the phone. As I started to call Maddie, I saw the icon that indicated that the phone had good reception, opened the browser and navigated to the website with my horoscope.

September 26 🖼️💟⭐

One step forward — two steps back. Don't worry too much about any setbacks. With Venus in your fourth house your goals may be well within reach, and you'll find a way to meet them. Go with your first instinct — it could prove to be the right one.

Seriously? With this leg, I didn't see myself stepping anywhere for a while.

"Go with the first instinct," I said to myself, "Yeah, right."

"Go where?" Marcus asked as he came back through the door with the cushion from the kitchen bench.

"Oh, nothing. It's just my horoscope," I said. "It's full of shit. Or 'scheise', as you say."

"Here you go," he lifted my leg up before sliding the folded cushion underneath the cast.

"Did it tell you about breaking your leg?" he asked teasingly.

"Nope. It said to go with my 'initial instinct.'"

"Initial instinct?" he repeated.

"First instinct." I tried to clarify.

"*Ah, ja.* OK." He nodded as it clicked. "And what is your first instinct?" he asked, fluffing up a pillow and guiding my shoulder to lean forward.

I thought about it for a second while I leaned toward him, closing the space between us.

"Oh shit," I started, but our eyes locked, and I realized how close he was, and suddenly, I could hardly breathe. He laid the pillow behind my back, and I froze, not able to take my eyes off him, and as I leaned back on the pillow, he followed.

"Stay with your first instinct," he whispered right before he kissed me.

And to my surprise, I kissed him back.

He pulled away and looked at me, his eyes darkened, barely breathing as he held me carefully on my cheeks and kissed me again.

I tangled my fingers in Marcus's hair, pulling him tightly towards me and breathed in the scent of him. The scent that had been driving me crazy for days now. Only this time it wasn't in bed sheets or on clothes and my heart was pounding, and I shifted my legs. A move which let the cushion under my foot slide off the bed, making my casted foot fall down with a thud against the bed frame.

"Oh!" I yelped softly.

"*Ganz ruhig,*" he whispered, backing off.

"Just go slowly," he said, stroking my hair. "I don't think you need another accident."

My heart pounded, and I thought I should run in a completely different direction, if I could only run.

Marcus crawled up over to the other side of the bed and put his arm around me, guiding my head toward him.

"Come here," he said softly, "it's late."

I lay motionless with my head on his chest, scared to ask any questions, scared of saying anything that might make the moment end, and as I listened to the rhythmic beat of his heart, somehow, I drifted off to sleep.

****

The next morning, I woke up again to rhythmic sounds, only this time to the clang of the masts that resembled the thoughts that came rushing back into my consciousness: leg,

168

cast, pain and Marcus, who was not there, but I heard him talking somewhere far away.

I got up and limped to the opened door, and saw him sitting half-in, half-out of the kitchen in the hatch above the stairs. He was rambling on in German on the telephone and disconnected abruptly when he saw me.

"Good morning," he said, jumping down from the hatch. "How are you this morning?" he added.

"So-so."

"*Ja*, I guess it was a little too much last night. Still, you might take one of the pills you got if it hurts too bad."

"Look . . ." I closed my eyes. "Again, I'm sorry for the big circus last night. I don't know what . . .," I trailed off, shrugging my shoulders.

"Hey, it's OK," he nodded, "Here, I have something for you," he said, changing the subject, handing me a small brown paper bag.

I took the bag and looked inside. *Oh my God!* I thought. Looking back at me were two chocolate covered doughnuts.

"Yum!"

"And this is also for you if you want," he continued.

Did I detect a hint of hesitation in his voice?

I looked at him cautiously, and peeked in the second bag, where I found a clear, see-through travel case in it, complete with travel-size shampoo, toothpaste and a *toothbrush*. How embarrassing, but how perfect!

"I guess I look pretty bad, huh?"

"Not too bad," he winked, and I cracked.

"Stop doing that!" I said unexpectedly.

"You, you just said something about a toothbrush last night, so I saw one and thought you probably can't get out very easy, so . . ."

I said something about a toothbrush? In my sleep? Or was he lying? I couldn't remember and decided it didn't matter. There was *a toothbrush*!

"OK, well, thanks."

"Besides, I just talked to Fritz. There's supposed to be bad weather coming in the evening, so we need to get going. I made a coffee. It's on the table . . . and you can wash in the lavatory. The water tanks are full."

With that, he jumped back up on deck and left me alone.

The aroma of coffee drifted through the cabin mixed with the salt sea air. The tape deck with the Italian music was on. I could still hear the hypnotic sound of the water lapping up on the side of the boat, the creaking of the rudders and the seagulls calling from the sky.

I grabbed my backpack with all my stuff in it, held on to the door and hobbled to the kitchen table when the break in my leg said "good morning" with a vengeance. Suddenly, I was in deep pain. Maybe the blood rushed to my foot? The pain radiated quickly throughout my entire leg, and I started feeling sick, and figured eating two pain pills with two doughnuts should tackle all the symptoms and somewhere in the back of my head, I also had real intentions of using the time to try to think of some advertising strategies for Oktoberfest.

The pills, however, started to work quickly on my near empty stomach, and any signs of creative thinking were quickly wiped out and replaced by a dreamy drowsiness, and I found myself instead pondering why Marcus's suddenly blurting out that he had a girlfriend. Was she around? In the states? Or maybe he meant back in Germany. Or maybe she worked with us? The possibilities were now endless . . .

But why didn't he just say something?

I wondered what Sybille or Bree would say when I got back — if I got back. I wondered about this guy who was out there sailing this boat, and I thought about those kids who stole my purse.

With my legs out on the booth I leaned up against the back of the wall and watched through the window as we left the little marina, gliding out of the slip, down the fairway and back into the sea.

****

Marcus was stood over the bed with one foot on the end, closing the window hatch above the bed.

"Are you awake, *Schlafmütze*?"

"What did you call me?"

"A sleep . . ." he paused. "What do you say? Sleeping hat?"

"Sleepyhead?" I asked with my eyes closed.

"Ja, OK, sleeping head. You were asleep the entire way back." He jumped down from the wooden frame.

"Oh." I looked around, trying to gather my bearings, comprehending slowly what he'd just said.

I must have also contracted narcolepsy.

I just wanted to sit down and think about Oktoberfest, and instead, woke up a couple of hours later, just as we were gliding into the slip in the marina in Santa Cruz.

"We should get going, I guess, huh?" I asked, not feeling the need to prolong this any further.

"If you feel good enough, I will help you out. But there is no rush. Just when you are ready."

I looked outside the small window and the hatch to go above deck. It was already becoming dusk, and I didn't want to risk another incident happening on a dark dock.

"Yeah, I'm ready when you are." I slowly started up the steps, and Marcus struggled to help me up through the opening, then turned around to close and lock the hatch. He jumped off the boat and again picked me up and sat me on the dock.

"Wait here," he said.

He jumped back on board, grabbed my bag and came back on the dock. He looked around, I guessed to see if another wagon was around. There wasn't.

"So, up you go." He hooked one arm under my knees and one around my back.

171

"I guess this is probably fastest." His words were strained as he started off, me in hand, to the parking lot.

"Right," I said, hoping he would somehow know that I actually felt like a complete idiot for having to have someone actually carry me but too tired to respond any more than that.

He started off, and I saw his face from the close proximity. His blue baseball cap was pulled down low, keeping the evening sun out of his eyes. His long, dirty-blond hair was pulled back into a ponytail, and the two-day stubble had now blossomed into a full-blown beard. His face was chapped and sun-kissed, but a scar over his right eye was still noticable. Was his breathing getting heavier? I was glad that I hadn't eaten the ham and cheese sandwich yet.

"Here we are," he groaned.

"Yours?" I asked when he sat me down with a careful thud in front of an old post office jeep that had been painted green.

"Borrowed," he said unlocking the passenger side door and slid the door back.

"So, where should I bring you?" he asked, not bothering to shut his door.

"Home is probably best."

"Just go up Ocean Drive to the big intersection."

The old jeep rattled down the busy street, and we stopped in front of Maddie's white frame house. The lights were on, and I could here the TV through the open screened door.

"Are you doing better?" he asked quietly.

"Yeah, I think I was a little sea-sick back there. Solid ground might have given me a little strength back. Still a land-lubber, I guess. Anyway, it's, like, I . . ." I paused, trying to think of the right words, still feeling embarrassed over the whole last few days.

"Stop," he said, cutting me completely off.

Oh shit, I thought. What have I said now? I looked up at him to find him looking intensely back at me. He turned to face me and moved toward me in the green jeep.

172

"You are not at work or drunk or broken and knocked-out, and I've waited a long time now to do this. So just . . . stop talking."

He pulled me in and I got the distinct feeling he was going to kiss me.

"I think you have a girlfriend," I said quickly, reminding him of the bomb he had dropped the night before.

"What?"

"Your girlfriend. I thought you said you have a girlfriend."

"Had," he corrected just as quickly. "I had a girlfriend." He leaned back in the seat of the car and looked out the window.

"We broke up not long ago."

"Oh," I said, registering what that now meant. "Me, too," I finally added.

"You had a girlfriend?" he asked with wide eyes.

"A boyfriend, I mean."

"Oh."

"So, now, I guess, you don't have a boyfriend or a girlfriend?" he smiled.

"Presently? No." Was this going where it sounded like it was going?

"Hmmm. Then it might be OK if we went to eat or something."

Eat. Something. No Fraternizing. Job.

"Yeah, I think that would be OK."

"Good, then maybe Friday?"

"Friday might be good," I said, blocking out any and all thoughts of work.

"OK. Friday," he confirmed, "Then wait, and I will come help you out."

He came over to my side and supported me as I hopped back to the Maddie's house. Noise from the TV was floating out of the screen door, as Maddie reclined on the sofa.

"Knock-knock," I said through the screen.

Marcus opened the screen door and helped me into the living room as Maddie quickly sat up on the sofa.

"Hey, stranger," she said, doing a double-take. "What happened to *you*?" she asked, her eyes jumping back and forth from me to Marcus.

"Boating casualty. I'll explain later. Marcus, this is my roommate, slash, cousin, Maddie. Maddie, this is Marcus." I said, giving a short, hurried introduction.

"Marcus? Oh. Nice to finally get to meet you! Lilly has said so much about you."

I cringed internally while he shot me a questioning look.

"Nice to meet you, too," Marcus said politely, "but I think I better get going. — I'll pick you up on Friday. Is seven o'clock OK?"

"Seven it is. I'll see you then," he said, as he walked out the door, and was gone.

I wanted to simultaneously exhale a sigh of relief and scream at the top of my lungs.

"What was that?" Maddie demanded. "What happened to you?"

"I fell. Kind of hard, kind of overboard."

"Knock-knock." Marcus was at the door again.

We quickly quit talking when we saw him re-appear at the door. He opened it and stepped inside.

"Your things," he said, lifting my backpack up, showing proof, as he handed it to me.

"I'll see you on Friday."

"OK," I said suddenly. Our eyes locked for a second before he turned and left again.

"OK, so what's that all about?" Maddie asked, not trying to hide her curiosity, "Sybille called. And your Mom. And your work."

"Oh shit, really? Mom?"

"Yeah, what's going on?"

"The police?" I asked.

"No, shit, Lilly, what's going on?" she asked, her patience wearing.

"Well, long story short: When I got to work the other day, he was there, working at the festival. When it was time to go, I got mugged by a couple of local boy scouts, so he brought me home on the boat which I fell off of and broke my ankle."

"What a weekend. And you went to the police?"

"Yeah, but they probably won't find them. Sybille canceled my cards already. At least I think she did, and I have to go to a local doctor for this tomorrow," I showed my foot. "And today I spent the day escaping pain in a med-induced coma," I explained. "God, why does shit like this always happen to me?" I asked rhetorically.

"Does it?" Maddie asked quickly.

"Does it what?" I asked back, caught off guard.

"Does shit like this happen to you a lot?" A look of concern was suddenly on her face.

"No. Not really a lot. I was just thinking out loud."

I tried to change the subject while I started towards my room, and Maddie followed me with my backpack. I emptied the contents, my notebook and some advertising, which now looked like it had gone through the wash, and then turned on the laptop to check my emails. But before I could read them, Miss Teri's horoscope popped up:

September 28

Have you been sailing along without a map? Sometimes you have to lose everything to know what really matters. But don't worry. Neptune goes direct today, helping you pinpoint a long-term direction that satisfies not only your heart but also your soul.

I read it, then read it again.

"Look!" I screeched. "She's there again! Exactly like she says!"

The synchronicity of the horoscope and my reality were starting to get spooky, as the entry, again, had a real resemblance to my life. Sailing along without a map?

"Oh no. Not that, again." Maddie was pained at the sight of the horoscope.

"Read it and weep," I replied showing her the phone.

Maddie thought I was crazy for reading.

"You have to admit, it looks like my life."

"It's a metaphor. It could be anyone's life."

"Sailing without a map? Swept off your feet." I challenged. "Explain that."

"It is a coincidence, OK?" she said impatiently. She shook her head in disbelief. "Tell Sylvia. I think she's more sympathetic to things like that."

But swept off my feet? What if these things had a literal meaning? I probably should have read the horoscope a few days ago, I thought. My broken ankle was broken. How much more confirmation did anyone need? Maybe some of this could have been prevented.

"In any case, there's so much I have to do tomorrow. I need to call the bank, go to the DMV and to the doctor and get some crutches. Can you help me?"

"I don't know. I'm off tomorrow. So, I guess I can."

She smiled before she shut the door, and I was glad.

I lay on my bed where my to-do list was spinning through my head, and each minute, it seemed to get longer. A thousand things ran through my exhausted head, and somehow, I thought about the upcoming Carnival festival. I examined the fliers that had barely survived the water incident and began to get angry that the others I'd collected weren't there. Then, eerily, I saw the faces of the little boys that took me down in the garage.

****

"How much money did they get?" Maddie asked me the next morning as I told her what had happened in detail.

"None, thank God. I got the three hundred for the weekend after the fact, but my nest egg is nowhere near built back up, and I can't afford to be out of work for six weeks." I took a sip of my coffee. "And how am I supposed to go to the doctor without my insurance card?"

"You'll have to call your provider. I'm sure you're not the first person to have your purse lost or stolen," Maddie replied.

I called the insurance company and the bank and made sure my credit cards had been canceled. The DMV wasn't that far and the lady on the phone said an appointment wasn't necessary to get a replacement license.

"OK, then we'll come over this morning," I told her.

Two hours later, with an official, new California state license in hand, we drove over to the clinic.

The sterile blue and white doctor's office was cool in appearance. I filled out more forms in the examination room until Dr. Singh, a middle-aged man with Indian origins, came it and hung up the X-rays from the hospital in Port Morrow and explained them to me in greater detail.

"The good news is that the fracture is minimal," he told me as he offered a set of crutches. "The bad news is that because it's a vertical break and not horizontal, you won't be able to put any weight on the foot, or it will probably cause it to go ahead and break altogether where the top part could slide down and make things much more complicated."

My stomach did somersaults, and I assured him this was also not in my interest and I would gladly hobble around with a crutch and cast for the next six weeks.

Now I only had to explain this to Fritz. I went to the Black Forest Restaurant, hobbling in through the back door. I could tell immediately that Fritz was there, because I already heard him yelling something about the '*hella sosuh*'.

I took a deep breath and went in the kitchen where he took one look at me, turned on his heel and started a new round of yelling with his arms flailing through the air.

I stood there, too scared to move, when Liesl came in.

"*Oh mein Gott!*" she cried out in a shocked voice that gave me the feeling that she didn't know anything about what had happened, although I thought for sure Fritz would have informed her.

"Look at you! What has happened to you?"

"Just a little fall." I said.

Fritz looked at us, and I got the feeling that he was about to implode right there before my eyes. Suddenly, he went off again, incoherently saying something tight under his breath, unable to keep it in.

"Hush! Let her explain. Hush now!" Liesl snapped at Fritz. He looked at her and then at me, giving us both a look that said "futile" before turning around and leaving the kitchen.

"Man, he always scares me when he acts like that. I always think he's going to have an aneurysm."

"I tell him also, Fritz, please don't have a heart attack. It is really not good for him to get so excited like that. But? What can you do?" She gave her own "futile" look and shrugged her shoulders.

"Don't worry too much about Fritz. Marcus called this morning to tell us about your fall. Good that Marcus was there to help you."

What was that supposed to mean? I wondered what exactly he had said.

"Don't you worry. We will work something out."

Liesl guided me out of the kitchen into the still darkened club room. The lights were off, and the tables were not yet set. No tablecloths, no plates or silverware. Just plain wooden tables.

"Here, sit down, dear. Lilly, I have an idea for you. You know, I told you Oktoberfest starts for us next week, yes? For this we need a second cashier for the beer garden. Normally, I would do this, but I can also go behind the bar. My ankle is much better now. Would you be interested in that? Being the cashier? Like this, you can sit down when you work."

She looked at me expectantly and I was so relieved, I didn't know what to say.

"Of course." I spit out.

"Good. Then you can sit down while you work. That would be good for you, or?"

Or? They always said that at the end or their sentences. I had worked there for several weeks now, but it still caught me off guard. Or what? I didn't think about it long. I was just glad to get the offer.

"Fantastic. Thank you, so much!" I laughed. The cashiers didn't make as much money as the servers, but I jumped at the chance.

"Come in for a few hours on Thursday for training on the register," Liesl said before getting up. "You just come in your regular clothes for training. The cashiers do not have to wear the dress, anyway," she added.

No dress! I pressed back a little tear of joy.

"I'll be here," I promised.

She smiled and went out of the club, and I got my crutches and went out the front door, dodging any more encounters with Fritz.

10

October

It's funny how much you take for granted when everything is in proper working order. But then, in one fell swoop, with one little crack, routine things, like getting dressed, become tasks of epic-proportions. And everything immediately changes.

Suddenly you're limping, and you have to rely on crutches and other people, and with overwhelming clarity you feel every ounce of your vulnerability – and this, clearly, can suck.

Sometimes, however, you get showered with care and love by people you know, and some you don't, which balances out all the pain and inconveniences, and you think that maybe, just maybe, the world is OK after all. I found myself in a constant balancing act, a kind of see-saw mode, constantly teetering between happy and sad: sad because I'd broken my leg, but happy, because I didn't have to wear the dirndl at work. Sad, because two pairs of my jeans had to be destroyed so that I would have some pants to wear at all. But happy, because at least I could go to work – even if it was in torn jeans.

Today, however, was my picnic date, and I decided to go with something completely different. I looked though my closet and found... (wait for it)... my black skirt, as it was just easier to be in, *and* was long enough to partly hide the cast, and hide any razor stubble from my other leg that I might not have caught, as bathing and shaving had also taken on unforeseen difficulties.

I slipped my free foot into my slipper just as Marcus rang the doorbell.

"See you later!" Maddie called from the kitchen.

"Yeah, see you later!" I called back as I grabbed my crutches and opened the door.

"Hi!" he said, with an over-aspirated "H".

"Hi. Are you OK?"

"Yeah, are you ready to go?"

"I am. I'm ready."

"Then, shall we?" he asked in that voice that allowed him to say "shall" and get away with it.

"We... shall." I answered. But felt like a real dork using proper verbiage that was probably perfectly normal in some parts of the world – just not in mine.

We drove down Water St. and over to the marina, where the wind was gusting so hard that the boats were bouncing up and down, up and down with each wave, and all the masts and chains from all the boats were clanging and echoing over the harbor.

I wiggled my way over the railing and scooted down the seat as Marcus handed me my crutches over and then jumped on board himself with ease. One quick turn of the key, and we slid down into the cabin of the Star Struck.

"You like spaghetti, or?" he asked.

"Or yeah," I assured him.

"Then, *Spaghetti marinara,* it is."

A basket was on the table filled with wine, a package of spaghetti noodles, a baguette, and stuff to make spaghetti sauce.

"Spaghetti alla marinara it is," I smiled.

"No, not spaghetti alla marinara," he said. "That's something else, with, what is it? Muschels? No. Well, seafood anyway. This is a basic, simple kind."

"Oh. I guess I'm not up-to-date with my recipe names."

"Well, *Spaghetti alla marinara* is Italian, it means 'mariner's spaghetti', which is made with seafood, but this is just a simple, normal sauce. Anyway, since we are here, in the marina, I thought, or I hoped, this would be the right thing."

"Will I be tested on this?"

"What? Uh, no," he answered.

"Then simple spaghetti, it is," I said, as a wave pushed the boat up and I held my stomach as the it floated up, and down.

"Then, while I open this, you can start cutting these," he said as he handed me an onion and took out a corkscrew.

"Of course, if the weather was better, we could've gone out on the water a bit and had our picnic on deck. As it is," he steadied himself on the table, "we'll just have an indoor picnic."

Through the wind and clanging, we heard voices from outside, and the expression on Marcus' face changed from happy to one of concern, and he leaned over the table and closed the curtains on the left side.

"Never know when someone might come around. A lot of people know Fritz here, you know," he said.

On the one hand, I was disappointed that he wasn't trying to up the ambiance, but on the other hand, I felt kind of excited, that we were doing something *forbidden*.

He handed me a cutting board and a knife, and I began quickly chopping as he started opening the wine bottle.

He offered me a glass, but with a strange look in his face.

"What's the matter?"

"What are you doing?" he asked in disbelief.

"Chopping onions?"

"Yes, I see, but, it is...it is an onion, not your ex-boyfriend."

He took one of my hands in his, still holding onto the onion, and the knife if the other.

182

"When you cut the onion – you have to *prepare* to eat it, not destroy it," he said, slowly moving the knife back and forth, down and through the vegetable.

For a moment the thought of it being my ex-boyfriend sounded funny, but I didn't want to think about that. Not here with him. Not at all, really. My eyes started to water.

"You are alright, *ja*?" he asked with concerned.

"It's the onions."

"Good. Alright," he said relieved.

"Just leave out the ex-boyfriend jokes. We don't want to go there."

"Of course. Sorry," he said.

I continued *preparing* it as he sat down, also with a cutting board and a knife. As I wiped my tearing eyes, I held out the other onion for him.

"No. You are in charge of the onions – Not that I want to see you cry, but I take the garlic and basil."

He picked up the cloves and inspected them before methodically pealing each one, squeezing them through a garlic press into a small bowl with olive oil, and then he pulled out a serrated knife and some tomatoes.

"Stolen from Liesl's garden," he confessed.

I gulped, then quickly continued cutting, slowly, as he started to cut the tomatoes, also very methodically.

Everything was fresh, homemade, by hand, and I felt like it was something very special. But then, he pulled out a can of tomatoes.

"What's that?" I asked, as the illusion evaporated.

"Tomatoes," he answered. "Why?"

"I'm just surprised. I thought you only used fresh stuff."

"Ah, you are a purist cook!" he exclaimed as if he finally had me pegged.

"I'm not *any* kind of cook. I just..."

"Oh, so you think I'm the dogmatic chef."

"What? No! That's not what I said. I just thought..."

"Do you not ever use canned tomatoes?"

"*If* I cooked, I would probably *only* use canned tomatoes," I said, somehow defending myself.

"Lilly?"

"Yeah?"

"I'm joking. The ripe summer tomatoes are gone, and I think canned ones have more flavor than these, so I mix them. I hope that's alright with you."

"Um, OK. I mean, I guess I can accept that." I said and took a drink of the wine, and exhaled, glad that that didn't escalate into something weirder.

Marcus took out a large skillet and began mixing the ingredients one by one: the garlic, then the onions, basil, spices, and finally the fresh and canned tomatoes before letting it all simmer.

"And to top it off, a bit of Spätburger," he said as he poured a dash of wine onto the mixture, and then pulled an old, broken ladle out of the drawer.

"And now, we just keep stirring till it thickens up."

"I see."

He poured some water in a pot and let the spaghetti boil as the boat kept rocking back and forth, and up and down. But as the waves increased, I was concerned that it would not only be the aroma flowing through the cabin. And no sooner had I thought that when suddenly the boat rose more than usual and there was a crash on deck.

"Scheiße!" he exclaimed. "Here, stir this. I just go have a look."

"Sure."

He unlocked the hatch and went on deck as I scooted out of the bench, hopped to the stove and stirred the bubbling sauce.

There was some rumbling around on deck and thunder rolled through the marina as he called down into the cabin.

"Winds are picking up. Some chairs blew over. Just keep stirring!" he called from the deck.

"I'm stirring!" I called back.

"*Ja,* I have to secure some things. Just keep stirring."

I stirred and stirred as the rumbling continued and finally, he climbed back down the stairs into the cabin.

When the spaghetti was done, he strained it off into the sink and portioned it out onto two plates before topping them off with the sauce.

"Ready," he said calmly, placing the plates on the table.

"Looks good," I muttered.

"And you said you can't cook."

Embarrassed, I could feel the heat start to rise in my neck as the windows started to patter from the oncoming rain.

"Guess we won't be able to go on deck," I said.

"That's OK," he said with a wink, "There's enough to do in here."

I twirled the spaghetti on my fork and took a bite of the noodles, a perfect *al dente,* sucking the last bit up between my lips.

****

Carnival in the States is mostly celebrated in New Orleans, and it was months away. But as I researched all things "carnivally", I found that in Germany, for whatever reason, it officially started next month, November 11, to be exact. At 11:11 o'clock, to be even more exact. Did it get any more exact?

It didn't matter. I obviously needed to get started, but my head was still in the clouds from yesterday. On the one hand, I was worried that someone might find out. Or already knew. On the other, I got all warm and fuzzy just thinking about it. One the other, it was one time – and it wouldn't happen again, not as long as I worked there, and besides, I was looking for a real job.

My sketchpad was full of thumbnails of potential flyer designs, but like my bedroom, my desk, and my head, they were very chaotic.

My desk, in fact, was running over with mail from different doctors and bills that needed to be paid. Co-pay here, co-pay there, fees for this and lots of worries about money, rent, money, bills, money . . .

"I have to go back to work," Maddie called from the living room, "If I'm going to bring you, we need to go."

"I'm coming."

As Maddie drove quickly along Ocean Drive through light traffic, my phone went off.

beep beep

October 4 ☖☵☆

Are your feet no longer on the ground? Borders between your work life and social life could be blurring, making you wish you had clearer boundaries. Take some time out to clear your head and draw clear lines if you need to.

Mesmerized, I read it out loud.

"Can you believe that?" I asked, stunned. "I mean, I'm really not on the ground, and, well, one foot *is really not* on the ground!"

"What?"

"Right here, it says it," I continued. "But, oh, wow. I need clearer boundaries," I said more to myself.

"It makes me nervous when you keep reading those, you know that?" Maddie grumbled as she turned the corner on the way to the Black Forest.

"Why's that?" I asked.

"I just think you need to be more in control of your life, and when you keep relying on that, it makes me think, you know, maybe you're not. Or don't want to be. I mean, look at you," she said pointing to my leg.

"Well, if you have a secret success coach or guidance counselor that you'd like to introduce me to, well, I'm all for it. And if not, don't worry about it. I'll be fine. Just listen, it even says it here: Take some time . . ." I read it out loud.

186

"Earth to Lilly," she cut in, "I feel like you're in need of a major reality check," she stressed as she stopped the car. "Now go to work."

"I'm going already."

I got out in the alley behind the restaurant just before three o'clock, and my mind was really kind of blown away.

As my evening shift neared, I shuffled in through the kitchen which, to my surprise, was empty again. With nobody there, I was extra careful to get through the quiet, germ-free environment, the whole time scared I might fall and crack my head on the stainless-steel counter-top and even more scared of Fritz's fury at the sight of my blood contaminating his impeccably white tiles.

No, this was not the right place for me. This was another accident waiting to happen. Best to get myself to the beer garden as quickly as possible. At least there, should I trip on a partially exposed root or electrical wire, the blood of my injury would much easier go unnoticed as it would seep into the dirt and gravel on the ground, thus saving me from the wrath of Fritz.

I made my way through the kitchen and dining room and went out the opened wooden door to the beer-garden. The large yard was enclosed by an ivy-draped, six-foot cedar stockade fence, and it was completely decorated in blue and white. The long, wooden tables and benches were covered with authentic Bavarian blue and white, diamond-checked, plastic tablecloths, and blue and white flags that were attached from one tree to another, hung overhead with party lanterns. Oom-pah-band German music, that somehow reminded me of a mariachi band, played throughout the restaurant and also in the garden.

The bar and a register were set up between the trees and I hopped over to my work spot and propped my crutches up while Liesl, obviously nervous for some reason, was running on about the specials.

"Lilly!" she called anxiously from the doorway with Gerri right behind her. "Good that you are here already. I have a bar-stool here for you, so you can sit down while you work."

"Here are some lemons and limes," Gerri added. "Can you cut them up? It's getting' late." She handed me a bowl and placed a knife and cutting board on the check-out where I was sitting.

"Sure," I said, taking the bowl from her.

Unlike the 4-star menu that usually reigned here, schnitzel, bratwurst, huge pretzels and a kind of German pizza called a Flammküchen, were the specialties of the day.

Liesl oscillated back and forth between the garden and the kitchen before coming over to me in a nervous rush.

"Is everything OK? Do you have your drawer counted out already?" she asked in her voice of authority which was starting to make me nervous as well.

"Yes and — umm, yes," I lied, because I didn't.

"Did you check the credit card machine? It needs to be working out here, too, you see. The people will be coming in shortly and you must be ready."

"It's all under control," I lied again, looking for the credit card machine.

I pulled open the drawers. No machine. I looked underneath in the cabinets. Shit! No machine. Why was I responsible for setting the machines up in when it was completely obvious that I was having trouble getting around at all? *Why me? Why me, stuck at the register?* I thought as I saw Marcus coming in, and then it dawned on me that he would be working all evening at the outside bar. Which was right next to the register. Maybe there were worse places to be stuck.

I took out the bills and started to count my bank.

"Twenty-two, twenty-three, twenty-four," I whispered to myself.

"Fifty-six, eighty-one, fifty-two" sounded a familiar voice from the door, as Marcus stood in the doorway, succeeding in his efforts to sabotage my counting. Thank goodness he didn't know that he didn't have to say a word to accomplish that. For some reason I stiffened up just knowing that he was in the vicinity.

"Be quiet, or I'll . . ." I trailed off, unable to think of any threats that I could say in public, not to mention any that I could make good on.

"What?" Marcus asked, "What will you do?"

"You know, they have a pretty strict work policy here" I whispered as he walked around the bar.

"No, I've not heard about it." He leaned in closer to me. "But maybe later, you can tell me more about it," he whispered.

Suddenly I was in a warm-fuzzy thought bubble as the thought lingered as I sat down on the bar stool, envisioning me and Marcus discussing the silly work policy, possibly over a nice glass of Gewürztraminer or some other unpronounceable vintage... Maybe just one more time. Maybe it was be worth the risk.

No. Stop.

It was almost time to open. Again, I tried to concentrate on my bank and control the influx of internal dialog in my head.

"Get out of the way, Marcus," Liesl huffed as she came back outside with a tray full of monster one-liter mugs, and Gerri was right behind her.

"These are the real beer steins, imported," Liesl said breathily while she awkwardly let them down on the counter and I wondered if beer glasses of this proportion were legal.

"Are you sure you should be carrying that? It looks heavy," I asked, not knowing which might topple over first, the glasses, or Liesl.

"They're not gonna walk out here themselves," Gerri pointed out sarcastically.

"Fritz will be bringing another keg of beer, so that you have it here when you need it," Liesl panted.

"Good. What kind? The Franziskaner?" Marcus asked.

"Ja."

"What is Franziskaner?" I asked.

"One of the oldest beers in Germany," Liesl said. "It was first brewed by monks in Bavaria, over seven hundred years ago!" she called as she walked back to the restaurant.

"Hey there, darlin'!" I heard Johnney's voice from the open door, catapulting me back to here and now. I looked up to see her, even more bodacious than her usual self.

"Hello, Johnney," Marcus replied, smiling.

And that was it for my warm and fuzzy thought bubble.

Gerri's eyes widened when she looked at her, then she looked at me and then at Marcus.

"Hey y'all! Hey, Lil'! You back on your feet? — No, just joking," Johnney said, tossing her hair back. "Seriously, what happened to you?" she asked and at the same time adjusted what seemed to be a severely padded push-up bra under her dirndl, which must have been altered to be even more low-cut. She casually walked behind the beer bar and sat down on a bar stool — *his* bar stool.

"My stars, what has *she* done?" Gerry whispered, surprised.

"What happened to me?" I answered Johnney. "What's happened to *you*?"

"Oh, this?" she asked innocently. "Just a little help from 'Aunt Vikki'. Helps with the tips," she said and gave me a wink.

Now she was winking, too?

"I'm thinking about getting it done permanently, though," she announced. "What do you think?"

Nothing was left of my warm, fuzzy bubble.

"Are we gonna get 'em all drunken up again tonight?" she asked Markus with a laugh.

Had I missed something?

"I think that is why they come here," Marcus answered her, still smiling.

"Well, they sure do tip better when they're drinkin' the hard stuff," she said and laughed with a high pitched, honeyed voice.

190

The exchange between them went on for what seemed like forever. I, meanwhile, sat there, my feet not on the ground but chained to my bar stool, unable to escape while my giddy mood morphed into something else, something not so giddy.

Liesl came back, saw Johnney and walked by her, speechless as the first customers were following her.

"Here is your table," Liesl said to the three men in their late twenties. She waited for them to sit down and handed them each a menu.

"Gerri will be with you in just a moment to take your order," she informed them in her 'hostess-with-the-mostess' voice. "Be sure and try the Paulaner Pils. Or maybe a Maisels Weiße, it's a nice wheat beer. They are the beer specials for today."

Mike came in with a tall, dark man, still in a work suit walked up, "What do you have to do to get a beer around here?" he asked playfully with a nasally voice

I thought the man looked vaguely familiar, probably a regular who I just hadn't seen that often.

"Hey, Emilio! I wondered if you'd be here." Johnney asked and got down from the bar stool.

"Hey, good-lookin'", came a flirty greeting from Emilio as he walked toward the beer bar. "It's Oktoberfest. And you know I can't miss that. And then I heard the music and had to come in."

"Be right back," Johnney said as she walked away to one of the tables.

"Who's that?" I whispered to Mike, glad that Johnney would have someone else to focus on.

"Emilio? Just another alcoholic," he laughed and patted him on the back.

"So, you like the music?" Marcus asked.

"Oh, sure. And I even play the accordion," he proclaimed.

"Well, you play in a band, don't you?" Gerri asked.

"Sure," he answered, taking a drink, "mariachi. We play around here sometimes."

"I thought some of the music here sounded like a mariachi band," I said.

"Yeah, I was stationed over there in Kaiserslautern for several years. Used to play every now and then with a couple of guys."

Marcus gave me a look of confusion and leaned over to me. "Of all the German musical influences to follow, they chose oom-pah," he said confidentially, and my bubble kind of came back.

"But you know what I was wondering?" Emilio asked, "Why do you girls where those dresses? I mean, if this is the *Black Forest* Restaurant, why do you where Bavarian dirndls?"

"What? Um, I don't know." I said. "I guess there must be a difference, if you're asking about it."

"Heck, yeah, there's a difference. I don't think you'd find too many women wearing dirndls in the *Schwarzwald.*"

"Ask Marcus. He must be the expert in that department."

Marcus looked up, nodded his head, but shrugged his shoulders. "You're right, but I don't know why they mixed that here."

"Ask Liesl," I suggested.

"Yeah, there's probably some story behind that mystery," Emilio concluded.

"Hellloo," Johnney called as she handed me a ticket to be rung up.

"Two Paulaners and a Bitburger," she called the order to Marcus.

"Got it," Marcus started searching for the right bottles.

"I'll take one of those Paulaners, too, while you're down there," Emilio called.

A muffled response came from Marcus who was half inside the refrigerator. When he came up, he opened four bottles with a metal bottle opener.

"Here you go," he said, giving three of the bottles to Johnney, who put them on her tray and left to deliver them.

"And for you." Marcus handed a Paulaner to Emilio who looked thoughtfully at the beer.

"*Prost*, as you say over there, right?" he asked lifting the bottle.

"Yeah, Prost," replied Marcus.

"I learned that when I was in the army. Didn't get off the base much, though." He took a drink and gave Johnney a long once-over as she made her way back to the bar, her boobs arriving a good two seconds before the rest of her.

"Johnney, did you get a new — . . . dress?" he asked, obviously noticing her enhanced shape.

"I got *lots* of new things," she answered, not missing a chance to mention her new unmentionables.

"If I didn't know better, I'd think you were the real thing, a real-life *Mädel*," Emilio chuckled.

"Ah, Emilio, what do you know about German girls?" she asked.

"They've got interesting dresses." He turned back to Marcus. "Isn't this what the girls look like over there?"

Marcus looked at Johnney. "Not where *I* come from, but . . ."

"I mean, you two, you might look good together," Emilio added as he drank his beer, looking back and forth at Johnney and Marcus.

"What?" Johnney laughed. "Really? Well, whaddaya think, Marky? Me and you?" Johnney laughed. "Guess one should probably take their chances," she whispered at me before she walked back to one of her tables.

Marky?! I thought I'd misheard them all. Suddenly my stomach hurt, my heart rate accelerated, and I was scared I might break out soon. I tried to concentrate on the register but couldn't help hearing the exchange going on under my nose.

"Here you go. I got two to tab out." Johnney shoved two tip trays on the counter, each paying with credit cards. I looked under the register but saw that I still didn't have the machine. Shit. I grabbed my crutches and slid off the bar stool.

"I'll be right back."

"Are you alright?" Marcus asked.

"I'm fine. I'll be right back," I said tautly.

"Where are you going? They want to tab out!" Johnney called.

I hopped slowly back inside to the bar. First stop though: the bathroom. I knew the credit card machine wouldn't be in there, but neither would Johnney, Emilio or Marcus. I took out my phone and re-read my horoscope: *Take some time to clear your head.*

At this rate, I figured I would need a long time before my head was clear and wondered how long I could stay there before they would notice that I was gone longer than need be. But it was no use. I had to go back. So, I grabbed my crutches and hopped to the bar to go find the credit card machine as Liesl accosted me just as I opened the restroom door.

"Lilly! What is the matter? Why are you not outside?"

"Oh, I just have to finish setting the register up. I need to go to the bar for a second," I said, trying to shimmy past her, which was almost impossible with crutches.

"Hurry up, the garden is already full, you see."

I looked through the opened door, and indeed, almost all the tables were full. I searched through the cabinets of the bar and found the credit card machine next to an opened bottle of schnapps. More temptation? Fuck it, I thought. There was no need to struggle even more. I was struggling enough just trying to deal with the circus that was buzzing around me outside. Extreme conditions called for extreme measures, I rationalized. I opened the bottle to guzzle a few shots of the dark liquor when Fritz's penetrating voice rolled through the bar.

"I'll be right back!" he called, spontaneously appearing out of nowhere, just when I least expected it.

"Lilly!" he roared as I threw the cap and the bottle back into the cabinet.

"Have you seen Liesl?"

"Outside," I coughed. "She's outside."

Regardless of what a master cook he was, he was maniacal and, more often than not, had large knives in his hand. He didn't seem like a person I would want to provoke, at least not in my current condition. I would at least want to be able to run. I opted against the schnapps and closed the cabinet before limping back to the register but kept the schnapps in mind, just in case.

"Here are the tickets to tables six, eight and three. Table two wants to tab out, so, could you kind of hurry?" Johnney asked wrinkling her nose.

"Sure thing," I replied flatly, pushing the tickets into the slot of the register.

"You were gone so long. Did you find what you needed?" Marcus asked.

"I did. Things are just getting really crazy, know what I mean?" I asked, trying to contain the contempt in my voice.

"Well, this and carnival. The two big events of the year. *Mantau!*"

"Ehm, what's that?" I asked impatiently.

"Just a greeting they yell around carnival time. Another event to drink a lot of beer. Only then, they get dressed up like Halloween, but not so scary," he said handing me a ticket. "Can you ring these up?"

"Of course."

The tables were full, and the beer was flowing. Even Johnney was also sneaking a drink or two between tables, and before long, I felt like to be able to endure an entire night of this, I would probably also have to be wasted. Maybe this explained why the monks invented beer in the first place. Maybe they were just as frustrated. Maybe Mother Necessity just helped them concoct the first self-preservation brews to help them deal with ruthless medieval shape-shifters.

For the rest of the night I focused on adding and re-adding the tickets, covertly smoking a cigarette and taking in the money. Emilio had gone, but the conversation between Marcus and Johnney kept repeating in my head, and I was relieved when my shift was over. I cleared out the tickets, finished counting my drawer and went to call Maddie to come and get me.

"Where are you going?" Marcus asked from behind me.

"What do you mean? I'm going home," I answered as casually as I could.

"You leave already? You have it good."

"Maybe so. See you tomorrow."

I put on my backpack and left through the back door of the kitchen, where a light fall breeze carried the rotting scent of the dumpster through the alley while I hobbled over to a bench down wind of it as I sat down and heard a couple of kids further down in the alley. I held my breath but exhaled when they got closer and I realized that their mother was with them.

Fuck, I thought. *What the hell am I doing here?* I pulled my cigarettes out of my purse and re-read the day's entry. As I closed my eyes and inhaled the newly lit cigarette, the heavy kitchen door opened behind me and I heard footsteps over the gravel way getting closer.

"Out of the way!" Carlos called and walked past with a bag of trash. He was wearing just a T-shirt and I almost didn't recognize him without his usual chef's jacket on, which showed just how inked-up he actually was, tattoos over his entire arms, and some kind of scary ones at that.

"Wow. You're like a walking canvas."

"Yeah," he looked critically over his arm, "but I'm getting some of them taken off. Some things just aren't meant to be forever, know what I mean," he asked on his way back to the door.

"Yeah, I hear ya," I agreed as Carlos walked in and Marcus walked out.

"Hey, you are still here," Marcus said.

"Yep. Still here. Can't get out of here that fast," I said, raising my leg a little.

"Is everything alright with you? You seem . . . don't know, in a bad mood," he said and sat down next to me.

I felt the urge to run, and then it disappeared. I figured it was my amygdala kicking in and wondered what he would think if he knew about my disorder.

"I'm OK. Just tired. I just need to go home. I hear I need to clear my head, regain my perspective." I tried to sound convincing and showed my horoscope as supporting evidence.

"Ah," Marcus said after he had read the entry. "Your life is a blur? What is a blur?"

"No," I answered defiantly, "It's when it all foggy and mixed-up, kind of."

"Well, yesterday is not a blur," he said confidently.

"Shh!", I hushed him immediately, "They'll hear you. There really is the work policy, and I still need my job," I said as Maddie pulled up in her blue Mazda and parked behind the dumpsters.

"Hey there," she said obviously irritated, "traffic is absolutely terrible. It took me forever to get here for some reason. Are you ready to go?"

"Yep." I got up, wrestling with the crutches. "Bye," I said to Marcus. "I gotta go."

"Or . . ." he started with raised eyebrows.

Or what?! I thought.

"Maybe I come with you?" he asked with a risky look.

I couldn't believe it. He finished the question. Both   came unexpectantly, but not necessarily unwelcome.   Johnney's voice suddenly rang through my head in the background. *Take the chance*, she'd said.

OK, I thought.

"Right, come on," I said, daring him to join me, although I knew he had to go back.

He inhaled, acting like he was taken aback, and hurt.

"Too bad." I said as I hopped off.

"Wait," he said, walking to me, "listen, um . . . maybe you want to go out this week, you know, we could talk me more, about the policy."

"You mean, strictly business?" I asked, looking around to see if anyone could hear.

"Of course. Strictly business." He patted my arm, and again, I struggled with my amygdala disorder.

"We could probably do that" I managed to say before going off to Maddie's car.

"Then I call you tomorrow."

"OK. Have a good night."

"You, too." he said with a wink.

11

November

The house was so quiet when I walked into the living room that at first, I didn't even notice Maddie sitting at the table.

"Morning," she whispered, eating her breakfast.

"Morning. I didn't know if you'd be up, or still here, or whatever."

"I got a few minutes," she said. "How're things going?"

"Going OK."

"OK?"

Did she expect more? "Yeah. OK," I answered. "Why?"

"I don't know. Just seems like I haven't seen you much lately. You seem to be spending a lot of time with Marcus, that's all."

"Oh, does it? Yeah, I guess maybe I am."

"Maybe I am," she repeated with a knowing smile.

"What?"

"Oh, I don't know. 'Maybe I am.' Lil, you're spending a lot of time with this guy, that's all."

"We're just hanging out on the boat, that's it," I said, careful not to reveal too much.

"Oh, right. Like 'If this boat's a rockin', don't come a knockin.'" She smiled again.

"Shut up," I said, embarrassed.

"It's your story, Lil. You tell it any way you want to." She got up, smirking. "You're doing alright, though, hm?"

"I'm doing good. You?"

"Right now, I'm doing good. If I leave now, I'll still be doing good when I get to work. I'll pick you up at three, right?" She pulled her bag and coat over her shoulder.

"You're taking me to the doctor. Yeah. I almost forgot."

"Almost? You did forget. Have a good day. I'll see you at three."

"Yeah, you, too."

Was I doing good? I couldn't even bring myself to say it.

November 4

Having trouble seeing the forest for the trees this golden autumn? Well, the view gets a lot less dense now. This week brings perspective to matters that have kept you confused for the last few months. Plan some travel, a study or even a social gathering.

The view was clearing up. On one of the first sunny days in weeks, I looked at my cast with relief. Maddie would pick me up after work to take me to Doctor Singh, and I was happy that today, it would be taken off. *Putting things into perspective.*

Yeah!

Table-tents, menus and flyers of festivals past lined my desk as I looked out my window. A golden autumn hadn't yet materialized. El Niño had been awake for most of October, and instead of a golden autumn, the gullies were stuffed from leaves and branches that had been blown off the trees and swept down the foliage-littered streets which were now flooded from days of non-stop rain. The weather, however, had actually lent itself to my situation in that respect, as I was forced to sit indoors, which actually had some advantages. Being the cashier, there was no way around learning the menu — free from pressure. I just rang everything up and let the names of the items and their prices sink in. Plus, I got a chance to see everyone's orders, so I even knew which plates went to which unpronounceable name.

At the same time, though, the boys from Santa Barbara still haunted my thoughts. I saw various versions of them on a regular basis in the alley behind the restaurant, and sometimes from Liesl's garden when we were collecting the herbs that miraculously hadn't gotten swept away by the rain.

To my surprise, the "carnival campaign" was almost ready. I printed out the table-tents and mock menus in several different versions, one which included an idea for a gardening project with a local community center. I didn't know if Liesl and Fritz would be open to any ideas like that, but I thought it might be worth a try.

Fritz had been gone a lot, but I'd heard that he might be there today, so I put all samples in a folder and carefully adjusted it in my back-pack, along with my right shoe that I would finally be able to put on after my doctor's appointment.

When my shift had ended at work, I was getting ready to show my ideas to Fritz and Liesl when Maddie called me.

"I have to work late. I'm sorry, but I can't take you to the doctor."

"Oh, fuck," I said, totally disappointed. Plan B?

"Sorry, maybe someone from there could take you? Or we go tomorrow?"

"No . . . I'll think of something. I just want this off! I'll try to call a taxi. OK, I'll see you later."

As I hung up, Miss Terri went off again, and I read the message with frustration. What happened to "the forest for the trees? The view gets less dense?" I needed that right now! The "confused for the last few months" part was completely accurate, but a bit of clarity would be quite welcome at this point.

"Everything OK?"

I looked up to see Marcus standing there.

"No, not really," I said with a grimace. "I need to go to the doctor. Today's the day, but Maddie can't pick me up."

"Oh." He paused for a second before asking, "Where do you have to go?"

"Fifth Street."

"Could I maybe take you there?"

Clarity came! My heart jumped just a little, and I carefully answered, "Would you?"

"I'm also off, so, sure. Why not?"

I grabbed my bags and crutches and followed him out to the postal jeep. Or did I float?

Plan a travel, and get perspective to matter? Yes! I thought.

We left through the back door, and the windows of the jeep rattled while we traveled across town, but traffic was crawling on Water Street and had come to a complete stop.

"Come on, damn it! I don't want to wear this stupid cast for one minute longer than I absolutely have to!"

"Relax," Marcus said in his usual calming voice. "You will be there in plenty of time."

The light changed and we drove on, pulled into the parking lot of the clinic for what I hoped was the last time.

Despite the warm apricot colors, the full waiting room felt sterile and anonymous. There were several people already sitting in the room, making it uncomfortable to talk. I picked up a magazine, but couldn't really concentrate on anything long enough to actually read it.

"Lilly DuMont," called out a nurse in blue scrubs.

We got up and followed her to the examination room where we had to wait again, this time alone.

Marcus picked up a stethoscope that was hanging on the wall.

"Maybe I should examine you?" he asked, directing the stethoscope to my chest.

"You could, but that might seem strange to Dr. Singh, since it is my *ankle* that is broken."

"Pleas—" He stopped in mid-word because the door opened.

"Good morning." Dr. Singh walked in, looking at my file. "So, you are ready to relinquish your cast?" he asked.

"Are you kidding? I almost took it off myself."

"Better that you came here."

Marcus took a step back and leaned against the counter where he discreetly laid the stethoscope down behind his back. I sat on the clinic bed, and Dr. Singh came over with an electric rotary saw.

"Ready?"

"More than ready." I suddenly felt a wave of self-consciousness. Didn't casts stink when they came off? Weren't the limbs all shriveled and icky? Did I really want Marcus to see this much of me?

"You sure you want to see this?" I hoped he might opt out to leave, but he was just smiling, so I guess it didn't matter to him.

After cutting through the cast, Dr. Singh took another instrument and pried open the cast, revealing a shriveled, hairy, very white leg. Icky? Yes, but luckily nothing too grotesque.

"It looks good," Dr. Singh diagnosed before letting me go. "Be for the next few weeks just be careful. You can make an appointment at the front desk for a check-up in two weeks."

I was elated and marked by perma-grin as I slipped in both of my shoes. We walked over the parking lot back to the car, *sans* cast and crutches.

"So, you want to go jogging home now, I guess?" Marcus joked. At least I hoped he was joking.

"I actually feel like I could."

"Well, maybe you should take the doctor's advice and take it easy for a little longer."

"Wouldn't want to risk a re-laps just out of the box, would I? You don't mind taking me home, do you?"

"Ah, the things I have to do for you."

When we left, the sun was blinding, which prompted Marcus to put on his sunglasses. I looked out the window and noticed the beautiful fall foliage. Besides a chance to shave my very hairy leg, what else could I want? Everything was going in a wonderful direction.

I turned to him. "You know, I was thinking that the whole Oktoberfest thing introduced me a little bit to your culture, right?" My heart started beating fast enough for me to feel it.

"And, well, Thanksgiving is coming up. I thought, if you'd like, maybe you could come over, kind of get an official taste of something truly American."

"And I thought I had already tasted something truly American."

"Ha ha. Seriously. I mean, I'm not a super cook, so I don't want to promise too much, but I just thought, maybe you'd like to come."

"Thanksgiving?" He smiled and looked at me through the mystery-making sunglasses. "That's the festival with the goose, right?" he asked without a trace of humor.

"Turkey."

"Ah, turkey. Might be nice. I think I would like that. When is it, this Turkey Festival?"

"The fourth Thursday in November, like every year."

He looked out the other side of the window as if deliberating something, before he turned around to me with a serious look on his face.

"I think it is a great idea," he said, choosing his words carefully, "but Lilly — can I tell you something just between you and me?"

Wait. Was he confiding in me? I waited for the rest, the suspense killing me. Calm down, Lilly, I told myself, desperately trying not to be overcome by the thrill of what might be a "yes".

"The thing is, that I am perhaps no longer here at that time."

Wait.

"What?!" I'm sure I heard wrong.

Burlaps sewn along here with that twine.

"I mean, I probably will be, so I would say 'yes', I'd love to."

OK. I exhaled. There was a "yes." Cloud Nine.

November 17 ♥☺☼

We know you're grateful, especially with Thanksgiving right around the corner. Still, as the Holiday Season starts off, don't forget to plan in some much-needed R & R as you're planning everything else. When one closes, another one opens, and if anyone knows how quickly things can change, it's you.

R & R?

With only one week to go until Thanksgiving, finally, things were really starting to look up! No time for R & R! I was back at work and tips had never been so good. Suddenly, I wasn't just getting by, I was *actually making it.* My leg was fine, I knew my stuff, I got on the schedule more often, got better sections, and had finally kind of eased into the whole waitressing thing. My campaign was almost finished, too, which only left Thanksgiving dinner to tend to.

I had never cooked a Thanksgiving dinner myself, but I figured it couldn't be too hard. I mean, what would we have to do? Put a turkey in the oven? I could do that. It was even better that Maddie had decided to go along with me on this one, having Turkey Day with her friends who had become like extended family. Plus one.

I wasn't a domestic goddess by any means: wasn't into laundry, housework, decorating or even shopping for that matter. But, jeez, I'm from Texas! Although there was no shortage of women in Texas whose life goal it was to be a beauty queen to major in M.R.S., even today, I knew lots of intelligent, successful women who were also great at cooking and things like that. So surely, simply by heritage, there had to be an ounce of culinary goddess somewhere in me.

I tried to summon out the Julia Child in me — if I had one, but that didn't work too well, so I took a more conventional route and looked online. I checked all the latest on party planning and found tons of topics:

feast decoration, menus, party planning, main dishes, decorations, menus, non-alcoholic drinks, traditions, appetizers, side dishes, garnishes, hot drinks, pop-up name cards, desserts, alcoholic drinks, cold drinks....

Where to start? A labyrinth of details. I spent hours scouring though websites with all the latest on Thanksgiving planning, In a lot of ways, it didn't seem too much different from what was going on at work, only now Maddie and I were doing all the work by ourselves, and of course, we weren't getting paid .

I figured maybe this constituted the part of my horoscope that spoke of expanding my horizons, because, apparently, there was infinitely more to Thanksgiving than I had ever dreamed of, and just when I thought I was gaining some momentum, my search came to a screeching halt as the headline came up:

'The Thanksgiving Dinner Timetable Planner'
What to Do One Month in Advance

One month in advance?! I didn't have half a month to plan.
Were we too late for Thanksgiving? I thought, as panic attacks set in. Why didn't Mom ever start *one month* in advance? Or did she? Maybe I just didn't notice? Three weeks ago, I was definitely not making turkey stock or cranberries. Three weeks ago, I was up to my ankle-challenged ass in wiener schnitzel and sausage. And now, Thanksgiving was only a week away, so what could I do? Obviously, it was time to wind down the "research and development phase" and go get some practical experience.
"Maybe you could ask Fritz. He seems to be the event-planning-guru," Maddie suggested.

"Don't be stupid. I'm not making him think I'm any more incompetent than he probably already thinks I am," I snapped.

My protest revealed more of my impending meltdown than I wanted. And besides, he'd been increasingly nervous lately. It had something to do with the trial. Even Carlos was more quiet than usual, so I figured he had enough on his mind.

"What about my mom? I think I'll just give her a call," Maddie announced, exaggeratedly calm. "She's made enough Thanksgiving dinners, and I she never started a *month* early. I don't think."

I didn't have the energy to protest, so, while she talked to her mom, I went to the back porch, still happy about not having the cast on but still feeling a panic attack coming on. That was at least the one good thing about breaking my leg: the pain medication had stifled any sense of caring so that panic attacks hardly possible. I didn't have any now, so instead, I lit up a cigarette while all kinds of scenarios played through my head:

Could I postpone Thanksgiving?

Could I do Thanksgiving take-out style without anyone noticing?

In a surge of buyer's regret, I even tried thinking up a reason why Thanksgiving was suddenly cancelled this year when the back-screen door opened and Maddie came onto the porch.

"Everything is OK. You can come in now. Mom is sending us her traditional, 1-2-3 method of easy Thanksgiving. She said to tell you that we never had name cards, much less pop-up ones, so come on, let's roll up our sleeves, get our hands dirty and get down to business."

We looked through the pages we had printed out, and before too long, we actually had most of the dinner planned out, even with a few decorations and a list of who could bring what. We decided that we didn't really need name cards, and if anyone had trouble getting to know someone better, well, we had wine on the list for that.

****

The next morning, I packed the shopping list and my folder with my presentation for Liesl in my backpack and   made my way to work.

I walked along the mall where the store-front windows were already transformed into scenes of Thanksgiving and Christmas spirit.

When I got to work, I slipped into my uniform and tied an apron around my waist when I caught a glimpse of Johnney, who was squeezed so tightly into her dirndl that it pleaded for mercy, and she looked kind of like the balloons that man on the mall twists the long, skinny balloons into animal shapes. I suppressed an urge to go stab her to see if she would pop.

Instead, I went to the bar and pulled out the presentation, so I could show it to Liesl when she arrived. I wiped down the bar, and Carlos nodded silently when I walked through the kitchen to get the bar garnishes from the walk-in refrigerator. I moved some boxes of vegetables out of the way and propped the door, so it couldn't close. I popped a few strawberries in my mouth, hoping they wouldn't be missed, gathered some lemons and limes, and suddenly Marcus stood behind me.

"Enter at your own risk," I said, "it's freezing in here!"

His hair was disheveled, and his after-five shadow looked more like after-ten. He kicked the veggie box that held the door open to the side, letting it fall closed, and I could tell by the look on his face that something was amiss. Maybe he didn't like refrigerators?

"I wanted to come by earlier." His voice was tight. "I need to talk to you"

"Why's that?" I asked, alerted. "I mean, not that I don't want you to come by, I just could have straightened up a little, you know."

"I wanted to talk to you. Or, I need to talk to you."

All of a sudden, there was something in his voice that made me realize that it wasn't just the missing strawberries that were making him so serious.

"What's up? What's going on?" He had my nervous, undivided attention now.

"I got a call from my mother yesterday. I got a job that I had applied to, so I have to go home."

I looked at him, stunned. So far, the whole subject of "leaving" had been more or less taboo. He was leaving. We both knew it, but we never mentioned it.

I looked at him in disbelief, unable to change gears so fast.

"Is it getting colder in here?" I asked, starting for the door.

"I got the job offer at a very good restaurant in Stuttgart. It's advent season coming up, so they need me back soon. Sooner than I thought. There is much more work than expected, so I have to go back. I just wanted to tell you this as soon as I could, because of Thanksgiving and all."

I looked at him, able and somehow unable to register what he had just said. "Congratulations," I whispered. I stared at my shoes for a few minutes, letting all the words sink in. "Wh-When?"

"Monday."

"That's just four days."

"*Ja.*"

Suddenly I felt knots in my stomach in places that I didn't know I had. Whatever we had talked about previously, whatever had seemed to be important and meaningful ten minutes ago, had changed. Everything had changed.

"So, you're not coming for Thanksgiving dinner, then," I confirmed, stating the obvious, waiting for the feeling of someone twisting a sword through my heart to stop, while I tried to keep myself together.

"No, I'm afraid not. You have to go where your work takes you, or?"

To my surprise, he sounded disbelieving. Apologetic. Was he in shock as much as me?

"My train leaves for San Francisco on Sunday morning," he continued. "I have to get my things together." He turned away, running his fingers through his hair. "I really can't believe this," he confessed. "I thought this would somehow be different."

I shook my head, trying to fully comprehend what he was telling me.

"So, what are you saying? This is it?" I couldn't fathom that *this* was *it*.

"I'm not sure myself. It's all happening so fast. I didn't plan to go like this." He got up, looking around. "But, *ja*, I think so. Unless I can see you again? I mean, I want to see you again. I don't want to leave without saying good-bye."

"OK." I agreed immediately. No time for thinking. No time for games.

"When?"

"I have to pack my stuff, but I can pick you up tomorrow after work. OK?"

"Yeah."

He leaned over and kissed me, and just at this very moment, the refrigerator door opened, and Fritz walked in – and freaked. Of course, he did - but not in his usual freakiness. He was absolutely quiet and very serious.

"What?" he asked shocked. "This cannot be," he said as he glared through the door.

"Fritz," Marcus started but got cut off, knowing it was no use.

"Just go. Both of you!"

I hurriedly threw the lemons back into the box and slid through the refrigerator door.

"Liesl!" I heard Fritz yell from the back of the kitchen, making me go faster to the bar where I could see my red, flushed neck and chest in the mirror.

Liesl darted by me.

"What is the . . .?"

"Liesl!"

"I'm so sorry," I whispered when she looked at me stupefied.

210

I grabbed my back-pack and left, dashing quickly back out of the kitchen, through the alley and down the mall. I just wanted to get home.

When I walked in, I heard Maddie in the kitchen.

"Here you go — 'Thanksgiving Turkey', 'Delicious Dressing', and 'Yummy Yams'. All the perfect recipes for the perfect dinner," Maddie announced cheerfully, handing me several recipes we'd printed out.

"Mom emailed them over as quickly as she could, so you can quit panicking."

I looked away, not able to think about Thanksgiving anymore, and there was a long pause.

"What's wrong?" she finally asked.

"I — um — I don't think we need the recipes anymore," I whispered.

"What's the matter? What's going on?"

"He's going home," I sputtered, "and I got fired."

"You *what*?" she exclaimed. "You got fired?"

"He's going home, Maddie." I repeated. Wasn't that more important right now?

I told her what had happened and was really wishing for a compassionate ear.

"Damn it, Lilly! What part of 'no fraternizing' don't you understand? Seriously, Lil, in the refrigerator," she said with disgust.

"He's leaving." Didn't *she* understand this?

"Yeah, Lil. He's got a job. And you? You said you were just friends! You said you weren't looking for The One. Damn it, Lil. I'm sorry, but — you got fired!" Maddie repeated in disbelief.

I had just tripped and ran back into another wall, and the wind had been knocked out of me. I wasn't sure what I should do first. Cancel the dinner invitations? Go shopping for something hot to wear for our final encounter? Cry? Sleep? For lack of strength and direction, I opted for the last. I went to bed, rolled over and pulled the covers up over me. Too stunned to think, I closed my eyes tight and hoped that it would all go away.

****

November 17 ⬚⬚⬚

Gemini, Gemini, have you rushed into something, again? Acted impulsively? You may have learned some tough-but-sobering lessons about jumping into affairs. It's possible that you and your romantic partner could be kept apart due to work or family obligations.

Another über-accurate prediction. It didn't go away.

I got up the next morning and made a pot of coffee while waiting on Sylvia, who was coming over for breakfast. I was glad that she was coming over. She, if anyone, would understand.

I was still in shock and noticed I was beginning to feel the pangs of desperation when I recounted the horrors of yesterday and the predictions that were taking on pretty scary undertones.

"You got fired!?"

She had the same look as Maddie, but at least her voice had a more sympathetic tone.

"Aren't you listening?" I asked again. "He's leaving."

"Yeah, Lil, I understand you're upset, but," she suppressed a laugh, "in the refrigerator? What should the Health Department say?"

"It's not like we were *doing it* in the refrigerator, for God's sake!

"It was one kiss."

"Yeah." She took a sip of her tea. "A financially fatal one."

"How did this happen?" I asked frustrated. "How is it, that he's working for the same restaurant as me in exactly the same time? How does something like that happen?"

"Everything happens for a reason, Lil. Try not to be so sad, ya know," she tried to console me. "One door closes, another one opens. You may not know until much later what it was good for or what you're supposed to get from all this."

"Right. Literally, apparently." I said as I poured us both a cup of coffee. "But it's just *too* weird, you know. And now he's *leaving*," I said, my voice getting wobbly. "I always feel like it's just getting started, right when it's ending."

"Maybe there is no real clear-cut beginning or end."

"Do you really believe that? It sure feels like an end. I'm probably never going to see him again. I just thought you would understand."

"I think I do, but you know — what will be, will be, Lil," she said when she left.

Obviously, nobody was going to understand this. Me least of all. But, at the moment, he was still here. I looked at my horoscope in the paper to see if there were any more shockers on the horizon. Or maybe there was some good news, something hopeful that would say it was all a joke, a huge misunderstanding. Something like "get ready for someone to unexpectedly move in" or "don't be surprised when that certain someone makes a sudden mad u-turn and has decided to turn down the new job offer." But it didn't.

In fact, it was spot on. Once again. It was incredible. The accuracy was almost unbelievable, and to be sure, I didn't want to believe it. But there it was, in black and white. I tore the horoscope out of the paper and lit it with my lighter before throwing it into the ashtray. As I watched it burn, I lit up a cigarette. Stupid fucking horoscope. I sat there going through "what-if" scenarios how he might stay. At the same time, I knew I was feeling desperate, and no matter how well-meant, desperation is not sexy.

With no job to go to, I walked around the mall, and as I looked in the store windows, I saw a silver ladle in one of the windows of a kitchen and cooking store. It looked like the one on the boat and immediately I heard "Keep stirring, keep going," and I knew that was the right thing. I went in and browsed over at the different ladles that they offered. Inside the store, they had a small selection ranging from super cheap to super expensive. But the one in the middle that had a golden handle with a line of four stars going down it was just right. It stuck out and made my decision easy.

I purchased it, and outside, I put it in my back-pack when my phone rang.

"Hello?"

"Hi." Marcus's voice rushed through my cell-phone. "I have to hurry. Are you going to be around?"

"Where should I be? Why?" I asked back.

"Well, I'm on my way to the airport in San Francisco."

"You're where?" I broke in, my voice about to crack and my head suddenly spinning. "But you said, um, tomorrow." My voice trailed off as I wasn't sure what Marcus was getting at.

"I *am* leaving. Tomorrow. I'll be back at the boat around four o'clock. Can you pass by there? I haven't a car anymore."

"Yeah, of course," I said.

The rest of the day was a blur. I cleaned my room, washed some clothes and looked heartlessly through the job ads. At ten after three, I drove through the heavy traffic, and it inevitably took much longer than I'd anticipated to arrive at the harbor where the *Star Struck* was docked. When I finally drove up, I got out and walked over to the boat.

"Marcus!" I called. "Hello?"

There was no answer. It was too cool to stand outside, and the grey November sky promised it could start to rain at any moment, so I went back to my car and rested my head on the steering wheel, trying to ignore my stomach ache.

"*. . . you rushed into something, again? Acted impulsively? learned some tough-but-sobering lessons . . .*"

The words replayed in my head. Had I acted impulsively? Had I *rushed* into something? I'd known him almost a year. I would hardly call that "rushing". Maybe I'd rushed with the Thanksgiving dinner, but seriously — that?

My phone rang.

"How are you doing?" Maddie asked.

"OK, I guess."

"We're still on for Thanksgiving, right? I mean, I sent invitations -"

"Sure," I said.

"Good. So, I'm just going over some things on the list. What do you want for dessert?"

Dessert? I thought. What a question.

"Maddie, I'm sorry, but I can't do this right now. My mind is kind of somewhere else, you know. I don't really feel all that thankful to be honest."

"Lil, I understand that you're a bit disappointed, but I think you're going to be OK. And, hey, we did invite other people."

"You're right. Of course." I caught my breath and tried to do the right thing. "It's just that I read my horoscope and followed it. I listened to it."

"Well, Lil, maybe the universe is not always trustworthy."

"What?" I gasped.

"Knock-knock."

I looked up to see Marcus at the window.

"Oh. I have to go," I said quickly and disconnected.

"Hi there." Marcus opened my car door. "Glad to see you." He smiled, and I squelched a swell of happiness.

"Are you OK?" he asked.

"Not sure. Why?"

"I don't know, you just look a little . . . tired."

"Oh, maybe I am."

Keep it together, keep it together, I warned myself. Don't even *think* about getting all emotional! I got out of the car, and we walked back down the docks. I held on to the rope and jumped over the side while Marcus unlocked the hatch to go downstairs, where we sat in our routine places at the table and he made the usual pot of coffee.

"So, what were you doing in San Francisco today?" I involuntarily snapped.

"Ah, I took most of my belongings to the airport today and did an early check-in, so that I don't have to do all that tomorrow."

"And why couldn't you just take it with you tomorrow?" I pressed on.

"Hey, Lil, what's the matter?" he asked.

"You just —" I stopped, getting myself back together again. "You just could have said something, that's all. I just thought for a minute that you were . . . never mind."

"I see. You thought I was leaving today," he said in surprise.

"Are you crazy? No! I'm not going to leave like that," he said. "I'm taking the train to airport in San Francisco, and from there, I will take my flight home."

The look on my face must have divulged that there was still some information missing and that I still didn't really understand.

"No-one can take me back to the airport tomorrow, because it is such short notice," he continued. "See, tomorrow I don't have a way to get the car back here, so I took all my things and checked in today. That way, tomorrow I only need to have one piece of luggage when I get on the train."

"I guess so. I'm not the experienced traveler like you, I guess. I didn't know you could do that."

I thought about him trying to take care of everything on his own, trying to get ready to leave, and it hit me that this was really happening.

"But that is all taken care of. What about you? What about your job?"

"Good question."

"I don't know what to say about that. I'm sorry. I guess I shouldn't have . . . I talked to Fritz, you know. Of course, he can't fire me but only fire you. I hope he sees that it was my fault."

"I'm a little surprised, true. I mean, I've been looking for a real job the whole time, anyway. I'll just have to look a little harder now, I guess," I said as the pressure started to build in my throat.

"I'll be right back," I said, and I got up and went to the backroom. Maybe the stupid fucked-up horoscope was right after all, and I did jump in too fast. I took a few deep breaths and then went back out there.

"So, any last wishes? Anything you want to see or do one last time before you check out of here?" I asked as I sat down at the table.

"Are you serious?" he asked with that once-over look. "Yeah, I have a few wishes," he admitted with a half-suppressed laugh "But let's sit down for a while."

"All right." I sat back down and exhaled trying to seem as relaxed as he did.

"Wait here." He got up and jumped out on top of the deck. I could hear him doing something on deck, turning chairs over or opening and closing the seats. He jumped back down the hatch, carrying a few flowers in one hand and a bottle of wine in the other.

"Here. For you. A Spätburger for later and some autumn flowers. They're from around here."

He handed me the flowers, and for some reason, I felt myself blush, which made me more self-conscious, and I struggled with a tear that almost began to spill out of my eye. *Not now!* I told myself, drinking the last of the coffee.

"They need some kind of a . . . *Vase*," he said like vah-sah, "I mean, vase."

Marcus looked around in the cupboards and found an empty mason jar that he filled half way with water —and I had a flashback to the first time we met — and then put the flowers in the water and sat the jar on the table.

"They're beautiful," I whispered.

"*Hübsch*," he said, "like you." He smiled.

I didn't know what that meant, and it sounded really nerdy, but my neck started to burn, and I knew it must be flushed. Somehow, I guess I liked the nerdy part.

Marcus got a bottle opener out of a drawer and started to open the bottle he was holding. "Or should I open this now?"

"Fine by me. — I mean, that's great."

He filled up some glasses, and then he put the tape in the tape deck and pushed play.

217

"Cheers," he said smiling.

"Prost," I replied.

I took a long drink of the wine. It was almost six o'clock, and the time seemed to be racing by. "Don't you have any loose ends to tie up?"

"Loose *hands* to tie up?" He raised his hands and looked perplexed, trying hard not to laugh.

I re-worded. "Not loose hands, loose ends! You know, things you have to do before you leave — things to take care of, finish up."

"I already took care of most of the stuff. My things at the airport. I said good-bye to everyone, so, there's just one thing I still need to do."

"What's that?"

"You."

I laughed out loud. "What?" I asked, taken aback.

"No," he said, embarrassed. "I mean, you're the only thing left that I have to tie-up,"

"Oh, I don't know, Mr. Bergmann. You seem to have curious plans for," I could still hardly say it, "departing."

"The only thing left that I have to 'tie-up', as you say, is you. Can I say it like that?" he asked, sitting down next to me on the green booth and putting his arm around my shoulder.

"Stop already!" I laughed. "I think I know what you mean."

The music drifted out of the little black box and more dejà-vu flashbacks to the first time we listened to the tape together came. Flashbacks to when the tape was something exotic and foreign. Now it was familiar. Ours. Even if I still didn't know what it was saying.

"Hello?" came a loud voice from outside the boat. I looked at Marcus who was getting up, smiling.

"Hello? You in dere?" asked an accented voice.

"Who's that?"

"It must be Joey with dinner. Wait here." He smiled and jumped out of the hatch.

"Over here!" Marcus yelled from the deck.

Who was Joey?

There was some mumbling around on the deck, and seconds later, Marcus was back downstairs with a pizza delivery guy with a large, delicious smelling pizza.

"Thanks for the delivery," he said and gave him some money.

"Arrivederci," he said to me, climbing back up the ladder.

"Bye!" I called back, my eyes on the pizza. "Who's that?"

"That's Joey from the pizzeria. He imports wine and stuff with Fritz. Sometimes they are at the same food festivals. It's cheaper that way."

"Oh."

I found a round pizza cutter in the drawer and when I started to cut the pizza, it all hit me. The music and the pizza, the cut flowers and the wine. Definitely not all a coincidence.

"So, it's Hawaiian. You *do* like Hawaiian, right?"

"Yeah. I do," I answered, wondering how he knew that.

We didn't talk a lot more and ate in a strange silence. Not because the silence itself was strange or awkward but rather strange because the silence felt OK. Comfortable.

But maybe it was too perfect? Even though my catastrophe alert antennas were now relaxed, I couldn't shake off the feeling that the blade was about to fall and I kept expecting something to happen that would mess up the moment. Something catastrophic like a hot coffee would spill and cause third degree burns with an emergency visit to the E.R., or maybe a hole would suddenly appear in the bottom of the boat.

But it didn't, and after we ate, we moved back to the niche where we talked for hours.

"But seriously," he said suddenly, "there's so much more we could've done. We should stay in touch."

His blue eyes darkened, a mixture between anticipation and, what? Maybe sadness?

"We should," I agreed as I pulled him close, glad at least, that for just a little longer, time stood still.

"By the way, thanks for taking me tomorrow," he said finally.

My stomach tightened at the thought, and all I could say was, "Oh, don't mention it."

Please. Don't mention it.

******

"*Schlafmütze*," Marcus whispered.

"What?" I asked, realizing the night was over

"Oh my God, I'm still asleep. I'm sorry." I groggily tried hard to wake up.

"It's OK. But it's morning," he continued.

"No, it's not!" I could hear the clang of the masts, the birds crying overhead. I could see the soft morning light coming in through the window above. I couldn't believe I had fallen asleep.

"I let you sleep as long as I could, but the time is going," he informed me gently.

"Why?" I pleaded. I didn't want to sleep. I wanted to spend every moment I could with him, conscious.

I got up, got a drink of water and went to the table. The place was spotless. No wine, no pizza box, just my shoes on the floor, and the flowers.

"What time is it?" I asked.

"Eight-thirty..."

"What time do you leave?"

"My train leaves at eleven."

I put my shoes on, functioning in zombie-mode. I went up to the deck, where it was so foggy that I could hardly even see the lighthouse at the end of the harbor. Obviously not the best day to go sailing. No, probably it was a really good day to stay put, crawl back under the covers and sleep and snuggle for most of the day.

Marcus climbed up the stairs on to the deck, put the door in the hatch and locked it up.

So final.

"Should we go for breakfast?"

"Yeah. Where would you like to go? IHOP? McDonald's? Something truly American?"

"The café here?" he suggested. "The Hot Ham and Cheese Café?

"OK." I couldn't help smiling. It sounded so sweet, and he looked so sweet saying it.

"Hot Ham and Cheese Café it is."

We put on our jackets, jumped over the rail and walked back up to the parking lot.

"I just have to go for a moment — to the office."

"OK."

We walked over to the harbor office where Marcus laid a bunch of keys on the counter.

"These are for Mr. Neuhoff, slot 182. He will come by to pick them up this week."

"Have a good trip home, Marcus," said the very tanned, middle-aged woman with short, frazzled blond hair.

"Thank you again for everything," he answered and then turned to me again. "OK then. I guess we can go."

We walked down the walkway to the next building where the Hot Ham and Cheese Café was in a row of tourist shops. We went in.

Everything seemed very mechanical at this point. Meaningless small talk. Terrible weather. Eggs and coffee. And there it was. The time was up.

"Check please," Marcus said to the waitress who passed by us. He paid, we put our jackets back on, and went to my car.

"OK, next Stop — San José Train Station," he mimicked one of those electronic voices on the train.

"Time check?" I asked.

"9:32."

"We better hurry."

I started the car and drove down Water Street and over to Highway 17 to San José, when it started to sprinkle through the thick fog. I turned on the windshield wipers and drove north.

"Do you have to check in like that at the train station?" I asked.

"No. I just have to give them my ticket on the train."

He looked through his pockets and pulled out an envelope from the travel agency and confirmed the details of his trip.

"Looks like everything is OK," he said, but I had the feeling I was driving the wrong direction. There was still time to change this. He wasn't gone yet. *Go Back!* screamed a voice in my head.

"Looks like a good day to be above the clouds," I commented instead. "The weather down here is so bad."

"At least the traffic is good."

Sporadic small talk continued, and far too quickly, we were there, parking outside the train station.

"Time check." I looked at my cell phone. "10:52. I guess we better get you up there. Oh, but before you go, I just want to give you this."

He looked at me expectantly while I got the small wrapped package out of my bag.

"Should I open it?" he asked smiling.

"Well, I guess so. If you want to."

He opened the blue wrapping paper and looked at the silver ladle, smiling.

"Keep stirring, keep going," I said.

"Lilly," Marcus started, shaking his head, "you know I have to go back to start this job. But I also liked being here and being around you."

"Same here," I said breathless, unable to even look him in the eye.

He picked up my hand and kissed it. "I think the best thing would be to pack you with me," he said. "but you know you have to go where you can do whatever it is that you do."

"I know. I guess that's what you need to do right now, before you risk missing your train," I said quickly.

A group of people came and encircled the green mini-van next to us. Doors opened. Hatchbacks closed, reminding me that this *was* a parking lot.

"Thank you," he said as he smiled and grabbed his bag from the back seat. We got out, and I pushed the button on my key to lock the doors. We walked through the station, and when we walked up the stairs to the platform, the train was already coming to a stop. Within seconds the doors opened, and a uniformed ticket controller got out, allowing passengers to exit the train.

My heart was racing. I knew now that this was really happening, and how helpless I felt. *Make a good impression!* I told myself, fighting my brain defect. *This is the last time he'll see you! Your last impression!*

A few seconds later, other people began wrestling with their luggage and began boarding the train.

"I better get on board," he said as he put both hand on the sides of my face and kissed me.

I looked up at him and gave him a quick hug and breathed in one last time his sweet, spicy scent as the doors of the train started to peep annoyingly, warning would-be travelers that they needed to board — *now*.

I opened my mouth to say something, but nothing came out.

"Lilly, we should talk again soon," he said with a thick voice while getting into the train.

I watched him through the windows as he looked for a seat. Then he put his hand on the glass and motioned to me.

"Thanks!" he mouthed and smiled, holding up the ladle.

I walked along the platform as long as I could, as the train started to move and made its way through the thick fog.

And just like that, Marcus was gone.

12

December

I got up, made a coffee and took the paper outside on the back porch where it was freezing. I lit a cigarette, by-passed the job ads and opened it to read my horoscope.

December 2 ◎☆♔

To trust or not to trust? That's been a big question for you recently. You've been reluctant to get close to people at times, unsure whether their intentions were above board. Soon things clear up and help you see who's truly on your team.

Trust? Who or what was trustworthy these days? I sure couldn't tell. I couldn't see how anything was clearing up and decided, who cares. I turned Miss Teri off, finished my cigarette and went back to bed.

****

"Not doing so well . . . yeah . . . it's been almost a week . . . I know . . . well, if she would just eat, maybe."

"I don't think she's up to it right now. But I'll let her know that you called."

Maddie's voice was in the distance. Apparently she was on the phone, since I only heard her part of the conversation.

"I don't know, really . . . OK. I will. Bye." I heard her say.

I must have caught a terrible cold — out on the platform in the cold fog, and after two days in bed,I couldn't think. I couldn't eat. I could hardly move.

Maddie opened the door to my dark room.

"Hey there, Lil," she whispered, "You awake?"

"Kind of."

"How do you feel?"

"Feel? Numb."

"Your mom called again. She wants to know why you won't call her back. She's worried if you're so sick."

"Really? I'll call her later. I just need a little more sleep," I mumbled.

"Lilly ..." Maddie paused. "You've been asleep for almost three days. You know, I'm also getting a little worried here."

"I just need a little time, you know. A little more sleep. I just . . . I just can't right now."

There was no use in trying to explain. I curled up on my other side and held my knotted stomach.

"Can I get you anything? I can't stand seeing you like this, but I don't know how I can help."

"You can't," I whispered.

She stayed in the doorway, obviously reluctant to let me die in peace.

"What's the matter Lil? Does your head hurt? Your stomach? Should I get you a bucket?"

What's the matter? I didn't know myself. I couldn't begin to describe how I felt. Numb, stupid, hopeless, angry, shocked, lost. Not to mention unemployed. Can you fix that with a bucket?

"No," I said.

I heard the door shut and went directly back to sleep.

****

225

beep beep

I looked to see that there was a notification from Miss Teri.

"I know. I read you already," I said as I switched it off.

Maddie came in around six in the evening, turning on the light and opening the curtain. So much for suffering in silence.

"Yoohoo," she called softly, "Lilly, you *have* to get out of bed."

Her words were nice, but the tightness in her voice revealed that she was also getting annoyed.

"Come on. *You* have to help me plan this dinner," she reminded me, "It's in *two days*!"

"Maddie, I can't right now. I'm sorry — I don't want to leave all this on you. Can't we just cancel Thanksgiving?"

"Cancel Thanksgiving? No. Come on, you've got plenty to be thankful for," she said in a pep talk tone. "For one, you have a cousin like me to get you up and around. Now come on."

I could see that I wasn't going to get out of this easily. She was determined.

You can do this. Be strong, I thought to myself. I got out of bed, put on a pair of jeans and a black shirt.

"What do you think we need to do first?" I asked, unable to prioritize at this point.

"Why don't we just go down to the boardwalk and think it over. You know, clear your head a little, and then we'll see."

I swallowed, trying to get the words out. "Sure."

We drove through the cold evening breeze over to Ocean Street and the Boardwalk.

"I don't really feel like lots of fun and games, if it's just the same to you," I told her.

"Fine by me. I just think you need to get out of the house and see something different."

The rides at the Boardwalk were all closed for the season. Only the arcades were still open, but I didn't feel much like playing at the arcade. We walked past the Boardwalk out onto the wharf and sat down on a bench and watched the sunset in the crisp air.

The lighthouse was lit up. Newly decorated with Christmas decoration lights, it was glowing far more than usual. From top to bottom, it was so bright that it could be seen clearly from the wharf.

"Isn't it a little early to have the lighthouse all lit up?" I asked irritated.

"Not really."

"A little overkill, if you ask me."

"It's pretty, though, don't you think, Lil?" Maddie asked, attempting to brighten my mood.

"I don't know," I answered toneless. I sat down on a bench and wiped an unyielding tear away from my eye.

"Hey, Lilly, come on, what's up with you?"

"I don't know. I can't seem to get away from his . . ." I couldn't finish.

"Are you talking about Marcus? Lil, I thought he was only a friend.

"Me, too." I couldn't hold it in any longer. The tears raced down my cheeks, and I felt like an idiot. "I can't seem to get away from him. There's reminders everywhere I go."

"What do you mean?" she asked, "Where?"

"Everywhere. Here. My horoscope, the boats. The wine and stupid flowers. Who goes around picking flowers in winter, anyway? . . . And the lighthouse here. At home. On the streets. — And now he's gone." I hid my face in my hands. "I read my horoscope. I'm supposed to see signs of people I can trust, who are on my team. But I only see signs of *him*! How am I supposed to be thankful? Fuck the stupid horoscope! Just . . . fuck it."

Maddie watched the ocean as she contemplated the situation.

"Come on, Lilly. Let's go back." She gave me a tissue and took my arm. "And don't worry about the dinner. I think I can take care of it."

She guided me back to the car, and we both slowly realized that this was something that only time could take care of.

December 6

I gave up reading my horoscope. It peeped all the time, but I figured, I wouldn't be able to see the connections and I couldn't be reminded of so many things if I just let it be. I thought about deleting it from my phone, but I wasn't there yet.

When I got up, I had breakfast and finally even had the nerve to call the Black Forest Restaurant.

"Thank you for calling the Black Forest Restaurant, this is Gerri. How can I help you?"

"Hi Gerri, its Lilly. I just wanted to ask when I could come by to pick up my last pay check and return my uniform."

"Oh, Lilly. Hi. Well, Liesl isn't here right now, but pay checks are out on the fifteenth, as you know, so I would say around then. But you know we close on the seventeenth, so, you better make sure you come in pretty quick. The restaurant will be closed till January."

"Yeah, right. OK."

"How are you doing?" she asked carefully.

"I'm OK, I guess. I'll be in on the fifteenth, so, take care."

*****

Thanksgiving turned out to be a terrible fiasco where I had too much wine, which, inevitably, embarrassingly, led to too much whining and wailing, and Maddie decided that I needed a time out and a change of scenery. She took care of everything and scheduled a trip to go home for Christmas. The only problem was that the flight left on the fourteenth, and at first, I wondered if I should go at all. But seeing that I was now unemployed, it made the decision easier. I could exchange the dirndl for my check in January. Now it was time to go somewhere without so many triggers.

December 11

A string of southwestern red chili pepper lights bordered the windows, tin painted cacti and lizards hung on the Christmas tree in the corner of my parent's living room, along with the classic angels and snowmen. I was relieved that there were some things that didn't change.

In a way, the things that had been suffocating me before I left were now comforting, and I was glad that having so many people around distracted my attention, at least it did until they were gone, and the next morning, it was all there again.

Miss Teri beeped and beeped, and I almost lost my nerve and read her news, which scared me too, so I disabled the apps., silencing her though Christmas.

I went into the living room where Mom was making a list for Christmas dinner, simultaneously watching re-runs of *Marcus Welby, M.D.*

God! *Marcus* Welby?! Figures. The good doctor looked serious he examined the cranial x-rays of a young woman. Why didn't I run? I wondered if he knew how to treat a Hijacked-Amygdala.

"Do we have to watch this?" I asked.

"*We* don't, but I am," Mom answered dryly. "It'll be over in a few minutes."

Obviously, watching this wasn't going to pull my thoughts in a productive direction.

"Then just tell me what we need for dinner, and I'll go do the shopping. What should I put on the list?" I asked impatiently.

"Let me think about it for a minute," she said, waiting for a commercial break. "Well, I guess we'll need some yams and potatoes. A turkey and a ham, of course," she added. "And don't forget the eggs for the egg nog," she went on, "and go ahead and get an extra carton of eggs for the deviled eggs and for the stuffing."

"What?" Sybille asked surprised as she walked into the living room. "*She's* doing the Christmas dinner shopping?"

"I guess so," Mom said, "I don't know why not."

"I'll go with you," Sybille said quickly. "*This* I gotta see," she said aside to Mom, but not out of my ear range.

"As if I never went shopping for a holiday dinner before," I shot back. "I could single-handedly cook the entire Christmas dinner, I'll have you now."

"Yeah, right."

I didn't press the issue, because I knew I had already said too much.

"Come on, if you're coming. I need to get out of the house."

I parked my dad's Lincoln in the grocery store parking lot and took the list out while Sybille got a cart. We walked down Aisle One — the "Milk and Produce" aisle and stopped to pick out potatoes when I looked up and saw a stand for "Marcus's Salsa".

"Oh, come on! Seriously?" I exclaimed to the display. I could still hear Sylvia's voice saying, "There are no coincidences", and I slowly got the feeling that maybe she was right, but more like someone was playing a joke on me. I looked around, but there wasn't anything that seemed conspicuous. Only Sybille with the perplexed look on her face.

"Are you OK?" she asked suspiciously.

"Sure," I answered, hoping I didn't look as paranoid as I was beginning to feel, and I made a mental note to put Sylvia's bracelet back on.

We continued our shopping looking for eggs, hams, stuffing ingredients, yams and everything else that was on the list and after standing in the long check-out line, we loaded up the car and went back home.

Marcus Welby M.D. was over, but I still wondered if all the incidences were really just coincidences. Or could there really be something more? I decided I was probably just overwhelmed with the holidays and that, at most, maybe I had some heightened perceptions, probably related to my Hijacked Amygdala Syndrome. I promised myself I would go to a doctor about my amygdala soon. For now, it would probably be best to just keep on concentrating on planning Christmas dinner.

****

Being home was more comforting than I had anticipated. I tried to be of help, but honestly, for the most part, I stayed in my old room and slept.

"When are you going to get up?" Mom asked.

"I don't know. Is there a reason why I should?"

I slept most of the day, and woke up around 8:00 in the evening, just in time to watch a movie with my mom.

"Have you seen Bree?" she asked.

"No. She's not here. She said she'd be around next week or so."

My inner clock was completely turned around and at five in the morning, I was still up. I resisted looking over my phone and opted for the television. That must be safe, I thought, as I flipped through the channels, I stopped at an infomercial.

"There's still time to get the perfect Christmas present, folks." The TV screamed at a low volume, "Right here, Ninja Knives! Nothing cuts cleaner or faster than the Ninja Knives! And if you order now, you'll receive this set of Super Ladles direct to your home!"

Click.

I didn't need to hear about the Super Ladles. It's just a coincidence, I thought. and flipped a little more, stopping at a music channel.

"Next up some Christmas cheer with Marco . . ."

This is absurd. Or I really am going nuts. I turned off the TV. This *can't* be happening. Even *I* couldn't make this up. But I had no idea how to explain it, and it was getting so strange, that I thought it would be weird to even try to talk to someone about it. They would probably think I was obsessed or crazy or lying. Who knows. And besides, what would it help?

I took a shower, got dressed and went to do some Christmas shopping at the mall. At least at 8:30 in the morning there aren't so many people around. I found a train set for Jaird, a doll for Emmy, and hoped that they liked that kind of thing. I found some perfume for Mom, and some golf balls for Dad, and was relatively happy that things seemed, for the moment, to be somewhat normal.

December 25

Christmas music played in the CD player. At least that way nothing could happen.

"Merry Christmas!" Mom said as she came in the kitchen. "You doin' alright?"

"Could be better. We don't really need sauce, do we?"

Between culinary steps that I could hardly keep up with, I'd snuck off to the back porch to smoke a cigarette after nearly burning the duck sauce.

"Here." Mom put a ladle in my hand. "Watch this."

Just keep stirring. Marcus could do all this with his eyes closed.

"What is it about cooking that is such a mystery to me?" I asked.

"Well, maybe you take after your Grandma. You know, she was also not the best cook on the block. I had to learn a lot on my own. But it's not that hard, really."

"Maybe it's one of those things that skip a generation," I said, making a mental note that it was just something else I could add to my list of disorders: Recessive Culinary Gene.

"Sorry I'm not more of a help," I apologized to Mom, "I actually wanted to try to do this, but I guess I'm just not up to it."

"Don't worry about it. Just keep stirring, I'll be right back." She gave me a knowing smile.

"Where are you going?"

"Just keep stirring."

"No! I mean, why did you just say that?" I demanded.

"What? So the sauce doesn't stick to the bottom of the pan!" she shot back.

"I mean, this isn't one of the gas-lighting things, is it?"

"Lillian, your mother is not in the habit of gas-lighting you. Now wait here," she said as she left.

Get a grip, get a grip!

I stirred fast and suppressed the knot in my throat until she came back a few minutes later, with a present.

"Give me the ladle for a minute," she said, exchanging the ladle with the present she'd brought in. "I should make you wait like everyone else, but I think you might need this now."

I took the present and unwrapped a black apron, printed with big letters: *I Kiss Better Than I Cook.*

I let out a big laugh as I read it.

"What's this?!" I asked.

"You can't be good at everything, you know," she said.

"I know. Thanks, Mom."

"That doesn't mean you're excluded from helping though."

She handed the ladle back to me, and I started stirring the sauce again, while she tied the apron around my waist.

"When you're finished, why don't you take charge of the drinks? That seems to be more your forté."

"I can do that."

I set the table for nine, put the salad plates on the dinner plates, the silverware in its proper spot, and the glass tumbles to the upper right of the plates.

Sybille stepped in behind me, carrying the potatoes and gravy, and Mom behind her with ham.

"I could go swimming in the potatoes!" Jaird cried out.

Mom had rescued the dinner, as always.

December 28

On Tuesday, Bree also got back into town, and I was anxious to see her after such a long time, so Maddie, Bree, Sybille and I decided to go out for dinner to catch up.

"Where should we meet? There are two new restaurants off I-40. An Italian place, Angelo's or some kind of home-style cooking?" Sybille asked.

"Angelo's," I chose.

"Sure. Then text Bree to meet us at seven, OK?"

"Alrighty."

I went into the new restaurant, a family-owned place, very modern and with no less than 5 televisions in the dining room. Sybille and Maddie drove in together, and Bree showed up in a black outfit, looking fantastic, as usual.

And as usual, we started off at the bar, where Bree told us about her new job in Tulsa.

"I'm getting used to it. There's still a lot to learn, but it's fun, and for Christmas, I'm thinking about getting a bigger apartment, now that the probation period is over."

"Good for you!" I said, glad that at least *her* life was actually shaping into something.

"What can I get you?" asked the bartender when he finally came over.

"I'll have a Zinfandel," I answered.

"You're a wine drinker now?" Sybille asked surprised.

"Make that two."

"Three," Maddie said.

"I'll have a Baileys and Coffee," Bree said.

"I had to go through a complete six-week apprenticeship just to wait tables at that restaurant. And that despite having a college degree! Part of the job was knowing your stuff when it comes to wine. So I might as well use it."

"So, you're integrating your knowledge into your lifestyle," Bree added.

"Sure."

"Well, I'm glad to see that you're taking the 'lifelong learning' attitude seriously," Bree joked.

"Here's to lifelong learning," I toasted.

"So, who was this guy, anyway?" Bree asked.

"Marcus."

"Marcus...who?"

"So, tell me again, what's the difference between a connoisseur and a sommelier?" Maddie cut in as she lifted her glass.

"One drinks wine and knows a lot about it, and the other gets paid to drink wine," I said.

"Which one gets paid?"

"The sommelier," I answered.

"Sounds good to me," Sybille agreed. "Maybe I also need to rethink my career goals. Maybe you could become a sommelier, you know, looking for a job and all."

I exhaled, when the music in the background changed.

"I'll be damned," I said.

"What?" Maddie asked,

"Do you hear that? Listen! It's the exact same song as on the boat!"

Italian tunes – the exact same one, right there, playing in Angelo's.

"Would you stop at once?! There's nothing there!" I called into the air, as they all three looked at me with blank faces.

"Lilly? Are you OK?" Sybille asked, and I realized how they must think I was completely overreacting. "I've never heard it."

I exhaled, again.

"It's just a few things I learned while I was working there. You don't have to make fun of it," I said with a sudden seriousness in my voice that surprised me, but I didn't feel like taking it back.

"Alright, don't get all bothered, Lil. It was just a joke." Bree said

"I got it."

"OK, sorry. So, seriously, what happened? Why'd you get fired?" Sybille asked.

"We kissed."

"In the meat locker," Maddie added dryly.

"In the meat locker? You can get fired for that?"

"You can if they have a strict 'No Fraternizing Policy'," Maddie said.

"It was the walk-in refrigerator," I corrected.

"Oh my God. That's a new one," Bree said, suppressing a smile.

"OK, let's change the subject, shall we?" Sybille interjected. "You could try to guess who I saw the other day, in case you're interested in things like that."

"Joe?" I asked, anticipating that one of them would mention him.

"Yip," she said.

"Well, come on, out with it. No need to be all suspenseful over him, too," I said. "What is it? Is he getting married or something?"

"Hardly!" she laughed. "Nothing like that. I just saw them a while back. At the Oyster Bar. He and Jack were all bummed out because one of their favorite dancers quit. They said she's trying to get a real job somewhere, and they were just pissed off about it. But get this: remember their friend Ben 'the poser'? Well, I heard he also started dancing. Marcia saw him at a bachelorette party a couple of months ago."

"Oh my God," Bree laughed.

"Be glad you got out when you did, Lil," Sybille said.

I was. An image of Patty's Oyster Bar surfaced in my head, one of the last times I'd seen Joe. Apparently, that hadn't gotten any better, and we didn't need to bring that up again.

"Bergmann," I said suddenly.

"What?" asked Bree.

"His last name. It's Bergmann."

"Oh, that's cute," Sybille said, "You're both 'from the mountain'."

"I'm from here. The only geological change around here for fifty miles is a great big hole in the ground," I reminded them. "There's no mountains."

"Not that you're from the mountains, but your names. DuMont means 'from the mountains' and Bergmann is 'mountain man'. It's kind of a cute coincidence, that's all," Sybille mused.

"Oh. Really?" I asked, my thoughts reeling at yet another coincidence. "Do you *see* this?" I asked, nearly begging inside.

"Sure, but what about it?"

"Ugh." I said exhausted as my phone beeped, and I touched the button, relieved for the distraction, and Miss Teri popped up.

$\mathcal{D}$ecember 28 ©♡✉

News from distant places finds you ready for a fresh start. An important relationship could hit a turning point and evaporate any doubts you might be having. Be brave and go with that one thought.

That was too much. I was stunned. I re-read the entry and couldn't move as my mind was raced and my jaw must have nearly hit the floor.

"That does it. I'm going back," I declared.

"Yeah, I'll go with you!" Bree joked, drinking her wine.

"Here. Read it yourself." I showed them my phone.

Sybille stared at me.

"You're not going anywhere. Stop this, at once. What about New Year's?" Bree asked, "We just got back here!"

"I know," I said, "I mean, I don't know. What about this song? The ads on the TV? And now this? How do you explain all this?"

They all looked at each other.

"OK, it is kind of strange," Sybille admitted. "But, do you want to miss New Year's Eve?"

"Are you really going to miss something if you stay?" Bree asked.

"What if it was him? Is that what you want?" Sybille asked.

"I don't know, but if I don't go and see, I know I'll regret it. And I think, I'd like to find out."

"Well, there's only one way to do that," Maddie said.

****

December 30

In the morning, I didn't take time to read Miss Teri. Instead, I called the travel agent to see if they could re-schedule my flight. The agent wasn't sure and said she'd call me back. I waited and thought about the prediction for most of the day, unable to get the thoughts out of my head, and as in most of my moments of doubt, there was always one place where I could go to clear my thoughts. The canyon.

It was six o'clock in the evening when I decided to get out and drive around. At a whopping twenty-five degrees outside, it was bitterly cold. I drove out through the dark, clear evening, got on the highway and drove out to my thinking spot.

Was I delusional? Was I sick with hope? This wasn't me doing this, I thought. I'd ran as far as I could – but everywhere I went seemed to be I was feeling apprehensive, suspicious that I could just be extremely delusional and sick with hope that something wonderful might happen, and that these thoughts were driving my actions. I tried to shake my head, shake the thoughts away, shake off the bitter cold. But the pull was too strong.

I gave in to the thought, to what I was hearing for a moment and realized, *Something* is there. *I can feel it.*

And with unexpected clarity, I knew. I knew it was *something* and I had to go back.

I drove back to my parents' house and called the travel agent again to change my ticket. It would cost me, she said, but it was do-able.

"Then do it," I said quickly.

"So, you're serious? You're going back already?" Sybille asked, not sounding all that surprised. "I mean, what do think this is?"

"I don't know, but I have to. There's something there. I *have* to go."

"Are you sure you're going to be OK?" Maddie asked when she called.

"I'll be fine. I have to go back a little early, that's all. Thanks for everything, Maddie. I'll see you when you get back next week, OK?"

"See you next week," she said hanging up.

I packed my bags and presents and for the first time in weeks went to sleep early, and the next morning my dad helped me load my things into the back of the car and drove me out to the airport.

"What are you going to do there with no job?" he asked.

"I'll find one. I have a little saved up again, and of course, thank-you you, the Christmas money will help. I'll be OK," I said.

We stopped in the departure lane at the airport and I lit up one last cigarette before having to enter the smoke-free environment.

"One last one," I said, clicking the lighter.

"Let's hope so," Dad replied seriously. "You know, your mother doesn't get to light up every time you take off."

"What? Where'd that come from?"

"I'm just saying."

"Oh. OK." I hadn't thought about that. She was home, comfy in the kitchen, doing her thing. Wasn't she?

"I'll be back soon. I promise. I mean, maybe it's nothing, but I have to go see, Dad. I just... have to."

The freezing wind swept through the departure zone, and I put out the cigarette in the ashtray before lining up at the check-in counter. Dad waited until I was through, and we had a hurried round of good-byes as they were already calling out my flight. I went through the gate, blew a kiss from the other side, then walked quickly down the crowded, decorated corridor to catch my flight.

Epilogue

New Year's Eve

December 31

Beep!

No, Miss Teri, not now. I didn't answer her beeps because I was too scared that it would jinx everything. *Go with that one thought*, I thought.

After eight hours of planes, trains and automobiles, I was finally home late in the evening. I made a peanut butter and jelly sandwich and called my parents to let them know I was back.

"And, any word from Romeo yet?" Sybille asked, not leaving out an opportunity to give me a hard time.

"No," I answered. "Well, actually I don't know. There was a call yesterday by an 'unidentified caller', someone called today with a string of random numbers, nothing that I could make out. So, who knows."

Exhausted, I took a bite of my PBJ and answered with my mouth full, "I have to go to bed. I can't think anymore."

Around eleven o'clock in the morning, I woke up alone in an empty house in a city that I still didn't know well and where I didn't know that many people. And the ones that I did know were all either back home or gone for the holidays. My dirndl, hanging over the chair in my room, was the only thing that greeted me.

Guess I won't be needing that anymore, I thought. And then again, somehow, I did.

I tried to figure out the time in Germany, but me, mornings and math don't go together. Was Germany nine hours ahead or nine hours behind? I could never keep that straight. I looked at my phone and figured out that it must have been around eight o'clock in the evening in Germany. Marcus was probably at some party or dinner or doing something festive to get ready to ring in the New Year. Like everyone else in the rest of the world.

Everyone, except for me.

I got up and took a shower, cleaned up the living room and went to the grocery to get a paper, coffee and staple items to get me through the next couple of days. I went back home, made a pot of coffee, poured it, added a teaspoon of sugar, mixed in some milk and read through the paper, when I got slapped by a wave of doubt.

What if it was really nothing? What if this was just another stupid idea that I had dreamed up? What if it really was my amygdala?

I read the paper and before too long, it was three p.m. in California, which meant it was midnight in most parts of Europe, and as long as it was already New Year's *somewhere*, it must have been OK to open a bottle of Mumm.

"Happy New Year," I said, taking a long drink.

I got dressed, spent some time in front of the mirror primping, just in case I decided to do something. I put on Mom's apron, took a picture of myself and posted it, and soon it was already getting late. Eight o'clock, nine o'clock. In Germany, it must have been around six o'clock in the morning. Should old acquaintances be forgot? No. Or maybe? Maybe it really was nothing.

I felt a little disappointed and silly that I had thrown caution to the wind and actually followed something so ridiculous as my horoscope.

It was ten o'clock, and I had started channel surfing, unable to make the incredibly hard decision between *New Year's Eve Around the World* and *Memorable Moments of the Year.*

RING

I bolted upright and jumped to the kitchen. My heart was beating nearly out of my chest. I picked up the phone, looked at the display and exhaled after realizing that I recognized the number immediately.

"Hello?" I answered.

"Haappy Neeww Yeeaarr!" Maddie screamed over the phone into my non-suspecting ear. I could hear her smile, I knew she was having a good time, somewhere.

"Happy New Year!" I wished back.

There was a two-hour difference between Texas and California. Texas being two hours ahead, of course, they would now be ringing in the New Year.

"Are you at home?" Maddie asked.

"Of course. Where else could I be?"

"Here, for one. Lilly, you've got to get out. If he hasn't called yet, he's probably not going to, and he shouldn't expect you to sit at home on *New Year's Eve* to wait on him! Go out, Lilly! Go out!"

The phone had obviously been passed on to the next one. A noticeably inebriated Bree had the phone now.

"Lill, dear, I got a prediction for you: you need to get out! This is no fucking way for you to start the New-fucking-Year, sweetheart," she screamed. "Now I want you to get out there and find somewhere to go and go celebrate and paarrttay!"

"OK, thanks a lot, guys! Glad you are all having a good time. The T.V. is very good company, but I have to admit, you may

be right."

I hung up the phone and curled up back on the couch.

10:12 p.m.

I looked at my phone again, because maybe someone had tried to call *exactly* in the three minutes that I had just spent on the phone. I checked my messages. Nothing. Haven't I done this before?

Maybe I wasn't meant to be in California. Or maybe I just wasn't meant to be in there.

The more time went on, the more antsy I became. It had been New Year's Day in Germany now for a full seven hours, and if Marcus had been to a party anything like Maddie and Bree's, he was definitely not thinking about calling me. He was probably most definitely sleeping off his excesses of eight pints of beer.

So why was I sitting at home alone?

I called over to Rick's Café, but they were closed, so I looked through the paper but didn't really see anything that I would be brave enough to go to alone. Sylvia and Brooke had gone skiing with some friends, so that left me pretty much alone.

But sitting there alone with PBJs was also not really my idea of ringing in the New Year. I figured I would be a lot better off if it were joined by some of Comfort Food. Something yummy and filling like a nice pizza.

I called up to Joey's Restaurant to order a medium Hawaiian pizza and a bottle of red wine to be delivered.

"I'm sorry ma'am, but we do not deliver." The man on the phone told me.

"What do you mean, 'we don't deliver'? But you delivered to the boat?"

"We have been here for ten years, and we do not deliver, not even across the street," he said, attaching an 'a' on the end of every other word.

I couldn't believe what I was hearing, and I definitely didn't want to start my New Year with just me and a PBJ. So I decided I wasn't taking "no" for an answer. I know what I saw.

"Can I speak to Joey?" I asked, proud of myself for trying to stick up for myself.

"Sure," the voice said quickly on the phone.

The clanging of dishes and laughter and voices mixed together as they made their way into the phone. I waited several rings before I heard the receiver being picked up on the other end.

"Hello. Joey here," the guy said quickly. Maybe he was just a little busy? My confidence faded a bit.

"Hi. Um . . ." I felt like an idiot. *Don't back down! Just ask politely!* "Um, this is Lilly. I just wanted to ask if I could get a pizza delivered. I know it's. . . well it *is* New Year's Eve and all, but —"

"We don't deliver," he cut in, answering decisively.

"Oh. Is that something new? Cause, you see, a friend of mine, Marcus, had a pizza delivered from you not too long ago down at the harbor, and —"

"Wait," he cut in again.

The muffling sounds on the other end were getting louder.

"Who is this?" he finally asked.

"Lilly," I answered spontaneously. "Why? Wait — what do you mean?" I backed up, realizing I didn't know who exactly I was talking to.

More muffling sounds were on the other end.

"Look, it's alright. I can just go out and get something." I insisted quickly.

"Wait a minute, please," Joey said.

The background noise was still forcing its way through the receiver when he got back on the phone.

"Is this the Lilly from Marcus?"

Didn't I just say that?

Embarrassed, I had a sudden urge to hang up quickly. But I couldn't.

"Yeah, that's me," I stuttered.

"Yeah, listen, I remember that. It was a special deal, you see. Hang on." I could hear him talking and loud Italian music in the background.

"Where are you, Lilly?"

I croaked my address into the phone.

"OK — We don't actually *deliver* the pizzas, ya know, but, uhm, Lilly, listen," he continued. "We got someone goin' out that way, so we can go ahead and do it, just tell me what you want," he pressed.

"I'll take a…" What did I want? Where should I start? I wanted to be with my friends, I wanted some kind of sign that I was shooting in the right direction. I wanted to hear something from Marcus. No. I wanted to be with Marcus, and not just tonight or a phone call.

"Hello?" he asked again.

"A large Hawaii and a bottle of Merlot with that, if you can."

"Got it," he said. "It'll take a bit, ya know, its New Year's Eve."

"I understand," I said, "Thanks."

I poured another glass of Mumm, watched *New Year Around the World* and googled Italian music, and for just a moment, I was back on the boat.

Forty-five minutes later the doorbell rang, and I nearly tripped getting to the door, and then, I nearly fell over when I saw not Joey, but Fritz.

"Wh-What are you doing here?" I looked around with the suddenly feeling that this must be another joke.

"Delivering your pizza," he answered, holding out the steaming box.

"I mean… you're supposed to be in Europe," I asked stunned.

"I know. The trial got pushed up, so I had to come back early. Worked out good, though. We won," he said relieved.

"Congratulations."

"Can I come in?" he asked.

"Oh, of course." I opened the door.

"And, you're wondering why I brought the pizza, I guess," he said as he put the pizza and the bottle of wine on the coffee table.

"Well, yeah." I wondered if he would be going to give me the bill or start screaming at me. "What is it? You want the dirndl back?"

"No. Well, yes, but that's not why I'm here. I wanted to talk to you. After I let you go, I had some second thoughts, and I also have something else for you." He started pulling something out of his coat. A knife? A hatchet?

"About this." He showed me the folder with the ad campaign.

"Oh, I can explain that."

"You don't have to. I saw it. I mean, it fell off the counter, and I saw it, and I like it. Lilly, I can't hire you back for waitressing. You broke the work policy, you know that."

"I don't want to come ba—"

"Look, the thing is, I like what you did here," he broke in, "it's good, and I'd like to talk to you about it. If you want. Maybe we can work together doing something more that's in your line of work. Liesl and Joey also liked it, by the way."

"They did?"

"Yeah. It's not too bad. I mean, you're not so bad at waitressing, but what you did here was really good. And this idea of working with the community center, it's also not too bad. Have you ever thought about working for yourself?"

"For myself?" Inside, I hiccupped.

"No."

"I think you might have a real talent for this. Why don't we talk next week? You can let me know how much your rates might be. I have a lot of work throughout the year that needs to be done. Would you think about it?"

"Umm, I think I'd like to think about it, yeah, of course. We can talk about it."

"OK. Great. Then, thank you, Lilly."

Fritz and I stood there, awkwardly looking at each other.

"And this is also for you. Here," he said, handing me an envelope. "Your last paycheck. I thought you might need it."

"Should I get you the dirndl? I'd had planned to wash it first."

"Do that, Lilly. We'll talk next week. Are you going out for New Year's?" he asked looking around the obviously empty house.

"Oh no. It's just me this time. I like it like this, you know, a new start and all."

"Sure. You have a Happy New Year, then. You can come by on Monday if you have some time."

"Sure. Monday. I'll be there."

"Enjoy your pizza." He turned and shut the door behind him, and I stood there, stunned. Happy and sad at the same time.

Was that the person?

What had just happened? I couldn't believe that I had an opportunity to start my own business. I had to tell Maddie and Bree and Sylvia about this, so I turned on my computer and scrolled through all the pictures.

Fifteen likes of my apron picture, and one friend request. I clicked on the button and let out a loud laugh.

'Marcus Bergmann wants to be friends — accept or deny?'

Do I want to be friends? I thought. A month later and you finally contact me? Are you *crazy*?

Still bewildered from the last ten minutes, I quickly clicked the "accept" button and looked at his profile picture: a picture of him in some kind of kitchen, enthusiastically holding up a ladle. Underneath was written: "Gewonnen!".

What was that? What did that mean?

I looked it up: "Won!"

Won? Won what? I looked at the ladle again, and upon closer inspection, I recognized that it was not any ladle, *but the one I had given to him.*

It was too much, everything.

My eyes teared up and I didn't know if I hated all of this or if I loved it.

And what about him?

My heart skipped a beat, my head started to spin — and all that even without the wine.

Unbelievable, I thought. He made it. I quickly typed in "Happy New Year! And Congratulations!" just as he simultaneously clicked 'like' on my picture with the apron, and then came a comment with only one word: "True ;)"

I wondered why it hadn't been the other way around — Marcus at the door, and Fritz per email?

But it comes as it comes.

And Fritz came to me and liked my work.

And he wants to talk to me. About my work.

Would I also have a quiet triumph?

I nervously typed the news in a private post to Bree, Maddie, and Sylvia, and then hesitantly turned on Miss Teri and read her prediction.

January 1

Intentions that you begin with today can quickly bear fruit and a breakthrough convinces a distant connection to contact you. Like to travel? That job you've been working towards might get two birds with one stone — so why not take it and enjoy the ride?

1:02 a.m. I sat alone in the living room in Santa Cruz. A new day, a new week, a new month and a new year. I guess you never know how things are going to end up. Or which turns and curves your ride will take you on. Considering the last year, I was careful not to be over-confident, but this time, I thought, who knows? Maybe this year I'll also make it. It kind of felt like it. Maybe I already had.

And as I started to log out, my computer beeped: one new message. From Marcus.

I took a deep breath before I opened it. OK, I thought, just sit back and enjoy the ride.

Acknowledgements

I would like to thank my parents, Jimmy and Mary Ingram, for all their love, support, and being there when I need it most. Thank you to Jörg Erdmann, and to my children, Raiden, Cassidy and Drake, for all the patience and support and love that you have shown me.
Thank you also to Jill, Valerie, Barbie, Tina and Craig, Tina z.O., and Danni; to Margret Wagner, and to Martina Takacs for editing. And to many others, far too many to name – many I unfortunately do not know their names – but who knowingly or unknowingly – (so often I couldn't tell), who came out of nowhere and pushed me along for nearly ten years, who helped, supported, inspired and encouraged me. I am humbled and grateful.

It's been a long, long road.

Thank you.

About the Author

Nicole Erdmann was born in Oklahoma City and moved to Germany in 1998. This is her first novel.